ALSO BY Kevin Canty

A Stranger in This World

Kevin Canty

INTO THE GREAT
WIDE OPEN

Kevin Canty is the author of *A Stranger in This World*. He received the Pacific Northwest Booksellers' Association Award for *Into the Great Wide Open*, and his work has been published in *The New Yorker, Esquire, Details*, and *Story*. Currently, he teaches fiction writing at the University of Montana, in Missoula, where he lives with his wife, the photographer Lucy Capehart, and their children, Turner and Nora.

INTO
THE
GREAT
WIDE
OPEN

Kevin Canty

VINTAGE CONTEMPORARIES

Vintage Books

A Division of Random House, Inc.

New York

FIRST VINTAGE CONTEMPORARIES EDITION, OCTOBER 1997

Library of Congress Cataloging-in-Publication Data
Canty, Kevin.
Into the great wide open / Kevin Canty.
p. cm.
ISBN 0-679-77652-4
1. Suburban life—United States—Fiction.
2. Teenagers—United States—Fiction. I. Title.
[PS3553.A56I58   1997]
813'.54—dc21   97-6672
CIP

Author photograph © Lucy Capehart

Random House Web address: http://www.randomhouse.com/

Printed in the United States of America
10 9 8 7 6 5 4 3 2 1

For my family

INTO

THE

GREAT

WIDE

OPEN

He met her in a van, in the rain, on his way to the Girl Scout camp at Chincoteague. An afternoon in mid-October. Gray rainy light leaked through the windows. Kenny sat in the last seat of the van, without a thought, without a plan. Wentworth slept on the seat beside him.

Rainwater snaked its way down the window glass: a little shoot or finger, top left to bottom right, dashing along and then stopping, trembling; then leaping forward, darting from drop to drop, safe harbors, running until they were too heavy to stop, off the window and down onto the road. Kenny gave them names, like racehorses. He felt a pleasant sadness when they died on the pavement.

The girls two seats in front of him were talking softly with their heads together. The others read or dozed, stared out the window. They were LRYers, Liberal Religious Youth, and Kenny didn't know any of them but Wentworth. They looked clean and white and rich to Kenny, untroubled. There was another vanload of them, ahead or behind. They were interchangeable. You could move them from one seat to another, one van to another. What did Kenny's father call it? *Fungible*, from selling corn to the Germans, maybe: no significant difference between one ear of corn and the next. His father worked in the Department of Agriculture when he was well enough. His father was an economist, which gave him a distant view of the world. He was an expert whistler: "Honeysuckle Rose," "Cherokee," "How High the Moon." Kenny caught himself thinking of his father in the past tense. There was some feeling, anger and shame all mixed together, and Kenny turned his face to the rain and the window so the others wouldn't see it. Not that any of them were looking.

Empty fields, turnrows of mud. The farmhouses stood alone in skirts of brown lawn, black skeletons of trees, swing-sets. Self-reliance, Kenny thought. Miles between us. The cool clean smell of the rain, as opposed to the complicated human smell inside the van: coffee, deodorant, farts, gasoline.

Kenny's father wasn't doing well. Last seen asleep on the sofa in the living room of the apartment, three in the afternoon. Kenny shut the TV off, covered his father with a chenille bedspread, took the melted highball off the coffee table, out of harm's way. That was yesterday afternoon. Kenny had been living with Wentworth and his family for a week already. He went home to see if it was safe to return, found his father, covered him with the bedspread like a piece of furniture in one of those big mansions where they covered the furniture with sheets and then left. Why? Kenny only knew about this from TV, but he knew that feeling, leaving things behind. Too much like dying: pulling the sheet up and over the body . . . You morbid little fucker, Kenny thought. Cut it out.

It was the rain's fault, he decided, that and the black houses standing off from each other. He was a little stoned, suggestible. He turned his eyes away from the lonesome countryside. What would Kerouac say? But Kerouac would never find himself in a van full of Liberal Religious Youth. Kenny couldn't remember what religion, even—Unitarian? Your parents would let you go because it said *Religious* in the title, and you got to go on overnight trips with girls, etc., and nobody cared if you got stoned or not. That was the advance publicity, anyway. Kenny had always looked down on the LRY people, even Wentworth a little. Now here he was, not quite through his own choice. There was no way that Wentworth's parents wanted Kenny around if Wentworth himself was out of the house. Wentworth was the last of five children. Kenny could picture the parents, crossing off the days on the calendar until Wentworth left for college. They were perfectly nice and kindly people, though. Kenny overheard Wentworth's mom dickering with the LRY leader, trying to make a place for him. "Well, it's both his parents," she was saying. "No . . . No, the mother's not in the picture at this point."

Wentworth's mom sold real estate, a fast, efficient talker, all business. "If it's just the insurance," she said; then a pause. "No, no, I understand . . . Look, I could sign a release. I mean, if you just needed one."

Kenny had waited like he was being sentenced, sitting in her kitchen. Mrs. Wentworth was waiting for the other end of the line. Staring blankly into midair, she suddenly noticed Kenny. What was she seeing? A naked orphan. A vulture chick concealed among her own. A voice buzzed through the telephone line and she brightened all at once. "Terrific," she said into the handset. "I do appreciate it. Thank you so much for your help." She hung up the phone and looked at Kenny, brightly. "You're all set," she said.

Motherless children, Kenny thought. Her kindness had a public, professional face. Nevertheless she kept him, made a place for him at dinner. His own mother was trying her hand at Supported Living, for the second time. They gave her an apartment, sent somebody around to make sure she took her medications.

Nine of them in the gray light, ghostly, including the counselor who was driving and the counselorette riding shotgun, who kept playing the same tape by the Police. Blond collegiate androids. Kenny thought of shaking Wentworth awake, just to get out of his own head. The rain, the light, the black wet dirt. Death by water (drowning), by fire (burning), by air (falling), and by earth: disease, decomposition, rot. Oh yeah, Kenny thought, I sound like a Slayer song, Black Sabbath. I Am Iron Man. Still the memory of his own hands pulling the bedspread over his father, gently, trying not to wake him . . . Chenille, another mystery. Those little lines and deedlee balls of fuzz didn't make it warmer, they must be for looks. Which meant that somebody liked it: his mother, who had bought it or kept it. For the second time in five minutes Kenny found himself confronted with his mother, the lady of Baltimore, stranded for life. He gave up, surrendered to the gray light and the sadness. Sometimes it was easier just to let it go, let events wash over him and drop the struggle. Something pleasant in the gray light. Kenny could do nothing about his mother. God grant me the something to change what I can, the something to accept what I can't change, the wisdom to know the difference. *Serenity*, Kenny thought.

His eyes came to rest on the girl two benches up: a head, a neck, slender shoulders in grandmotherly black wool. Her hair was black, or almost black, and cropped short as a marine's, uneven. Brain damage, electroshock therapy. This was interesting, but who was she? He tortured his brain, couldn't come up with her face. Wentworth had been too stoned to introduce him to anybody before they left, and nobody else had bothered. Kenny wondered if she'd come by herself, too: the way she now sat, alone and upright, not talking, doing something with her hands—what? Reading probably. Knitting. Kenny hoped that she might turn, so he could see her face, but she sat and stayed there, still, unfidgeting, with her back to him. Shoulders set against him. She wasn't giving him anything.

He would take what he could, then. He didn't feel any particular obligation to these soft, settled boys and girls. He would take what he was given: whatever his ears could hear and his eyes could see, and all the oxygen they weren't using.

Her neck was a delicate, fluted . . . Her skull was a graceful shape, too, which was good: her hair was easily short enough to show the outline of the bone beneath the skin. My little coconut. Kenny thought of how her head might feel in the palm of his hand, the short soft hair and the hard bone. Drawing her down . . . a little boyish, too, a little masculine, which was scary. A girl with a boy's head. Kenny felt a little stirring, danger or sex, he couldn't tell, he didn't quite care.

The usual number of earrings, seven or eight in her left ear and three in her right. Her skin, what Kenny could see, was immaculately white, untouched by the summer that had just gone by; an accomplishment in itself. The fresh-dead look, Wentworth called it. White skin verging on green, bright red lipstick, was the form. Kenny wondered. He sent the thought in her direction: show me your face. She didn't, the standard fate of his attempts at telepathy. She wore a black wool cardigan over a black blouse of some kind, a little Peter Pan collar, Kenny could picture it. All this was normal, safe suburban rebel.

What set her off from the others was her hair: it was extreme, it was *troubled*. This was a code word for people like himself. Nobody safe would cut it quite so short; or, if they did, they would at least do a little better job of cutting it evenly. Amateur brain surgery, Kenny thought. It wasn't style. He pictured her under the bathroom light, lifting her own hair between her fingers and then scissoring it off, as close to the scalp as she could. Scalp/skull. The sudden boy in the mirror.

And then the white skin of her neck, the delicate tendons, the dark fuzz of her hair trailing off into short silky animal hairs and then to nothing. One small red spot on her skin, insect bite or fading pimple. And what if she had pimples? But none of the children were ugly, their parents wouldn't let them be. Blank sometimes, though, generic, she might have a face or she might not. I command you to turn. The usual result. She reached her left hand behind her back and touched the red spot, scratched it lightly with her nails, put her hand back in front of her: long-fingered, slender, inkstained. *Artistic.* Which was almost as good as, almost the same as, troubled. And the length of her hand made him consider her height, which he calculated from the seat back, touching his own shoulders to guess: his own height, or nearly. Long Tall Sally.

Kenny found himself with the beginnings of a hard-on, which happened sometimes in buses and trains. All the bumping and jostling, and his own untrainable dick. Down boy, he commanded. I'm doing something. But his dick wouldn't listen to him; his dick wanted to talk about this body he was looking at, about the *white stalk* of her neck giving way to the rounded, damaged head, the short hair against the palm of her hand, pulling her close, tall, *boyish* . . . You, he thought, I want you.

Then, when he was not expecting her, she stirred in her seat and stretched her neck and then, bored, turned and looked at the rain outside the window and then back at Kenny, directly at Kenny. He sat there, caught, immobile. Then saw that he knew her. It was Junie Williamson.

"Hey," she said to him softly.

"Hey," said Kenny.

"What are you doing here?"

Kenny couldn't think. It felt like he was wearing his dick on his face. He needed to say something but he couldn't think of what (the anonymous body suddenly evolving into a person; he wanted the blank body back, the empty place). "It was Wentworth," he said, just to say something. "You know Mike Wentworth?"

She shook her head; she couldn't hear him.

"It's sort of by accident," he said.

But she shook her head again, shrugged, a social smile. She couldn't hear him. She disappeared again, leaving him stranded. They could talk later. It didn't help. Kenny was stuck with a wooden dick, stuck inside himself again, staring out at the houses, black with rain, standing in their skirts of dead grass; but even his melancholy had left him, the comfort of the gray light. He couldn't take his eyes off her.

Kenny had a scientific approach to girls, a two-axis system. Girls were available, unavailable, or unknown. There were also desirable, undesirable, or unknown. You could plot the variables. For instance, he had just spent the summer as a lifeguard, at a country club, staring down through his black sunglasses at a pool deck full of desirable/

unavailables in seventy-dollar swimsuits. All summer he watched their bodies, aimed his desire at them; but they were impervious, waterproof, his gaze slid off them. By the end of the summer they were unreal as TV faces. Also: whenever they dressed or drove or talked to one another—they never talked to Kenny—they mostly turned to undesirable/unavailables. This was the biggest category: cheerleaders, young Republicans. They didn't care for Kenny, Kenny didn't care for them. They were fine, as long as they were bodies. They were beautiful.

Undesirable/available: it was a shifty line, especially at parties. Either half of the equation could change. That's what Kenny liked: the moment, the invisible line when things got unclear and suddenly things shifted into unknown. Available/unknown, desirable/unknown. It was like girls who wore glasses, they took them off when they were kissing, when they were doing things, or sometimes Kenny took them off. Partly they were in the way, of course, but partly the glasses came off because it was better not to know. It was better not to name things, just to let touch guide them, skin on skin.

Junie Williamson: unknown/unknown. There were rumors about her, that was all. Kenny knew what the hallways of his high school said about her, knew what they said about her at parties and not much more: the blank place, again, the place for other people to put their desires and imaginations and feelings. Kenny had never really considered her, never thought she might be available or really thought about her much at all. She was somewhere in the outer orbit. They had friends in common, he couldn't remember who, and they had maybe been at a few parties at the same time: Kenny in the kitchen, Junie in the living room. The haircut was new. Last time he saw her it was neck-length, blunt-cut like everybody else's. He had mistaken her for everybody else. Suddenly she was visible. He had this feeling: they had been circling around each other, not quite touching. Unknown. It was a disappointment at first to find out that he knew her, the girl in the van; but the more he thought about Junie

Williamson the more he thought that he didn't know anything more than the rumors.

Junie and Kim. Kim was a short solid girl, with a fierce little smile. She wore her blond hair short, no earrings, no makeup, and she always seemed to be wearing her brother's clothes: blue-and-white-striped buttondown shirts, blue jeans, penny loafers. Whether or not she had a brother, Kenny didn't know—she just gave that impression. He was in an English class with her once and they were allies, sitting in the back row and answering all the questions. They were almost friends, boy-and-boy friends though. They used to smoke cigarettes together at the break.

And Kim and Junie were friends, or something. *Friends:* he wondered what he meant. The word was like a blanket, it covered up rather than showing what was underneath. Kenny guessed at the outlines: he had seen them, Mutt and Jeff, walking the hallways together or talking at parties. Junie was a head taller, quiet, strict-looking. He thought of her as awkward without any real evidence. Kim was always the one who was talking, always moving her hands. That and Junie's new haircut, *boyish,* and he wondered if the hallway rumors were true. Girl-and-girl friendships had a dark side, Kenny had seen this before, a face that was permanently turned away from boys, from parents; turned away from the world at large, a private space between them. It didn't mean anything, usually, except you couldn't touch them. Kenny was jealous, a little. Men and boys couldn't manage this kind of friendship, they couldn't protect each other. Dick versus dick. Unknown/unknown. She was starting to emerge a little out of the fog: she was Kim's friend Junie. She had smiled at him. It didn't mean anything. He thought of her, tall, short-haired (not just short but butchered) and thought: maybe they were wrong, maybe they were right. He didn't know which way he was hoping for. In between, undefined, *unknown.*

They piled out of the vans at the Girl Scout camp, into the rain in clumps of two and three, wrestling their baggage out of the back of the vans and then racing for the shelter of the buildings. Junie was carrying a camera bag and a tripod, half-unfolded, like a broken umbrella. Kenny lost her in the chinese firedrill. He didn't see Kim Nichols anywhere, though. He looked.

All this through the window, waiting for Wentworth to come around. He was a committed sleeper, talented. Living in the same house, Kenny had him pegged for about twelve hours a night, fourteen when he tried. Even awake, Wentworth's eyelids were heavy, his eyes turned inward, his breathing soft and regular. He might drop off at any second. Teachers hated him.

"We're losing," Kenny said. "Everybody else is getting the good rooms."

Wentworth yawned, shook his head. "It doesn't matter," he said. "It's all boy-girl, boy-girl, boy-girl anyway. Unless you brought somebody along?"

"You, baby," Kenny said. "You're all mine, big boy."

Wentworth blinked at him, annoyed, and Kenny was momentarily sorry. Big, soft, pink boys like Wentworth were sensitive about fag jokes.

"Mostly this is prearranged," Wentworth said. "I mean that's the point—to have a place to go. Little mommies and daddies. We'll find somewhere to sleep." He slapped himself lightly on the cheeks, looked reluctantly out at the rain. He was shy about physical discomfort, a delicate boy. "Sometimes you can get lucky," he said, still looking out the window. "That's what they say, anyway. I don't seem to."

They ended up in the bunkhouse, a long dim single room with a permanent stink of mouse turds and wet paper bag. There was a wood stove at one end and about sixteen or eighteen iron prison beds, with the requisite gray-and-white-striped mattresses. It was them and two other boys, who stationed themselves at the opposite end, as

9

far from Kenny and Wentworth as possible. They radiated social failure. Kenny wondered if he did, himself. Like bad breath or something, you couldn't smell it on yourself. He dug his raincoat out, a faded black thriftstore London Fog, and his Hanshin Tigers baseball cap.

"You look like a flasher," Wentworth said. "Where are you going?"

Kenny knew where he was going, who he was looking for, but he didn't want to talk to Wentworth about it. "Take a look around," he said.

"It's raining out there."

"Right. I noticed that. Actually we were driving though it all day."

"Fuck you," Wentworth said. "I don't care if you get wet or not."

"Dude," Kenny said. "Actually this is the only raincoat I've got. This is the Lone Raincoat."

Wentworth looked at it, Kenny shrugged: it didn't matter. Poor boy, a long way from home. It gave him a kind of power, to know he could live through this. He went out into the weather, alone.

It was still blowing, misting. He could feel the ocean somewhere close, out past the dunes. The camp was a scattering of cabins with green roofs, everything brown wood or painted brown. Outdoor signifiers, Kenny thought. Smokey the Bear. The cabins sat in a pocket of sparse, wind-whipped pine trees, a little valley in the dunes. The sound of the wind through them was constant and lonely. In the pines, in the pines, where the sun never shines . . .

He went looking for her in the main building, where the vans were parked, a long bungalow of round brown logs. Inside, a fire snapped and smoked in the walk-in fireplace, rustic tables and benches, a half dozen of the fungible white children sitting around, playing dominoes, sipping cocoa, talking to one of the counselors.

There was a stereo already playing on the mantel and the same Police tape going again. No Junie. The counselor spotted Kenny and stopped talking, looking up at him with a broad inviting smile. "Hi," he said loudly.

Kenny nodded, not smiling. The other children looked up at him suspiciously, he had come for their dope, their girlfriends.

"I'm Dave McHenry," the counselor said. "Come on over, sit down."

"It's OK," Kenny said. "I'm going to take a look around outside, maybe go down to the beach."

"It's raining out there," one of the children said; and the words hung in the air, along with the noise of the raindrops clicking at the windows. It seemed to be contagious, speaking the obvious. Isn't that a roof up there?

"Later," Kenny said, and walked out the long way, down the line of bedroom doors in the corridor behind the office. Not here, not here, not here. He felt dislocated: maybe it was the wood fire burning, the smell of smoke and cocoa, the fancy mountaineering baby clothes that the children wore, but he felt like he was going to walk out into an Appalachian meadow. That and the darkness under the pines. Lonely something. Empty hallway. Why am I always leaving the party, Kenny wondered. Why do parties have to end? A picture of his mother's face, only for a second, in one of her manic phases: grinning like a funhouse clown, *happy*. Nobody knew if it was inherited or not. That was one of the first things they told you.

Outside she was still nowhere. The afternoon had darkened toward evening; Kenny pulled his two-dollar pocket watch out of his black jeans and it said four-thirty. The rain had thickened a little. He set off on one of the trails through the pines, past the outhouse, the little cabins set like dice under the trees. Yellow electric light through the windows, and Kenny outside in the rain. Familiar gray sadness, comfortable as flannel. Kenny was right at home, remembering his mother's face, the poem that Mrs. Connolly taught him in English class: I am lonely, I am lonely . . . Inside, the little mommies and daddies, two to a house. Kenny was outside looking in.

Not that it mattered, not that he had a choice. The pines tapered off in the sandy soil and then the dunes rose out of them, grass and sea oats. Kenny trudged up the path and into the deep, soft sand, which trickled down into his shoes, Chuck Taylor high-tops, black, wet with rain anyway. He reached down and took them off, and his ragged socks. Better to come to the ocean barefoot anyway, he thought: humble, a supplicant . . . He came over the top of the dunes and there was the Atlantic.

A greater sadness rose up inside him at the sight of the ocean. Kenny surprised himself: it was just wind and water, a gray indefinite sky. But there it was, his sadness; he stopped for a minute at the top of the dunes and let himself feel it, sink into it; reminding himself, at the same time, that he had been warned against depression. Too much crazy sorrow in his family already for Kenny to flirt with it. He heard a crazy preacher on the radio once: *you give the devil a ride,* he said, *he's gonna end up driving.*

She was right where he expected her, walking down the beach. He saw her from a quarter mile off, hundreds of yards, a black scarecrow dissolving into rainy distance.

He started off behind her, tracing her footprints in the sand. She was barefoot, like Kenny. Experimentally he slipped his own foot into the track she left behind in the hard sand but he was bigger, he wiped her out. Her stride was as long as his. A girl my own size, he thought, matching her stride—like the game he used to play with himself, walking down the sidewalk without ever stepping on a crack, the footsteps coming in alien rhythms. Walking to her pace. The sky went dark and then darker, the gray of a rainy afternoon giving way to evening, and still she didn't turn around.

Almost dark when they came near each other, almost cold. A

raw day, Kenny thought. A *cooked* day. He watched her turn, glad for
the distance between them. He didn't want to be accused of lurking,
creeping. A gradual certainty as she came closer that it was Junie
after all, and it was, and then they were within shouting distance.

"It's raining out here," she said. "You're supposed to be back
with the fire."

The wind took the words out of her mouth. Kenny stopped so
he could hear her.

"Why do people keep telling me?"

"What?"

"It's raining," Kenny said. "I mean, water from the sky."

"Am I being stupid?" she asked.

He meant to amuse her; instead he had annoyed her. He said,
"I'm sorry."

"I'm sorry," she said. "I shouldn't be so touchy, I just . . ."

"That's OK," Kenny said. "I think I was being sarcastic."

A sense of futility hung between them, a silence. Then, without
warning, she wheeled around him, where he stood in her path, and
started moving again back toward the camp. She flung herself into
the walking, like she didn't care whether Kenny followed her.

Which she might not. He followed a couple of steps behind her,
waiting for her to tell him to go, tell him to stay. The Atlantic heaved
and buckled on their right, crashing into the shoreline, lacy skirts of
foam. Storm surge, Kenny thought. Something clean about it. The
wind had swept the beach clean of birds, and now it was just the two
of them under the lowering gray sky, not talking. She was wearing a
fancy mountain parka, yellow and black, a little too big for her but
plainly expensive. Under it the black cotton of her dress rippled and
furled around her legs, a flag in the wind. Bare feet, bare legs. Kenny
watched as the wind blew her dress up around her hips, then just as
quickly down again. Quick glimpses of pale skin, white underwear.
She didn't fight it.

She slowed down a minute, to let him catch up. "It isn't you," she said. "It isn't you in particular, I mean. I just like to be alone sometimes."

"I'm sorry," Kenny said.

"I get off on the wrong foot," Junie said. "It's not your fault. I'm antisocial, is all."

Kenny couldn't think of what to say. He was losing her, needed a pill, a magic formula.

"I mean, don't be sorry," she said.

"I can't help it," Kenny said. "It's a what?—a syndrome, I have to apologize about everything whether it's my fault or not. I'm sorry about the weather. I'm sorry about Oliver North, China, the whole works."

Junie's face relented into a grim little smile. "I'll have to be careful around you, then," she said.

"I'm sorry," he said. "You shouldn't have to do that."

He kept himself from smiling, and she searched his face again, and then she smiled unwillingly. He had said the right thing somehow, some accidental miracle. He had not, for once, fucked up. They started walking again, slower this time, together, Kenny stealing glimpses of her face: rain-streaked, her hair matted down. She had been out with her hood down, letting the rain fall on her head, her face. A little self-punishment, he thought, mortification of the flesh.

"I didn't even know it was you," she said. "I left my glasses back at the cabin, because of the rain."

"I remember you wearing glasses."

"It makes your eyes weaker to wear them," she said, fiercely, like Kenny had been arguing against her. "Your eyes just get worse and worse. You need to build them up. I've got these exercises, I do them every morning and every night."

"I'd like to see that," Kenny said. "Eye exercises."

Quickly she looked at his face, to see if he was making fun of her; but he was trying to make her laugh, and she gave in. "I know," she said. "It seems silly, but it works."

"I'm sure it does."

"OK, I don't know whether it works or not," she said. "It's just the idea of your whole life wearing glasses, I don't know—I don't want to just give up, you know? I don't want to be wearing glasses when I'm thirty, when I'm sixty."

"Did you ever think about contact lenses?"

"I tried them," she said. "I gave myself an eye infection. I guess I left them in too long."

They walked along, not talking. Kenny was trying to figure out who was taller, him or Junie. She was trying to figure out something else, thinking about oranges, maybe, or Kim Nichols. He felt dissatisfied when he thought about Kim; the tens of thousands of confidences they had shared in the privacy of their friendship, hundreds of thousands, millions. Or maybe he was making it up. Really, he didn't know anything. The sky and the sea had turned the same color, noncolor, *pallid*. Night was coming down quickly.

"How did you end up here, anyway?" he asked.

"I'm being parked," she said. "My mother and my father are out of town, they thought that I'd be safe here."

Lips pursed in bitterness when she said the word *safe*. "How did they know to send you?" Kenny asked.

"Oh, I used to come to these things sometimes, a couple of years ago, I still get the newsletters. My mother puts them on the refrigerator door. She thinks these outings are a great idea. Little does she know."

"I've never been on one of these before."

"It's just a lot of fucking, a lot of dope smoking. That and a little nature business. Nobody really cares about that."

She sounded so dismissive when she said the word *fucking* that Kenny sank a little inside. His hopes diminishing.

She said, "I used to come on these things with Kim Nichols and we'd be the only ones who ever paid attention to whatever we were supposed to be doing, bird-watching or whatever. I learned to shoot a bow and arrow once, a real hunting bow. Do you know Kim Nichols?"

Kenny didn't want to talk about high school; he felt himself shrinking, but there was no way around it. He said, "I was in an English class with her, with Mr. Harris."

"Dirty Tom," she said. "You know what he does? He drops his pencils so he can look up your dress, right in front of your desk. Like underwear is so exotic and beautiful, I mean, look in the newspaper ads."

Kenny nodded, guilty. He could still imagine the white flash of Junie's own underwear, still touch it in visual memory. Still, he'd rather have that than nothing, even if it was guilty.

"I remember Kim talking about you," Junie said.

"That business with the sheep?"

"What?"

"Joke."

"Oh," Junie said. It wasn't exactly that she was having trouble keeping up but she wasn't used to it, the rough-and-tumble, boy talk. She was *sensitive.* "No," she said, "she thought you were a bright spot."

"A little sunbeam," Kenny said. "I'm glad to hear it. It was right after lunch, I was always pretty stoned."

Right away he was aware that he had said the wrong thing. The light was going, her face fading to gray. A sudden impulse to jump into the Atlantic, clothes and all, see if she'd follow. Returning, a moment's imaginary escape: the dark water closing over his head, kingdoms of oysters, kelp and mackerel . . . Meanwhile he was striking out with her again, and again he couldn't quite tell why.

"I like Kim," he said, hearing in his own ears how lame it sounded.

"A lot of people do," Junie said. "A lot of people don't know her very well."

What the hell, Kenny thought; then saw that it meant nothing, words to fill up the air, nothing more. She was gone again inside herself, her head still bare to the rain. *Penitent,* he thought. They walked side by side, on separate planets, and then Kenny's raincoat sprung a leak. He could feel the first cold trickle down his sleeve.

They were most of the way back when he saw the flashlights, then heard the voices calling her name. "Junie!" they shouted. "Joooooonie!"

She didn't say anything, to them or Kenny. In the fading light he saw she was scared, an animal fright, like she was about to run away from them; like they were hunting her. He loosened his arm at his side, ready to hold her if she ran, but she didn't go. She stopped walking, turned to look at the ocean.

"I'm over here," she called out, and the flashlights came together around her: McHenry, the counselorette, one of the others.

"We were worried about you," McHenry said.

"Don't wander off like that," the counselorette said.

None of them paid the slightest attention to Kenny, shining their flashlights in Junie's face, grinning like Miss America contestants, trying to reassure her.

"You're fine," the third one said. "We're not that far from the camp."

"Then why did you come looking for me?" Junie asked. It was a challenge; she was angry, distant, herself against the Others. Kenny felt himself lumped in with the Others.

"We were worried about you," McHenry said. "It was getting dark."

"I'm fine," Junie said. "I can do just fine by myself. You go on ahead, I'll be back at the camp in a minute."

They all just stood there, Kenny included.

"Go on!" she said; and she was angry with them, all of them;

and they left here there, barefoot, at the edge of the Atlantic. Kenny trudged along in the wake of the counselors; stopped at the top of the dunes and let them go ahead.

He thought of her, blind with water, down in the sand. He looked down into the darkness, trying to see her. The leak in his raincoat spread down his arm, cold water. Junie had a good jacket but she wouldn't put the hood up. He stayed there, hiding himself in a circle of dune grass, a little ways off the path, until he saw her go by, still bareheaded, penitent. *Trouble,* he thought. He waited until he was sure she was inside, then followed her down.

He had the feeling that came to him in dreams sometimes, in which solid objects dissolved—putting his hand into a wall, for instance, or the old favorite of the car crash, unavoidable, with the phantom car that on impact was nothing more than colored air . . . He was on the porch of the main cabin after dinner, rolling a cigarette out of his little pouch of Dutch tobacco and listening to the sound of the wind in the pines, the rain dripping off the eaves of the porch, the shouts and laughter from inside. The air was clean, cold, antiseptic. It tore the smoke from his mouth in rags and streamers. I am not lonely, he thought. I'm alone. Loneliness is in crowds.

Then Junie came out onto the porch. "They're playing *Springsteen* in there," she said.

"What did you expect?"

She shrugged, still wearing her mountain parka, and curled into the Adirondack chair next to Kenny, one leg tucked under; a dancer's movement. Kenny hoped she wasn't. Junie still didn't have her glasses on and he wondered if she knew who he was.

"I'm sorry I got mad at you, down on the beach," she said. "It wasn't you, it's just, I don't know. My *problem.*"

"I don't know anything about your problem," Kenny said.

"That's fine with me," she said. Something about the way she held her lips, as if she might crumple into grief, a sheet of paper crumpled into a ball, thrown away . . . Kenny felt himself vibrating along with her, sympathetically.

"It's cold out here," she said.

"It's better than in there," Kenny said, angling his head toward the door: shouts and laughter, bottles clinking, Tom Petty.

"There's nothing wrong with that," she said. "They're having a perfectly good time."

But she sounded unconvincing, as false as Kenny had sounded to himself with all his beautiful loneliness.

"The food," he said.

Junie grimaced. "OK, the food is awful."

"The music," Kenny said. "The beer competition, who can bring the fanciest imported this or that. The conversation."

"Getting high," she said. "Young Americans getting fucked up."

Kenny took this personally. "What's wrong with that?"

"Don't you get tired of it?"

Well, no, he thought; but this didn't seem to be the time to say so. "It's just a pleasure," he said. "It's just another thing, like decent food or cigarettes."

"Or expensive beer, or sex, or television." Now she put her glasses on, a pair of tiny round wire-rims that made her look like the class Marxist, common scold. "It just seems strange to me," she said. "So much time and money, just to get away from yourself."

"I don't know," Kenny said. He felt himself deflating, thinking about his father. Blue: the feeling that he was born broken, un-repairable.

"I don't mean anything about you in particular," she said.

Kenny tried to think of what he might say, came up with noth-ing, the sound of the rain. At least she had apologized; at least she noticed he was there, but she had put her finger on a place where it hurt. Getting high, getting drunk: sometimes they seemed like completely different things, other times they looked the same. They looked the same to Junie. He felt himself judged.

She said, "I don't know what I'm talking about, anyway. I shouldn't be talking about other people."

"Why not?"

Before she could answer, the door flew open and two boys came tumbling out, wrestling—Kenny couldn't tell at first whether they were playing or fighting, not till they backed away from each other and they were both laughing.

"The Transylvanian toehold!" one of the boys said.

"The flying scissor drop!" shouted the other, and then they fell onto each other again, grunting and shoving, while the others came out onto the porch to watch. Kenny stood to see the fight better, to watch the crowd: the counselor McHenry stood on the stairs with his arms folded, grinning, holding the other boys and girls back. The fighters were streaked with mud now, rolling in the pine straw and straggling bushes. The boys on the porch were clapping, shouting, grinning, while the girls were telling each other how disgusting boys were, how stupid. Kenny thought to look: Junie was folding her glasses, putting them in her pocket. She slipped through the fringe of the crowd and off the porch and into the darkness outside, sideways, graceful.

"Hey, wait," he said, but there was no way for her to hear him above the shouting and clapping. He tried to reach her but the angle was wrong, caught in the crowd, tangled in elbows and legs. She was gone when he got down the steps. Running? Something changed in the sound of the fight: the boys on the porch stopped cheering, one of the fighters called the other one a fucker, loud enough for Kenny to hear. McHenry's voice said, "Hold it, hold it."

Then he saw her outlined against a cabin light, walking away from him. Kenny didn't stop to think but ran after her, didn't want to lose her. Walking away from me, he thought, remembering her dark figure on the beach. Walking away from me. Before he could make anything out of it, he had caught up to her, breathing hard.

"Stupid, stupid, stupid," Junie said.

"That's sort of the point, isn't it?" Kenny said. "I mean, I don't think they were trying to show how intelligent they are."

She didn't slow down for him, didn't look at him after her opening glance at his face. As tall as he was, long-legged. Junie Long-legs.

"More good clean fun," she said bitterly.

"What's the matter with that?" Kenny said; then thought it might be a mistake. He said, "I'm just asking."

"Well, it's stupid."

"So are a lot of things," Kenny said. "I mean, work is stupid, school is stupid, getting along with your parents is stupid, not getting along with your parents is stupid. You go out with somebody, most of the time that's stupid, and then you break up with them and everything's stupid for a while. Either they dropped you, so you wander around with your stupid feelings hanging out all over the place, or you dropped them, so you feel superior, which is really stupid. Somebody puts you down, you feel like shit, being smart doesn't help. You fall off a fence, break your wrist. I mean, it's stupid but it's still happening, right? Do you know what I mean?"

"Kim said you were smart," Junie said.

They walked along. Kenny felt stupid. "Where are you going, anyway?" he asked.

"Just getting away."

"You want to go down to the beach?"

She thought for a minute; again, Kenny felt her judgment on him. Don't mistake me. She didn't want to be a body and he understood that. The life of the body: fighting, fucking, getting drunk. Junie wanted something else.

"I should leave a note at my cabin," she said. "In case they come looking for me again."

He wondered why they were worried about her, but he knew better than to ask. He wanted to keep her near him. Followed her down the path to one of the little toy houses, followed her inside, watched her handwriting, which was long and tall and carefully considered:

I've gone down to the ocean
I'm perfectly all right
June Williamson

Artistic, Kenny thought. A life beyond the body. Then they were back in the dunes, the saw grass rustling in the wind, sound of the waves. Junie was leading, Kenny following. The rain had let up and the clouds were breaking apart in the sky, edged in moonlight. A wind coming off the sea, bone-cold. They left their shoes on, stepping lightly, hoping the sand wouldn't seep in, which it did anyway; down to the hardpack at the edge of the water, and then she sat down in the sand and stared out at the waves. Kenny sat beside her, following her movements—like church, he thought. I kneel, you kneel. But following seemed like the only way he was going to stay with her.

"Next stop, Portugal," he said.

"I've been to Portugal," she said.

"And?"

"It was full of people speaking Portuguese, and gentlemen trying to pinch your butt. My butt, anyway. I don't want to sound like that."

"What?"

"Oh, those girls that go around the world and then come back and tell you how much they hated it. France is all right but it's not good enough for me."

"I've never been anywhere," Kenny said.

"Not even Canada? Mexico?"

"Not even Chicago. I went down to Daytona Beach for spring break once."

"What's the deal with that?"

"Oh, it was stupid. It was this girl I was going out with, she wanted to go, she wanted me to drive down there with her. We got into a fight. I ended up sleeping in the backseat of the car."

"But she looked terrific in a bathing suit," Junie said.

"She did," Kenny said. "As a matter of fact, she did."

"She had gigantic bosoms."

"Not quite gigantic."

"A voluptuous behind. I love that word, *voluptuous*."

Kenny wanted this part of the conversation to end. He said, "Where should I go if I do go somewhere? Pick a spot for me."

"I don't know what you'd like."

"A place that you would go back to, then."

Junie thought for a minute; glanced at him, and then back out at the Atlantic. She was wearing her glasses again, holding her legs in front of her, bent at the knees and circled by her arms. She was leaning forward, like she was looking for something in the waves. Her skirt was restless in the wind. All half-unseen, the faint light of the moon shining through clouds, reflecting. The ocean talking, edge of something.

"All right," she said. "I'm going to send you to Verona. In the summer, they give operas at the old Roman amphitheater in Verona."

"I've never been to an opera, either," Kenny said.

"Me neither, not till then," she said. "It doesn't matter. It's just where everybody goes on a summer night in Verona. And it's beautiful, you know, people have been coming to this same place to hear music for a couple of thousand years. Everybody waits outside like wolves, waiting for the gates to open so they can grab a place to sit. I mean, they leave their kids behind."

"Who were you there with?"

The question bothered her; she woke from her trance, decided to answer. "This was Kim and I," she said. "We were traveling around with her parents, last summer. The grand tour."

His question had somehow wrecked it, and she didn't go on. She unlaced her black boots instead and slipped them off, practical wool socks that she stuffed inside; and then, barefoot, she lifted her skirts and walked out into the water. This was unexpected, and Kenny didn't know what to do: rescue her, join her, stay where he was. The night felt like a small closed room, the edges invisible, but not far away. She waded in past her ankles, up to her knees, letting out a little shivery yip when the wave came in to meet her.

"Jesus," she said. "Cold!"

Then stood there with her back to him, holding her skirt bunched together in her left hand, clutching her jacket, close to her throat, with her right. Looking for something?—or going where he wouldn't follow her. He didn't know. The distance between them. Kenny felt how strange and apart people were from each other, how far he was from Junie, separate planets. He didn't know what she thought, or what she felt. He wouldn't know, until she took some action to show it: start to sing, or wade in deeper, to her waist, to her chin, over her head, Kenny could imagine that. He longed to close the distance. I want to be inside you, he thought. Both ways. The way that men's bodies were closed, his own body. Kenny ended at the skin, no way out; but women's bodies had a hole in them, a place you could enter. It wasn't going to happen, he guessed that much— not this night, not this girl. Which was all right, more or less, he was liking her company so far. Just the longing wouldn't stop, the isolation. He wanted to escape himself. He watched her, turning a little to one side and then the other, the way somebody will move when they are singing to themselves. Her bare legs, the round dark shape of her penitent's head.

She came out of the water, still holding her skirt away from her wet legs, and she sat next to Kenny again except closer than before. This seemed like the time to put his arm around her and he did—

quickly, before he lost his nerve. He put his arm around her waist and felt her tighten under his hand, through the heavy nylon of her parka, like he was going to hurt her.

He waited for her to relax but she didn't seem to. They stared at the ocean, not at each other. He shifted his hand and felt the sharp intake of her breath, felt the tensing.

"Is this all right?" he asked her quietly. "Can I do this?"

"You seem to be," she said; awkward. She didn't move away, didn't move closer. Separate planets. I want to be inside you, Kenny thought, and sent the thought her way, so she would at least know: I want to be inside you, I want to be inside you. Wondering what would happen if he tried to kiss her—wondering which should come first, whether he should kiss her on the lips or on her beautiful neck or not at all—when he felt her start to shiver under his hand.

"Are you all right?" he asked.

"I'm fine," she said quickly. The shivering didn't stop. What did she mean? The wind, though it had died down a little, was still cold and clean. Her wet, bare legs, he thought. But she wasn't cold until he touched her. She shivered.

"You're cold," he said.

She started to deny it but saw that she couldn't.

"We should go back," Kenny said.

"Maybe we should," she said. Apologetic, but already getting to her feet, his hand left to fall to the sand, wherever it fell, careless. Nothing was going to happen here anyway, he reminded himself. But still.

"I, um," Junie said. Composed herself while Kenny got to his feet. "I don't mind, what you were doing. I mean, that's not the reason."

"No," Kenny said.

"I'm not doing anything to hurt your feelings," she said, although he had accused her of nothing.

"Nobody said you were," he said.

"Apparently I can't be trusted with other people's feelings. That's what they tell me."

"Let me tell you about my feelings," Kenny said. They were walking back, and he knew he was losing her, and he didn't know why. Her own internal drama. He didn't know if it was right or not, to talk about his own difficulties, but it was the only way toward her Kenny could see.

He said, "I came home last week, I don't know, Tuesday or Wednesday and my father was home early from work and he was drinking again. I guess he went out to lunch and had a couple and just kept right on going. He was sitting there at the kitchen table and reading the paper. So it's like Hi Dad, Hi Kenny, and I go off to my room because I don't like to be around him when he's drinking, nobody does. He gets to feeling sorry for himself."

Suddenly he didn't feel like telling the rest of the story, which ended with his father pissing in bed and calling Kenny a bastard.

"What?" she asks.

"I don't know," he says. "Various shitty things happen. I'm sorry."

"Let's spend the evening apologizing to each other," said Junie.

"For things we have no control over," said Kenny.

The magic word, apparently: she slipped her hand into his, their fingers laced together and they walked back through the dunes that way. Touching. Leaving the ocean behind them, the wild sea. Kenny saw her again, wading out toward Portugal, holding her skirt in her hand, bare cold legs, and wondered what she meant to do then. He had the sense of calling her back from her home under the sea. Half the year on land and half the year drowned. They left the sea behind and then, dropping down into the pine grove out of the dunes, they left the wind behind, except for the noise of it in the trees. There were electric lights, the smell of the outhouse, the distant sound of laughter, loud talk, Springsteen.

At the door of her cabin, while he was getting ready to let go of

26

her, she turned instead and kissed him: briefly, awkwardly, but still. Smack dab on the kisser. The sudden reality of another body. He felt the damp wool of her sweater with his cheek, coarse nylon of her parka, the *fullness* of her: as tall as he was, breasts pressing through the layers of cloth. Then the awkward, disentangling. She blinked, sleepily, still caught in some dream.

"Well . . . ," she said—the opening to some drab good-bye, so very nice to meet you, what a pleasure, let's do it again. Kenny didn't want to hear it.

"Can I come in?" he asked.

Sparrow startling out of a hedge, birds taking flight: Kenny was sure she would fly away. But no, she opened the door of the little cabin, she held it open wordlessly, she followed him in, and the door slammed shut behind them. A bare bulb racketed to light, casting crazy shadows into the damp corners of the room. "It's cold in here," Kenny said.

"There's a little stove."

"Is there any firewood?"

"I don't," she said. "I mean, I don't want to be always making rules and so on. But I don't want to, not tonight. I mean, I don't want to give you the wrong impression."

"No."

"But it's OK if you stay, if you want to. I mean, I'm not trying to get rid of you, I just don't want to . . ."

Prick-teaser, Kenny thought, the word rising up into his brain like some stinking bubble of swamp gas. He didn't want to be like that, wasn't going to. But still . . . some ugly suspicion, male pride she was messing with. You owe me a fuck. This whole side of himself that he didn't like and didn't make. Inherited from his father, from everywhere, Fred C. Dobbs. De Niro, *Taxi Driver*. Being a man felt like a sickness sometimes.

"I'm sorry," she said. She lit a kerosene lantern, shut the bulb off, and the room went soft, the damp still lingering in the corners.

"You're apologizing again," he said. "I'll build a fire. We can make s'mores."

"We don't have the ingredients."

"Take two Girl Scouts and rub them together," he said; and saw her face go dark again, just for a second, suspicious. There was nothing much that Kenny could do about it. He was feeling his way in the dark, chutes and ladders, unexpected holes in the floor. A little stack of dry wood, out on the porch, and some kindling. A copy of *Details* on the floor next to the stove.

"Can I use this?" Kenny asked her.

"I don't know," Junie said. "It belongs to Cindy."

"Who's Cindy?" Kenny asked—his turn to be suspicious, what if she really was? What if Junie really did fuck other women? But even forming the words in his mind made him feel coarse and ashamed. Knowing it was a sickness didn't keep you from getting it, no more than the common cold.

"She's an idiot," Junie said. "You know, the one with the Police tape?"

"Jesus."

"Well, that's her. She has to dump her stuff in the cabin with me so she can pretend she's not sleeping with McHenry, I don't know why. I mean, nobody's even *looking,* right? Some little fig leaf, I don't know."

"More like a bay leaf," Kenny said, carefully ripping out full-page BETTER SEX ad and crumpling it into a ball; then laying the kindling carefully on top, smaller then larger, then a couple of dry sticks. The fire caught on the first match. He knelt on the wooden floor, watching the paper curl and chatter as it was taken by the flames, the dry twigs burning quickly, the flame mounting. Troubled by a quick memory of the sea, the immense wild thing. From there to this little house, safety, fire and comfort, and he felt for a second that he had stolen her from the sea. The wind in the pines. The smell of kerosene, of age and abandonment and damp. Something, Kenny thought, anything. Be my sister, be my girlfriend and I'll be yours. Anything but the same old boys and girls. She came to him and sat on the wooden floor next to him, cross-legged, and in the apron she made from her dress, tented between her legs, she poured a package of M&M's. Bright green, red and yellow, they shined brightly against the black cotton of her dress. "Vice," she said. "Do you want some?"

She lay facedown, eyes closed, the black dress open to her waist, a little beyond. The smooth curve of her back—a lovely, natural shape, like the spine of a canoe—was broken by the white bra. Kenny's hands tangled in it, working his thumbs down the individual vertebrae, loosening the long muscles of her back.

"I can take that off if you want," she said, without opening her eyes. "If you think that's a good idea."

Kenny considered, or tried to; drowsy in the heat, the tin stove glowing cherry red. "Maybe not," he said. "If we're going to be good."

"Maybe we should stop," she said halfheartedly.

"It doesn't feel good to you?"

"Oh, no," she said. "It feels fine."

"Then I don't mind," he said, and dug his thumbs into the loosening muscles of her shoulders. Her body relaxed under his hands. Silence. He felt himself concentrated in his hands, in the place where it met her skin, nothing else. She shifted under them, breath coming in time to Kenny's rhythm; half-conscious, eyes closed, she let herself go. He made spiders of his hands, drawing then releasing, touching the hollow of her spine, all the way down to where it rose again into her ass. His fingers shifted the white cotton of her underwear out of the way for a moment and she didn't flinch, didn't draw back. She trusted him. She let him. Kenny thought he could do anything with her at that moment and, just to see, he kissed the back of her neck. She didn't stop him, didn't open her eyes. He felt the sharp stubble of her hair under his cheek, closed his eyes, kissed her again. She tasted like nothing, rainwater. He could feel her hips shifting, small movements. Let his hand trail down her back again, down and under the band of her panties, bare skin, and she was responsive, a live thing moving with him. Now, he thought, now or never. Wanting, not quite daring, afraid that he would break the connection between them. At the same time knowing he should try, take it all the way, take it inside. She wanted him to. She wanted him to stop. Before Kenny could decide, the chance was gone.

A trembling started somewhere inside her, the way she had been shivering on the beach, but here it was smaller; a fine tremor that barely reached the surface of her skin. He let his hand trail off her, pulled his body away from hers. She had not opened her eyes, but he saw that she was holding her lower lip between her teeth; she was biting down so hard that it must hurt.

"We should stop," he said.

She didn't say anything, didn't move, but Kenny knew it was over. He stood to put his own shirt on again and found his dick hard in his pants. Of course it had to be. The feeling had been somewhere else: in his hands, the surface of her skin, the look of her bare back in the light of the kerosene lamp. Now his dick was hard as wood. She was light-years away, another planet. Kenny was stuck inside himself again. He tasted old dried sweat in his mouth, and blood.

His father was sober when Kenny got back from the beach. He sat at the kitchen table with coffee and the Sunday paper, looking whipped, contrite. He asked Kenny, "Where the hell did you go off to?"

"I was at the beach," he said, against his will. He didn't owe his father a thing.

"All week?"

"I stayed with Wentworth a couple of nights."

"What did you do that for?" his father asked.

It was a two-faced question: either Kenny told the truth—you were drunk, disgusting—and started a fight, or else he lied, and made it his own fault—did it for fun, adventure. The lie was easier, always. The lie was tactically superior, too: his father would be grateful for letting him off the hook. The Tinkerbell theory: if no one mentioned it, if no one said the words, then nothing was wrong.

But that afternoon the lie stuck in Kenny's throat. Something has happened to me, he thought. "I made it to school all right last week," he said. "I was half an hour late on Wednesday but apart from that I was 100 percent."

"That's good," his father said. "I don't want to talk to Ralph J. Briscoe again. Did they give you homework for the weekend?"

Kenny's mouth was full of the truth, he longed to speak it: I don't know if they gave me homework or not, I wasn't paying attention. I left the house because you were falling-down drunk by noon. Something happened this weekend with a girl. I am the Burning Bush, he thought, I am the Mack Daddy. He looked down at his father from a great height, feeling the secret in his chest, feeling pity for him.

"It's good to see you back OK," he said; then left, before his father understood what he meant. It was about six-thirty or seven, already night outside. He went upstairs into the hallway, into his room, feeling his way in the darkness instead of turning on a light. In his room, Kenny sat in the dark for a minute. I seem to be different, he thought. I seem to be full of surprises—but then he stopped himself, he didn't want to think it into the ground. When the lights came on he would be stuck in his room again, stuck in his life, exactly where he didn't want to be: paperbacks and ashtrays, empty Cokes, the sheets in a wad at the bottom of his bed.

They had lived there six or seven years. Kenny spent his childhood somewhere else, farther out in the suburbs, a house where somebody else lived now. They came here after the divorce, after his mother's first adventure in the hospital. Kenny, his brother, his father. Now his brother was gone, too, given over to the care of another family, who had taken him to Australia two years ago. They had invited Kenny along as well, but he had decided not to go. It was hard to remember why. His brother's room was across the hallway, Kenny could picture it exactly, if he wanted to: the souvenirs and relics of a twelve-year-old: baseball mitt, Cindy Crawford poster. Exactly as he left it, like the room of a dead boy.

He stripped his sour clothes off, still in the dark, and felt his way down the hall in the dark; not real dark, but the deep end of twilight. The difference made a difference to him, why? Something about the shadows, the soft gray light, the exact color of depression. *Give the devil a ride,* he thought. Don't mess. But the temptation was always there, the easy way out. In the bathroom, he started the shower and let it run till it was hot. He was tired, worn-out, dirty, he needed a shave, he hadn't slept long the night before, lying next to Junie, the two mattresses from the camp beds pushed together on the floor. Kenny closed the door on the glass shower stall, letting the water run down over his head in the darkness, eyes closed. He was tired: the inside and the outside of his body, especially his head, felt like different sizes. His inside was too big for his body to contain. Gradually he worked the water to as hot as he could stand it and a little beyond, feeling the sting on the skin of his arms, his neck, his belly. Kenny was still thin, still faintly tan from a summer of lifeguarding. He was *young, attractive.* A woman at the country club had told him. Kenny felt like sex.

He eased the hot water open, another eighth of an inch, another. The steam was thick, the water scalding. He scrubbed his body with yellow soap and a coarse cotton washcloth, scouring himself clean, making himself ready for her. Her breath was like nothing, rainwater, neither foul nor chemical. Her neck. The memory of her skin was still in his fingertips, the feel of the coarse stubble of her head against his cheek as he bent to kiss her. His dick stirred at the memory of her, a feel of luxury and sex, and Kenny almost gave in to it; but that wasn't what he wanted. He shut the hot water off all at once and the cold poured down on him like ocean rain, his body cringing away but Kenny stood to it, saving himself for her. The cold chased the luxurious feeling out. His body was tight, glowing. He turned the light on, reluctantly, and stood in front of the mirror, shaving, trying to imagine Verona: the crowds gathered for the opera in the Roman amphitheater, the old stones and the cats. When the thunderstorm came, they scattered for cover; when it passed, waiting for the sets and lighting to be reset, they passed the time by doing the Wave. So Junie had said, and so he believed.

When he came out of the bathroom, still naked, still in the dark, he saw that the light was on in his bedroom. Kenny went back into the bathroom and grabbed a towel and wrapped it around his waist, like he was ashamed of his own nakedness, which he was not. He was tight, stoic, alive.

His father was sitting on the edge of Kenny's bed, looking infinitely weary. "Look," he said, "I'm sorry, I've got to ask. Are you taking drugs or something?"

He would have laughed, but the memory stopped him: memory of his father's enormous hand, raised back and ready to strike.

"I'm all right," Kenny said, hiding his real face: the blank mask.

"You come into the house," his father said. "I haven't seen you for a week. You don't say a damn thing and what you do say, it doesn't sound like you."

A sense of embarrassment, growing, like she was standing in the room watching the crude movements of his father's mind. He felt himself stripped, the purity slipping away from him, the cleanliness already gone.

"Then you're up here in the dark, I don't know what you're doing," his father said. "So you can see, I've got to ask."

Kenny tried to think of what he might say. His father seemed prepared to wait. He stared up into Kenny's face from his perch at the edge of the bed, and his head was ponderous, his eyes deep and dark-rimmed, injured. He looked like the survivor of some big dangerous experiment; except, Kenny thought, this experiment wasn't over yet.

"I can see you thought you had to ask," Kenny said at last. "I'm fine, though, really."

"I've heard things about this friend of yours, Wentworth, too," his father said.

"I'm sorry," Kenny said. "I'm fine, really, I'm all right but I'm tired and I want to get my clothes on. I just don't want to talk about whatever Ralph Briscoe might have said to you in some conference."

"He's not a complete jerk," his father said. "I know you don't like him, but it seems like he's trying to help you."

The thought of his father and Ralph J. Briscoe, his guidance counselor, teaming up to set Kenny straight was funny at first but scary afterward. Eagles, sharp talons. Blind to themselves. They wanted Kenny to live their way, they wanted victory. Kenny was *prey*.

"I'm just trying to ask you if you're a doper," his father said. "You can get in over your head. I've had my problems, you know that, and your mother even worse. I don't want to see you go through the kind of hell we've both been through."

"Well, thanks," Kenny said. "I'm all right, though. Can I put my clothes on, now?"

His father rose from the bed, and for a moment Kenny was afraid that his father might strike him; the way the hurt place shies away from danger, years later. Kenny broke his arm once, second grade or so, and still went to protect it whenever he was falling. And he had stepped on his father's John Wayne speech.

"I'm trying to help you," his father said angrily. "I'm trying to keep your life from turning to shit. Do you understand that?"

Kenny's voice was softer and softer. "I do," he said, turning his face away. *Now*, he thought, expecting the slap, it wouldn't be the first time. But it didn't come. His father sighed, a long mechanical sound like a train engine. You are the King, Kenny thought. You are the Elvis of depression, center of the known universe. He was small again, and dirty.

When his father left, Kenny put on the last of his clean clothes: tan corduroy jeans, a purple golf shirt with alligator, motley that his mother had bought him in the hope that he would turn out to be a social success after all, a popular student. Laundry time, he thought. His father sent his laundry out but Kenny did his own. He started to sort, white sock/black sock, then slowed down and finally stopped. He stared out the window, listening to the cars go by. It must have started to rain again: the streets were black, the noise of the cars exaggerated by water. He was thinking about his brother: lying in the next bed—they shared a bedroom in the old house—and watching

35

the shadows that the headlights made crawl across the ceiling, whenever a car would pass. Ray was asleep in Sydney, or eating breakfast, Kenny never could keep it straight. It was almost springtime there. If Ray was here, if Kenny was in Australia, they would be fighting about something—a pair of pants, what channel to watch, something, it was hard to remember but Kenny made himself remember. It was easy to get into some kind of daydream where everything would be fine and beautiful between them. And their father would be fine, their mother would return from Baltimore, the sun would shine and the birds would sing . . . Ray was just another boy, just another little dick. Kenny needed to remember this, not to make it worse by pretending it was different.

It was interesting, how much of adult life consisted of pretending. At the country club, for instance, where he worked the summer before, everybody did a lousy job of whatever they were supposed to be doing. The pool manager, for instance, forgot to switch the chlorine and filter kit on the Jacuzzi and two dozen people came down with an ugly skin rash. Kenny himself almost let a baby drown when he was lifeguarding stoned. The grounds crew ran over the sidewalks with the mower blades, leaving white scars in the cement. The Coke from the pool's concession stand was flat. Nobody was fired, nobody was criticized. They all *respected* each other. Everything was fine.

Or the food, which Kenny got to eat at lunch, whenever he had an eight-hour shift and he felt like eating it. A table in the kitchen for the help. The food was cafeteria food, and at first Kenny thought they had some special shitty meals for the help but it turned out, no—they were eating the same as the people in the dining room, the ones who paid American money and lots of it, the ones who told each other over and over again what a fine meal it was. They said this to each other on their way to eat lunch; they said this on their way back to the car, or lying out by the pool, how the kitchen was getting

36

better and better. It was Tinkerbell again, he thought, but it was powerful. Nobody wanted to break the news.

When he was younger, fourteen, fifteen, and just starting to see the adult-world, Kenny thought this was all bullshit. He wanted plain speaking. He wanted honesty. Lately he didn't so much.

When he went to visit his mother in Supported Living, for instance, and the attendant said how much better she looked, Kenny chimed in eagerly, though she looked no better and in fact a little worse than she had in the hospital. There were neatness issues. Nevertheless, he added his little voice and they all sang along together, the song about how everything was fine. Sometimes he was moved by it, this massive substitution of good wishes and hopes instead of the truth.

The part that bothered him . . . there were a couple. Riding his bike through traffic and seeing all the expensive, candy-colored cars, the Lexus in pearl white, like pearls in milk, you could reach your hand down into the finish . . . it just didn't make any sense, the million different boxes with one person each. It seemed like pretending had gone too far then, like we were building a world in the shape of our own pretending, based on nothing. The office towers rising in Bethesda, for instance: what were they there for? Some dream of height, of the future, of progress. The dream, in itself without substance, was now clothed in glass and steel. This felt backward to Kenny.

Also: people pretended not to want what they wanted. Pretending tried to hide the will. That was the secret of adult life, the undisclosed motor of the whole thing. People wanted what they wanted. They did what they could to get it. It wasn't complicated. Kenny knew that was the last step he needed to take before he could be an adult: he had to learn what he wanted, then had to learn to *want* what he wanted. He was too soft, he knew it.

———

Mrs. Connolly said, "What about it? Why do you think this story is told through two different narrators, Nelly Dean and Mr. Lockwood—who is a drip, right? Your basic nonentity."

A surly silence, combined with the sound of dripping October rain, splashing down from the leaf-clogged gutters onto the concrete sidewalk. The smell of bodies, washed and unwashed, Kmart perfume and English Leather.

"This is strange, right?" Mrs. Connolly asked. "I mean, can any of you think of another book that's like this? Can any of you think of a reason why it's told this way?"

Even the front-row butt-kissers were stumped by the question, which hung in the air above their heads; one of the girls halfway back made a gesture, passing her hand above her head with a whooshing sound, that made her idiot friends giggle. We don't know, we don't care, you can't make us, my mom and dad both make more money than you. This must be something she learned in teacher's school, Kenny thought: the way she let the question hang like that. Which was supposed to do what? Kenny didn't care enough to try to figure it all the way out, went back to the contemplation of Mrs. Connolly's nipples, which were not quite visible under the cotton of her blouse. *Implicit*, Kenny thought; and though the jocks and the girls that hated her would say for certain that she wasn't wearing a bra that day, you couldn't really tell, or Kenny couldn't anyway. He was trying to be polite, trying not to stare openly, make her any more nervous than she already was. Plus she was so small and small-breasted (her lithe little body, monkeylike) that it didn't matter what she wore beneath; it was just the thought of her bare breasts against the cloth of the shirt—some kind of cotton or linen, a slightly rough weave—the thought of the soft skin of her nipples rubbing on the coarse weave of the blouse, gently hardening, a little irritated (nothing Kenny couldn't kiss away), this was the thought he kept circling back to, until he looked up, to see if it was safe to stare at her, and found her looking straight at him.

"Kenny?" she asked.

He froze; he didn't want to make things worse. *Please don't:* he sent the thought her way but she kept bearing down. Maybe she had caught him staring, stealing her body, maybe she thought he had the answer. A quick flush of shame crossed his face, a hot, angry knowledge.

"Kenny?" she asked again.

"I didn't read it," Kenny said, in a soft surfer's monotone. He wasn't stoned but he sounded stoned. A quick burst of laughter followed what he said, and eyes meeting eyes around the room: did you hear that? Did you hear that?

"Why not?" asked Mrs. Connolly.

Because I've got better things to do, he thought, embarrassment flowering into anger, at her, himself, anyone handy—and then out of his anger, he said it: "Because I've got better things to do."

A wave of nervous giggles, poopoo-caca laughter. Kenny's anger spent itself, as soon as it was released. Mrs. Connolly looked puzzled, lost. She had not expected Kenny to let her down. She was what?—ten years older than Kenny maybe, twenty-seven or so, and in her confusion she was the same age. I'm sorry, he thought, and almost said it; but it was too late. He could feel the waves of anxiety and anger rippling around the classroom, *get him, get the slacker* from the butt-kissers up front, *you can't make me* from the jocks by the window, *I didn't read it either* rising out of the sleepy untroubled middle, wondering what this fight was about. A sudden eruption of real feeling, against the rules.

"I don't know," Mrs. Connolly said. "Maybe you should be doing those better things."

Kenny shrugged, caught, sheepish.

"Meanwhile," she said, "why don't you wait out in the hallway? You're not going to do anyone any good sitting here, not if you haven't read the book. OK?"

She was angry with *him,* Kenny realized—him in particular, for no reason he knew about. And this baby punishment, sit-out-in-the-hall, this was meant for him alone; and Mrs. Connolly was momentarily visible, human and mysterious, before the eyes of the class got through to him and he realized they were watching.

"Sure," Kenny said, and gathered his things, and went out into the hallway; and both of them knew, as they passed each other, that this wasn't what they were talking about, this wasn't what either of them meant. Events, they couldn't be unmade. Put the toothpaste back in the tube. Mrs. Connolly looked at him finally as the door closed: I'm sorry.

And then he was spread out with his ratty raincoat and his gasmask bag on the floor of the hallway, legal unless he moved, and Kenny wished for a cigarette.

And then, out of the two thousand one hundred boys and girls in this high school, it was Junie.

"Shit," Kenny said to himself, and sat there stymied, trying to wish himself invisible.

"What are you doing here?" she asked. Black dress, a giant red imitation ruby (or stolen from Mom?) dripping at her throat, black Chuck Taylor All Stars, high-tops. Oh, you, he thought. What are we doing here? I don't go to high school, I don't have parents, I came from the sea to be your husband.

"I'm being punished," he said, "for failing to read *Wuthering Heights.*"

"You didn't like it?"

"I just didn't read it," he said. "I don't know."

"You'd like the book," she said, and Kenny felt himself shrinking. He flipped the cover around of a book he was holding, casually he hoped, so that she could read the title: *On the Road.* I am not an ignoroid, he thought, and beamed the thought in her direction—I am a person like you, just a little smaller here.

"Yourself?" he asked. "Shouldn't you be studying something, somewhere?"

Her turn to avert her eyes. Next: Blushing and Stammering. "I'm off to be counseled," Junie said. "I'm being shrunk."

"By who?"

"Some idiot," she said. "It's automatic—you do a certain thing and they have to send you to counseling for so long, you know, punch the clock. It's punishment, but they don't call it that."

She was being bright, cheerful as she could, but she was unhappy. A certain thing, she said.

"They made me see a counselor for a while," Kenny said. "It was bad."

"For what?"

Oh shit, Kenny thought, don't make me say it. "It was a drug thing."

Junie frowned. "What?"

"It was nothing real," he said. "It was just, they asked everybody who came in for advising who they thought smoked dope and so on. And, well, I guess my name came up pretty often. They called my dad in and so on."

"He was pleased."

"Actually he was drunk," Kenny said, measuring out the words, watching her reaction. Pity was poison. But he hadn't felt it from her, not so far. "He was having a bad week himself. He has never quite forgotten, though. To have a son voted Most Likely to Smoke Dope by his whole class, well."

"A proud parental moment," Junie said—but she was still standing, staring down at him, calculating his worth. A suburban girl, out for a little adventure with the class loser. A *little* adventure. Maybe not; he wanted to think better of her; but it made him angry, if she was interested in him because he was broken himself. Suburban girls were easy that way, they wanted anything but what they already had (safety, money, good clothes, an uneventful life), which made them sitting ducks for a boy like Kenny. The usual transactions involving Camaros, tattoos, bad

41

dope. He felt himself losing the frequency, called himself back: so far she was innocent.

"I'm going to be late," she said.

"I want to see you," Kenny said. "When can I see you?"

The words surprised her, as Kenny had surprised himself.

"You can come over," she said. "People seem to."

"What does that mean?"

"Only my mother. You'll see. She has a somewhat more active social life than I do, at least with the high school crowd." Her mouth screwed down around the words, a secret core of bitterness.

"She likes your friends better than hers?" Kenny asked.

"I don't have any friends," she said, still twisted. "I have my *problem*." Then, at the last minute, when he had nearly given her up, she raised the back of her hand to her forehead, stared into the distance and sighed. She said, "Poor me!"

"You look OK from here," Kenny said.

Phantom: she dropped her hand, quickly, secretly (PDAs were against the rules, ugly besides, passionate freshmen and pimply Christians behind the fountain), and touched his upstretched hand, left the memory of her own fingers on the tips of his as she left, tall, somewhere between awkward and graceful, both of them mixed together, he thought. Everything all mixed up.

Walking down the lines of lockers, the students streaming from class to class or rushing for the bathrooms, gossiping in the stairwells, every kind of human smell of bodies awoken too early in the morning and stuffed together, too many in a small space: the bodies washed and unwashed, coffee breath, cigarette smoke clinging to jackets, the sour smell of wet paper, dust, cafeteria cooking (taco meat for taco salad), Old Spice and English Leather, Kenny could close his eyes and maneuver his way by smell alone: the formaldehyde stench of the biology lab, burnt coffee from the teacher's lounge, past the shit-house stink of the boy's room, down the stairwell under the portrait of Horace Greeley and under the one window that was always mysteriously open, a sweet smell of outside, escape, a kind of torment to Kenny always when he passed under it and remembered there was a world outside, people were making money and making lives and making love and just driving around going places while he was stuck in high school . . . but the thing was, *here* they stepped aside for him, they saw him coming and edged out of the way so that he moved through the slipstream easily, as if the others were only pretend, phantoms of the imagination, extras, they moved aside for him because they felt the pressure of his little magnetic field of trouble, his father's trouble, his own, this morning's fresh trouble with Mrs. Connolly, this was the only weight he had in all the world, the only power or force; and he only had it *here*, between these pale green walls, the last place he ever wanted to be . . .

Junie's house was a long low ship of wood and stone, set back among trees and shrubs and stone Chinese lanterns, a little mechanical brook that ran through the yard, pools of koi. Kenny saw it for the first time on a slate October afternoon, four o'clock, after school. A suburban fairyland, where all the trees had been left standing, the houses trying to blend into the natural landscape. Not my house, Kenny thought, driving up in his father's Reliant station wagon. Driving that car was like wearing your underwear on the outside of your clothes, but it was too cold to ride his bike, threatening to snow or sleet, indefinite mid-Atlantic gray. He left the Reliant parked in the street, but it was past autumn, the leaves had fallen, the bushes would not conceal it from the house, a faded, dirty maroon. Bruise. He left his schoolbooks on the seat, too. Too much evidence, the incredible shrinking man, boy, schoolboy. He was nervous.

Now he stood at the front door, rang the bell, nothing happened. This was a fool's errand. Junie's car sat in the driveway, a red

Accord. Girls who drove shiny, damageless Accords did not have time for boys who drove Reliants. Girls who lived in shipwrecked houses.

He rang again, and this time there were footsteps. A young man answered, tall, slender, with long elegant hands. "You're looking for June," he said.

Kenny couldn't answer at first: he thought he was seeing Junie, couldn't quite tell what he was seeing. The young man—it had to be her brother—wore a white dress shirt, black slacks, black shoes. His dark hair was short on the sides and back, long on top and drooping down over his left eye; a dandy in the English style, pale, slightly sinister. He was a year or two older than Kenny, older than his sister. A fag, Kenny thought—instinctive high school fear—then corrected himself: gay, maybe not even that. Kenny wanted to sympathize with any difference, anything but the big bland weight of the world, but this boy didn't want his sympathy. He didn't approve of Kenny, maybe of anything.

"She's down in the sewing room," the brother said. "You know where it is?"

"I've never been here before," Kenny said.

"You're looking for June?" the brother asked again, and Kenny nodded. The brother angled his head toward a corner of the hallway. "Well, the stairs are over there," he said. "You can't miss it, once you're down there. If you end up in the garage, turn around."

He nodded, having done his job, and walked away down a dark corridor that ran along the spine of the house. Kenny was alone in the flagstone hallway, a glimpse of the kitchen to his right. The house of homosexuals, he thought, with a little glimmer of fear (but fear was where the live thing was, he knew it, he wanted to walk right into it). The living room ahead was sunk down a couple of steps and dominated by a wall of gray fieldstone, a fireplace cut into a square in the middle of it. Everywhere were long windows framed in dark wood,

and through them a series of views of the garden. Even th[r]
bare branches of late fall, there were no other houses to b[e]
cars, no swing sets. The house seemed to exist to bring t[he]
world inside, to welcome it, everything long and low and graceful.
Like walking inside a piece of classical music, Kenny thought. *Beautiful*. He wasn't sure if he liked it or not but he owed this house the
word: beautiful. Lovely in its bones. He felt the contrast.

Beautiful and frightening—any trouble that Junie had, it started
here, he could feel it. Why? A faint bitter smell, maybe nothing more
than kitchen cleaner. Mr. Clean, Formula 409.

He wore his black high-tops, black jeans, a red plaid shirt unbuttoned over a t-shirt. He felt like he had wandered into a concert,
an art gallery by mistake.

Downstairs, then, before he lost his nerve. Mexican statuary on
shelves cut into the wall, obviously expensive, there to be touched,
handled, dropped. A goddess giving birth to something, hard to tell
what, squirting it out like a watermelon seed from big coarse vaginal
lips. Something to look at every day. Another hallway downstairs, lit
by an overhead window shining through plants; a dim, underwater
place, shifting light. The doors were all closed. Kenny tried them,
one by one, until he found himself in the garage. Then he knocked on
the opposite door.

"We're busy, Kyle," a woman's voice said. "We're talking.
What is it?"

"It's me," Kenny said. "It's, uh, Kenny Kolodny."

"Oh, Christ," the mother's voice said—it had to be her mother.
She said, "Come in, I'm sorry," and then, as he came into the room
and saw three faces looking back at him, "We were having a little
conference."

The room was dim, felt like it had been carved out of solid
granite with the dark wood shelves and drawers fitted in around the
living rock. That same underwater light, and it took Kenny a mo-

ment to sort out the faces: Junie, looking angry next to the window; her mother, unmistakable in the family resemblance but a little harder, a little sharper than Junie; finally a surprise, Jinx Logan from his high school, who was famous that year for getting pregnant and deciding to carry the child. They all looked caught, embarrassed, and in Junie's case angry besides.

"This is Kenny," Junie said, "a Liberal Religious Youth. I met him at the beach."

She said it like she was throwing him at her mother, trying to catch her off guard; and the mother cast a quick sharp glance at Junie before she turned to him and nodded her head. "It's good to meet you," she said. "I'm glad to meet Junie's friends."

She made no move to shake his hand, to acknowledge him at all except for a quick inspection. She was younger than he expected, still pretty in a hard way. The glasses she wore made her look quite severe, no makeup, and her clothes were natural and plain in the way that the house was. Something pursed about her mouth, drawn up. If you were my age, he thought. Beautiful/unattractive. The element of sex had been lost, which wasn't always a thing you could tell about other people's parents but Kenny could tell with her. Kind, probably, and pretty in pictures; but not sexy.

"I really like your house," he said.

"Oh," the mother said; flustered, like nobody had ever told her before. "We like it, I suppose. It fits us."

Junie looked at her, angry again. "Why don't you just get it over with and tell him?" she asked her mother, then turned to Kenny: "This is a Frank Lloyd Wright house, you know who he is?"

"Sure."

"It's not one of the famous ones but he designed it. The other thing is, it's a fake."

She kept her eyes away from her mother, who was the obvious target. So far Kenny's sympathies were all with Mom. So far Junie was acting badly.

"It was never sold as a Wright house," the mother said. "I don't know if *fake* is the right word."

June explained to Kenny: "I was looking through a book about him in the library downtown and I came across plans for the house, and then a picture, which was very weird—I mean, the furniture was all different, the stuff outside the windows. It was a picture of the living room."

"Did you see the living room on your way in?" the mother asked.

Kenny shrugged, sure.

"It's a very nice room, I think. But it's meant to be photographed as much as, maybe more than, it's to be lived in. There are a lot of inconvenient touches."

Some kind of competition, Kenny thought, with himself as the audience; though he had the feeling that any audience would do. He was *fungible*. Neither of them was looking at the other, neither of them was exactly looking at him. That faint bitter smell. The thing that felt odd to Kenny was that there was no attempt to smooth things over, keep the ball rolling. They both seemed to be itemizing some long internal list of disappointments, one by one. Jinx Logan, six or seven months pregnant by now, sat forgotten by the window, staring over the transom at the bare leaves outside, the gray sky. She had that inward look, like she was listening to Mars on her dental work. He hadn't seen her for a while at school, not that he was usually paying all that much attention. He wasn't stoned today, though.

"Kenny," Junie finally said, "come on. I want to show you my pictures."

"Thanks. It's good to meet you, Mrs. Williamson."

Junie started to laugh.

"What?" Kenny asked.

"Mrs. Williamson," Junie said. "Everybody calls her Jane. I haven't heard anyone call her Mrs. Williamson for a long time."

Jane Mrs. Williamson—as Kenny now thought of her—rose to the bait. "There's nothing wrong *in itself* with trying to be polite to others," she said. "There's nothing necessarily false about it."

"I didn't say there was," Junie said. "It's just that nobody calls you Mrs. Williamson."

"They call me *Doctor* Williamson at work. That doesn't seem to bother anyone."

"Why are you so worried about it?" Junie asked, and left before her mother could reply, pulling Kenny along in the eddy behind her. He was actively wishing he hadn't come. As naked as he felt himself with his shabby car and schoolbooks, he wasn't prepared for the family drama of Junie and her mother. Why couldn't they just keep it quiet? Her mother seemed like a perfectly reasonable person, Kenny thought. And the worst part, to him, was how schoolgirl Junie's bad acting seemed, how eighth-grade. He thought he had found a mystery at the Girl Scout camp, half-girl, half-woman, as tall as he was. Now he wondered if he had just gotten in the way of a bad mood. Incredible Shrinking Junie.

Out of place as ever and maybe worse, in his cheap clothes, he followed her up the stairs and past the Mayan goddess; stuck halfway through the birth, condemned to the most painful part forever. Or maybe past the pain, simply out of it. Kenny thought longingly of the joint in his backpack in the backseat of the car.

"I'm sorry," Junie said. "More family shit."

"If you figure out a way around it, let me know."

"The thing is, you liked her, right? Everybody likes her. I like her myself. I'm the only person in the whole world that can't get along with her."

They were in the front hallway, but she spoke like they were in private, like there was no chance of being overheard. He thought of the brother, the mother, the pregnant friend; though he had never known Junie to be a special friend of Jinx's. Really, he didn't know anything.

"I just feel stuck sometimes," she said. "Most of the time. You know, when you're doing something and you want to stop and you can't seem to?"

"No, I know," he said.

"You just want to break things," she said. "Let me know when I start apologizing again, unless you think I ought to."

"I'm sorry I don't have the magic words," he said. "You know, the words where you just say them and everything's all right again. I keep trying to find them, you know, with my father. I always end up saying the wrong thing, too."

"It's just embarrassing. Do you want anything? A glass of juice, coffee, beer, a glass of wine?"

"What are you having?"

"Chamomile tea."

"I'll try that," Kenny said; though he would rather have had a beer, by a mile. He had a feeling there were tests he had to pass: purity, cleanliness, single-heartedness, devotion. Was he making this up? He sat at the kitchen table—teak, slate, granite—and looked out at the bare winter bones of the garden, while Junie fussed around with the kettle, the teapot.

"She's a doctor?" Kenny asked.

"A pediatrician," Junie said. "Injuries and diseases of children. She only works half-time these days."

"What does your father do?"

She tensed again. If there weren't magic words to make things better, there were certainly ones that made things worse: *Mom. Dad. Happy family.* Incantations for the nervous life.

"He's a lawyer," Junie said. "He was last time I saw him, anyway."

"He doesn't live with you?"

"No, I mean, he does," she said. "We just don't see him all that often. He shows up, tells us all what to do, then he goes away again. I'm sorry."

"What?"

"Well, bitch bitch bitch. I mean, I have a family, you have a family, right?"

"More or less," Kenny said.

Kenny looked up from the photographs scattered on the table in Junie's room, and saw the first wet flakes of snow falling. They came down slowly, fat as parachutes, and melted in the black street. "I might have to go pretty soon," he said. "I don't want to get stuck in this."

"Whatever you think," she said. She wasn't going to try to get him to stay; wasn't even going to ask him. Not quite indifference; a matter of pride. Whatever she wanted was hidden down in the layers of camouflage.

"I just need to keep an eye on it," he said.

"Even if it starts to stick on the street in here, the avenue stays clear. You can always get back in and out of town, once you get to the avenue."

Kenny thought of the short, steep downhill onto the avenue at the entrance to her subdivision, and flinched: no picnic on four bald tires. Then realized that this was an invitation to stay. Be cool, he told himself. He sipped his chamomile tea, leaned over the table again. She shuffled through the pack of photographs, fortune-telling. Junie kept them in the bright yellow Kodak envelopes that the unexposed paper had come in. The prints came out with wavy edges, an uneven, handmade feel. They were chalky, sooty, grainy, out of focus; Kenny didn't know a thing about photography but he knew that most of them were no good. Once in a while, often enough to keep his hopes going, there was a good one. He wanted her to be good at this. He wanted her to be brilliant.

"This was when I was screwing around with this stupid gold

toner," Junie said. "You use real gold in the process, you know, I thought it sounded exciting. But everything just comes out brown."

The photographs were brown the way that shoes were brown: the trunk of a tree, rocks and shadows, a creek in winter where every stone wore a cap of snow like a nightcap. Serious, somber. The temple of Nature. Kenny wasn't in the mood. Kenny wanted rock and roll of some kind, motorcycles, Mexican prostitutes, something. Looking at these pictures was too much like being in church.

Also there was a body interference problem, a difficulty seeing through her aura. Ginsberg said it: what peaches and what penumbras! She was bent at her desk, looking over her own work, a little too self-absorbed. Wearing her glasses, serious. Kenny leaned on the back of her chair and watched over her shoulder, watching the photographs, the back of her head, her neck . . . This time it was her ears, too, which were delicate and pink. Something about the way the gold temple-pieces of her glasses wrapped around—she wore the kind that circled her ears, little restraint devices . . . It was hard to take the photographs seriously when he could look at the line of her back, bare naked ears, her shoulders. He forced his attention onto the pictures, hoping that each new one would be perfect.

They couldn't hold his attention, though. The pictures seemed to be *attention-resistant*. Bare branches, the sea in winter.

Junie's room was spare, monkish, the same totalitarian good taste as the rest of the house: burlap wallcoverings, teak furniture, picturesque windows, that faint Japanesy feel. No Barbie dolls, here, no Poky Little Ponies. He saw her for a moment as her mother's child: piano lessons, ballet, spinach. The room had a desk the size of a kitchen table, upon which the pictures were now spread out; a single celibate bed; a bookcase, which Kenny promptly judged by his own hard standards. *My Ántonia*, good. *Life on the Mississippi*, very good. *Slaughterhouse-Five*, eek! *The Trial*, very good, but only if she actually read it. In fact the whole shelf had the smell of schoolbooks.

Advanced-Placement English classes, either that or books her mother left on the shelf because she thought they matched the decor. Kenny would bet a hundred dollars that Junie never read *Red Cavalry,* by Isaac Babel. (He was wrong about this, as he was wrong about her photography, as he was wrong about everything else, almost. This is one of the places where it's still sore, looking back. He *underestimated* her.)

The interesting thing was, she kept shuffling unopened boxes of pictures back into the drawers. "Come on," he said. "What's in there?"

"Nothing," she said, a faint rosy flush creeping up her neck. She wouldn't look at him.

"It says Nudes right there on the box."

"Well, it's not exactly . . ."

"You can't just sneak them past me, Junie. I'm tired of rocks and trees."

"You don't like my rocks and trees?" Even this she said without looking up from the table; and he couldn't tell if she was angry or not.

"I didn't say that. I just meant, I don't know. I wouldn't mind some naked ladies."

Junie laughed, and for a minute it seemed to be all right. "These aren't exactly naked ladies," she said. "I bet my father's got a copy of *Playboy* somewhere, if that's what you're after."

"I bet he doesn't," Kenny said; remembering, with some murky, left-handed shame, that his own father had an almost complete collection dating back to 1965. His father in a velvet jacket, smoking a pipe. His father and bunnies. It was hard to imagine Hefner having a place in Junie's house. Jane wouldn't allow it.

"Maybe not," she said, and took a breath, gathered her nerves, spilled the packet of nudes out onto the table.

The ones on top were in the same brown-light and natural-shape mode as before, scarcely recognizable as human, closer to green peppers, tomatoes, folded pieces of cloth. After a couple of minutes, three or four prints, Kenny saw that the subject was a fat woman, bending, turning, reaching. The folds of her body shone in a kind of dim twilight. You couldn't tell, exactly, what was her ass and what was her knee, and which of these curves might be her breast. Kenny felt like a minor dog for trying, but on the other hand . . . They were safe, hygienic. All the sex had been boiled out of them; at least till Kenny thought to wonder who the model was. He never thought Kim Nichols was quite that fat but maybe, with all the bending and twisting, etc. . . .

"Where did you take these?" he asked her.

"These? Oh, this was in the class I took last spring, Lee Nye. He's a crazy man. He had the model come in and we all took pictures, she was sort of draped up there on this stand."

"That must be a strange feeling."

"I don't know," she said, shuffling to the next. "She was an old friend of Lee's, it must have been the hundredth time she'd done it. Really she was beautiful, just big."

"You never see her face?"

"That was one of the rules—no faces." She laughed, a little nervous. "I don't know if it was a jealous husband or what. Maybe it's just, you wouldn't want to walk into a coffee shop and see yourself buck naked on the wall."

"Buck Naked," Kenny said. "Sounds like a bass player in a punk band. Maybe I'll change my name."

"One of the things my mother says," Junie said, shuffling over to another sex-proof green pepper. "She started out in Wyoming, riding horses and everything. She says *crick* instead of *creek*. If she could go out every morning and chop her firewood with a hatchet, she'd be happier."

"Right," Kenny said.

53

"I'm not kidding," she said, leafing forward. "She's just not urban. I mean, she's not anything—she left Wyoming behind a long time ago, too. She talks about it. Oh, shit."

"What was that?"

"Nothing," she said.

"Let me see," Kenny said. A picture had come out of the pile but it was different; just a glance, a glimpse before she shuffled it back into the pile. What? The shape of a long, tall body, it had to be Junie. Something with the face, and a dark tangle of hair. "What was that?"

"I don't know," she said. "An experiment."

"Let me see," Kenny said.

A standoff. She wouldn't look at him. He saw the flush across her cheeks, the pink coloring her white lifeless skin. Restored to life, he thought. She turned and inspected his face, and when she spoke she was apologizing, pleading. "I didn't know these were in here," she said. "I didn't, I don't know. I didn't make these for other people."

"I can keep a secret," Kenny said. As he had been wanting to, he put his hand on her shoulder. She flinched away, then came to a tentative rest; a truce; OK for now, I guess, I suppose. She was wearing a black blouse of t-shirt material that was cut low in a kind of scoop, off her shoulders and across her chest, so that his hand rested half on cloth, half on skin. The architecture of bones and tendons at the base of her neck, a little hollow, shelter. You be whatever you turn out to be, he thought. I'll just fixate on your body.

"I'd rather not," she said.

"I'd like to see."

She turned toward his face, resentful now: she didn't want to show him, didn't have the will to refuse him. Turned her face away, and turned up the next picture, the next, the next, fanning them out like a fortune-teller's deck.

The pictures had all been taken at the same time, the same

place, a room with bare white walls and dark carpet. In the background, on the right, was a hallway that led to a bathroom, or so he guessed—it was dark and hard to see. In the left side of the picture stood Junie, naked. Naked as opposed to nude; nobody would look at these pictures and mistake them for art, he thought. No green peppers here. The strange thing about the face, the thing he had glimpsed in passing, turned out to be a sleeper's eyeshade, the kind you find in drugstores; a black, blind version of the Lone Ranger's mask, tied on with black strings that dangled. The light was hard black-and-white. Her hair was longer, shoulder-length as he remembered it, with too-short little-girl bangs. His eyes kept going back to the mask on her face, that and the tangle of her pubic hair, which was black and very thick. It spread in tendrils up her belly, down her thighs, unsuspected by Kenny. It was almost masculine, it had weight and presence. Kenny couldn't keep his eyes away, that and the mask, balancing off against each other. There was a black cord snaking out from under her foot. "What's that?" he asked.

"That's how I took these," she said. "It's this kind of bulb thing that you squeeze and the air trips the shutter, very rinky-dink but it works. I did it with my foot."

In a rush, nervous. Kenny saw why. In one picture, she stood like Venus on the half shell; in another, like a soldier, legs apart; in one that she quickly shuffled back into the pile, not quite before he could see it, she sat back on her haunches like a Vietnamese woman, two white calves and her vagina clearly visible between them, her head resting sideways across the tops of her knees like she was resting. No two of them felt alike, although the lighting, the room, the body were all the same. Different small feelings: secrets, some of them not polite. No mistaking these for art. Kenny didn't have any problem paying attention to these. Part of it was seeing her naked but there was another excitement besides: she was telling things she shouldn't say. Something she was working out, alone. These photographs were *evidence*. Also the grainy black-and-white, the mask, the surprising dark mass of hair—all reminded him of his first dirty pictures, a deck of pornographic playing cards, found in his father's bedside drawer. Dirty black-and-white; a world unknown, suspected but unplumbed. As she was. "What's the deal with the mask?" he asked.

"I don't know," she said. She wouldn't look at him. "I wanted to see what I looked like, I guess. I couldn't do it with my eyes open."

"I don't get it."

"It was just something I did one day," she said. "I shouldn't have showed them to you, I didn't mean them for anyone . . ."

"No," he said. "I mean, thank you. Thank you for showing these to me, it's like you trust me. I'm just trying to think of what to say."

And it felt like one of those moments—grace, the Holy Spirit—when something told him the right thing to say, and he said it, and it worked. Her shoulders relaxed under his hand and, still not turning her head, not looking up at him, she reached her own hand behind and touched his wrist, a soft, affectionate caress; like they had been married, for years and years. Wet snowflakes batted against the glass, like moths, a tiny sound.

"You don't have to say anything about them," she said. "You don't even have to think anything about them, that's the thing about pictures. They just exist. The eye sees them, that's it."

Kenny was instantly suspicious but now was not the time to start a war. He said, "I don't know why but I like these better than the others."

"There is a naked girl in these," Junie said.

Kenny decided to quit while he was ahead; there was peace between them, restfulness.

"Can I put these away now?" she asked.

"Sure."

And she didn't look at him again until the pictures were safely back in their envelopes, the envelopes stacked together in a file drawer under the desk, and the drawer closed. The room seemed dull without them; too brown, too natural. Junie was black-and-white, the thing that stood out. She sat on the bed, and Kenny sat next to her. He put his arm around her waist and she tried to put her arm around his shoulders but they got crossed up and banged their elbows together. "Ow!" Junie said.

"What are we supposed to be doing?" Kenny asked.

"What do you mean? What does my mother think we're doing?"

"Whatever," Kenny said.

"She doesn't care. She's downstairs doing good with Jinx Logan. That's her hobby, or maybe her vice—doing good. She just can't help herself."

The bitterness made her seem like a child, unattractive; but there was something else, a restlessness that Kenny recognized. What? He couldn't name it, couldn't pin it down. There had to be more, that was all; there had to be more than this. He closed his eyes and saw gardens, topiary shrubs, statues standing in pools of water; he saw a park, springtime, felt the sunshine on his shoulders and his neck. This was his future, the thing he was walking toward, every day another slow step. Will you walk beside me? Kenny thought; then saw her in grainy black-and-white, the pubic tangle. Will you let me inside?

Reached to kiss her, and Junie let him, and no more.

Kenny was opposed to the idea of the future: he was trying for Zen, where everything is the same, the past, the future, good luck and bad. He wanted to get off the wheel, samsara. Birth, suffering, death, rebirth. He didn't do much of anything to get himself off the wheel, but he thought about it.

At the same time, he knew that he was going to be somewhere for the rest of his life, however long that took, whatever ended up happening to him. Sunday in the park, with the sun on his shoulders. It was something to hope for, anyway. Other times he saw his father's face, the dark hollows around his eyes, like an electrical appliance had been socketed in his eyes and then unplugged abruptly, leaving scorch marks. Even when his father laughed, his eyes didn't. His father had found a way from his own childhood to his present location; Kenny had seen evidence, pictures of his father as a young man, grinning, with an oar in his hand. Kenny could find his own way. The easy certainties of the children in his class—school then college then work then marriage—felt silly to him but they appeared to work: it was Tinkerbell again, the children holding hands, singing together. Successful, interchangeable. *You have to believe . . .*

Kenny had a plan, a dream, a fantasy, something. It came to him one night, stoned: he would write a history of the future. Or maybe an archaeology, depending. When did the future start? Who first thought of it? What were the important events in the development of the future? He thought of the Trylon and Perisphere, the Apollo program. Rounded Packards, Hudson Hornets racing into the future. All that seemed to be over now. We were back on the wheel, samsara: birth, suffering, death, rebirth. The future was *dynamic*, the future was *nuclear*—they were going to get to escape velocity, escape the orbit of the wheel, blast off. In the future they were going to vacation on the moon. They were going to banish disease, they were going to banish suffering. Samsara was to be eradicated. They were going to be directional.

These suburban streets whirled and curved and dead-ended, intentionally; they were meant to keep outsiders from finding any use in them, to keep commerce away, to preserve the common peace. Boy lived in a house like the others. The neighborhood association prevented them from fencing their front yards, painting their houses certain colors, parking their cars on the street—they were to be inside, with the garage doors shut, a fantasy of order. Boy himself had been forced to sell a perfectly good Jeep when it wouldn't fit in the same garage with his father's Thunderbird and his mother's Crown Victoria. He was a year ahead of Kenny, out of high school but still living at home.

Seven at night, dark, a biting wind. Kenny parked the Reliant on the street, feeling like the neighbors were watching him from behind their closed shades—which they probably were, he thought, nothing to stop them. Boy had his own entrance, his own floor all to himself, down in the basement. Kenny let himself out of the cold and into the thick, jungle smell of Boy's house. "Hey," he yelled down the stairs.

"Hey," the parrot yelled back. "Hey mama!"

"Come on down," Boy said. "Leave the light off."

Boy was stretched out on the sofa, the room bathed in red light, barely visible. "Going on?" he said.

"Not much."

"I hear you're screwing a lesbian," Boy said. "Nice work. They said it couldn't be done."

Kenny stopped, exposed, embarrassed. I haven't screwed her, he thought; then realized that not screwing her was worse. He didn't mean to be out in the daylight with her, Kenny and Junie, didn't mean to be public property. Now here he was in the spotlight of Boy's attention. Boy was just trying to be a dick, same as always, but Kenny was ashamed anyway; like she was Kenny's dirty little secret, a side he didn't want the world to know about.

"Don't believe everything you read in the funny papers," Kenny said, just for something to say. It sounded stupid, even to him.

"Well, are you or aren't you?" Boy asked. "I mean, this is history in the making. I mean, not just any garden-variety lesbian but Junie Williamson, the famous one."

"I'll leave you to guess," Kenny said, stripping off his jacket, his sweater, his flannel shirt. It was maybe eighty-five in the basement, maybe ninety, and it smelled like Boy's basement and nothing else: the damp, rotting-leaf smell of a garden store, snake and lizard shit, marijuana smoke. Boy lit a joint and passed it to Kenny as he sat down across the coffee table from him.

"What's with the red light?" Kenny asked, and took a hit.

"I'm trying to get these snakes to breed," Boy said. "I'll be the first one in captivity if it happens. They're from Australia, though, so I've got to reset the clocks around here to the southern hemisphere. So it's, what? About three in the morning at Ayers Rock, almost springtime."

"What about the temperature?" Kenny asked. "I mean, this has got to be too hot for there."

"Too hot at night, too cool in the daytime," Boy said, taking the joint, taking a hit. A moment of silence, broken by the bubbling aerators in the fish tanks, the scrabbling of hard reptile claws along the metal floors of the cages. Time always slowed at Boy's house, you had to get used to the silences. Dope helped. Kenny drifted, thinking about Ray off in Australia himself, even as we speak . . . traveling upside down, sleeping when he should be waking, like a character in a Superman strip, backwardman, Mr. Mxyzptlk . . . a kind of dogged sorrow, low-down and blue, the thing that nobody talked about: it didn't feel that bad, being blue. Sometimes it felt fine. Boy let the smoke out in a thin stream, passed it back to Kenny. "Even in the spring," he said, "the daytime temps get over a hundred, way over that in the first inch off the ground, when the sun is shining. It can get to one-thirty-four, one-forty. The theory is it's a clock thing, day length."

"Science," Kenny said.

"I don't know," Boy said. "You try this, you try that. If it works, everybody thinks you're a genius." He waved the joint off.

Kenny settled back into his chair. Around him in the red-lit darkness were the usual denizens: a pair of Oscar fish in adjoining tanks, a clawed frog, Nile monitor, a saltwater reef aquarium, a ferret, a nine-foot rock python, frogs and fish and snakes without name—a continuous bench at waist level, all around the room, and every foot of it lined with cages or tanks. A preference for cold-blooded, what was the name? *Poikilotherm,* he remembered. Kenny always wanted to start a band, the Poikilotherms. What difference did it make if he couldn't play an instrument? He was getting high. The red light was cozy. He heard Junie's voice, scolding: *a bunch of young Americans getting high . . .*

"What do the rest of them think?" Kenny asked. "About the change in the clock, I mean."

"I don't know. I mean, we'll see. Most of them, their brain is just a wide spot in their spinal column. You don't want to go crazy trying to figure it out."

"Anything going on?"

Boy thought for a minute, then started to laugh. "You're it, man," he said. "You're the biggest news in town. Kenny Kolodny is screwing the class lesbian."

He felt himself blushing. The red light would hide it.

"I mean, that's so fucking great," Boy said. "That's unbeliev-able."

It got cold, stayed cold for two weeks at the end of November and the beginning of December, the last of autumn stripped off the trees. A couple of inches of snow was all but it stayed and stayed—not in town, where it rotted quickly to nothing, but out in the suburbs, in the playing fields and lawns and remnant pockets of forest. Along the river, the winter looked like it had come for good; a real winter for once. The river piled up in dams of ice around the edges of the rocks. The forest, stripped and empty, was quieted with snow. A gray sky kept the planes out.

And really, Kenny thought: why should I care? Winters past, a season of dead batteries and indoor drinking, of Christmas—reliably the worst week of the year in Kenny's house—and the shriek of tires spinning on ice. His sneakers leaked. The first warm coat in many winters was the one he bought himself from the surplus store downtown, a castoff of the Czechoslovakian army, black wool. It kept the snow off him but smelled like mothballs, defeat; he pictured winter as a long, painful retreat, a line of black skeletal men moving through the white fields . . . Kenny read military history sometimes, a leftover vice from deep childhood, and he had noticed that many of the worst things in the world took place in winter: Napoleon's flight from Moscow, the end of the Third Reich. Wars began in optimistic weather and ended in February mud. Even in December, it was nice at Pearl Harbor.

He let himself be seduced, though, by Junie. She had the clothes for winter, the cups of steaming cocoa to warm up with. She had snow tires on her Accord, and two or three poems by Robert Frost by heart. OK, he thought; I'll give it a chance. All the while hearing Rexroth in his brain: *pie glue! pie glue!*

(And his father, too: OK, I'll give nature a chance. OK, I'll give Europe a chance . . . that endless ability to judge, from a standpoint of nothing.)

A real winter, at last. Kenny and Junie went down to the canal one afternoon, four o'clock or so, after the indignity of high school. They didn't talk at school, didn't see each other more than they had to. Both of them shrunken, tiny versions of themselves. There were no other cars in the parking lot when they pulled up, which was a surprise to Junie. She said, "I guess it's the weather."

Kenny looked up skeptically. The sky was low and dark gray, pregnant. The temperature was right in between snow and freezing rain.

"We'll be fine," she said. "There's no problem."

Kenny had already made up his mind to follow her anyway.

They walked down through the winter woods. In her sweaters and her parka, with her head tucked into a stocking cap, Junie looked like a regular girl; a beautiful, regular girl. He forgot sometimes. Now that her hair was starting to grow out again, you could see her face more easily. Kenny was jealous: he was the one who had seen her, he had a prior claim . . . They came out onto the canal and it was perfect: hard-frozen, blown clean of snow. Somewhere past the next line of trees, the river was running along; he could hear it; one or two birds. "It's nice," he said.

"It's never like this," Junie said. "It's always crowded, or else the ice is bad."

She sat down on a flattened log and started to peel her boots off. Kenny followed suit with his sneakers. A thick heap of gray ashes inside a square of logs, a place where a bonfire had been. Kenny wished for one now. Some essential loneliness, a season for lonely Scandinavians. He longed for company, a fire, music (though he would have hated the music, certainly; the company, probably; everything but the fire).

Kenny laced himself into Junie's father's skating boots and wobbled out onto the ice. "I absolutely suck at this," he said.

"You don't have to be good."

"I didn't say I wasn't good," he told her, and fell on his ass. "I said I suck."

She glided out onto the ice in her white princess skates and in that moment Kenny hated her: the grace, the certainty of her movement. She had brought him here to demonstrate his clumsiness, the distance between them. He knew it wasn't true. He took her arm and stumbled upright again and there she was.

"Isn't this *fun?*" she asked, and Kenny gave her the finger.

"These things don't have any brakes," he said, leaning on her still, lifting one of her father's skates off the ice to inspect it. They were giant Bauer hockey skates, black and menacing. Even with a pair of cotton liner socks and a pair of wool socks over them, Kenny did not quite fill her father's shoes; a little joke that he had noticed right away.

"You don't need them, unless you're figure skating," Junie said. "Were you planning on figure skating?"

This: a flash of real anger, pure and unreasonable; he was being made fun of. No, I can't skate. No, I'm not one of you.

"Just glide," she said. "You don't have to go fast," and left him behind; slipping away from him again, leaving him pooled in anger. It passed quickly, leaving a bitter aftertaste. He wobbled slowly after her, trying to find a rhythm for his feet on the treacherous ice. One-two-three-oops-two-oops-two-three-one-oops-shit!—and he down on his ass again, Junie staring quizzically at him from twenty yards down the canal. Humiliation, the gaze of the graceful upon the clumsy. She said, "Do you want me to show you?"

"I just haven't done this in a while," he said. "I'll be OK."

Giraffe, gazelle, he thought; her white neck unfolding out of her scarf. For whatever reason, she was wearing her glasses today. Kenny hauled himself to his feet again and they started off, Junie in the lead, sometimes swirling back in a flurry of curves and stops. Not that she was that good but she was that much better than Kenny: he cursed and labored, flirted with bad sportsmanship. He reminded himself of his father. The ice was pebbled and cracked, rutted at first with the tracks of other skaters and then with sticks and leaves as they left even the marks of the others behind.

Slowly Kenny found a pace, a cadence of kick, glide, rest that he could settle into. The air, cold and damp when he first got out of the car, now felt soft to him, carrying in its humidity a taste of the ocean. The gray sky lowering. All right, he thought, if I learn to do this, can I be one of you? The doors of the club opening, to let him in; but it would never happen, there was too much she was born knowing that he would never learn, or learn too late, a lifetime playing catch-up and never getting there . . . They were half an hour from the car by then, a mile or two, it was hard to tell, and they still hadn't seen anyone; the river turning in and out of their sight, between the trees on the left-hand bank. Romance. OK, I get it, Kenny thought. Can we stop now?

On cue, she curled toward the bank, where there was an easy way up to the towpath, and a bench for the convenience of summer pedestrians. *A View of the Potomac, 1835*—the river running under cliffs of gray rock, making a big distant sound. He wobbled on his flimsy ankles up to the bench, where Junie was waiting for him, the blood risen into her cheeks, a rosy flush. Her breath was clear, while Kenny's came in clouds of vapor.

"Let's neck," she said. "Let's pet. Doesn't this feel good?"

"It's OK," he said.

"Don't be a bastard," Junie said; a surprise to Kenny, she meant it. Troubled again. She said, "Don't tell me you don't like something when I know you do. Don't fake with me."

"I'm sorry," Kenny said. "I like this fine. It's just all this nature, I don't know. I like it but I never know what to say about it."

"Then don't say anything."

But I didn't, Kenny thought; and didn't say it. This was where they started; where they always seemed to end up was here, a fallen cake of missed intentions. They were OK, they were fine together, just this was never going to be perfect. One or the other of them was always going to screw things up, he thought; but this blue, depressed half-light was where they felt at home. He kissed her on the lips, and she didn't object.

Her lips were warm with the blood running through her body, her breath was warm. He kissed her again, clumsy, lethal weapons on his feet. Kissed her neck, the hollow at the base of her neck. He could feel the loneliness of the winter woods everywhere around them; this small enclosed warmth between them, and the cold, the scattered scraps of snow, the empty branches. This little house of breath, with only the two of them in it; and the big cold world outside. He slipped his hand under her parka, under her sweater and found the warm bare skin hidden inside.

"Get that thing away from me!" she shrieked. "Jesus, that's cold. Get out of there!"

"Sorry."

"No, I . . ." Now it was Junie's turn to apologize, Junie's turn to wreck things. They were OK unless one of them started keeping score. "It's just so cold," she said.

"I know, sorry," Kenny said. He fished his plastic envelope of Dutch tobacco out of the pocket of his overcoat and rolled a cigarette, hands heavy with blood, swollen and clumsy. It was unfair that these hands should feel cold to Junie. No fair, no fair. The cold world was waiting for them, waiting for their little house of warmth to dissipate. Junie was looking off at the river.

He saw that the cold world would get them back. They were *temporary*. A trembling up the back of his neck, a certainty. They had not yet made love to each other then, he had barely touched her breasts. What do I do now? he thought. He felt like he was moving underwater, under a huge weight of water, the blue underwater light. But it wasn't even a question: it was too late to stop.

"Junie," he said.

"What?" Her eyes still on the river.

"Where are you going to be next year? What are you going to do?"

She took a minute to answer; he lit the cigarette he had rolled and watched the blue smoke trail off in the still air, a pleasant sense of violation. Not all Currier & Ives.

"I'm barely here right now," she said.

"What?"

"I didn't tell you," Junie said. "I was going to."

She stopped and Kenny, not sure he wanted to hear, waited for her. It was crazy that so much could be riding on a few words; that inside-out feeling that Kenny had sometimes, where everything was the wrong size. Small was big and big was small. He reminded himself to breathe.

"I was in the hospital, right before I met you," Junie said. "I don't know if you heard that or not."

"Where would I hear that?"

"I don't know," she said, and looked at him. She said, "I never know what parts of my life are public property. It was just for three nights, the hospital."

"What did you go there for?" he asked. "If you want to talk about it."

"I cut myself," she said.

"How did you do that?"

"No, I did it on purpose," she said; eyes away, her glasses still on, though. He saw her in the bed next to his mother and then realized that yes, that was the kind of hospital she meant, that was the kind of ward: the smell of piss, the burnt, electrical smell that the schizophrenics seemed to give off. Maybe he was making this up. A weight of sorrow, self-pity dropped onto him. Whatever else, she was supposed to be a way out.

"Where?" he asked.

"What?"

"Where did you cut yourself? Where on your body?"

"On my leg, my calf," she said, reaching down to touch a place on the outside of her left leg, the thickest part of the muscle. "Here."

"Let me see," he said.

"I don't want to."

"Let me see."

A momentary standoff; then, her face full of misgiving, she reached under her skirt and pulled the black tights down, bare skin on the cold wood of the bench, down over her thighs and knees until they lay in a loose puddle over her white skates. He saw the scar immediately, wondered how he had missed it before—a straight clean line, two or two and a half inches long, still red and slightly swollen along the edges. Lips, he thought. The lips of the wound.

"Why there?" he asked.

Of course she wouldn't look at him; he didn't expect her to.

"Because I'm left-handed," Junie said. "I don't know. If I could tell you why *anything* I'd probably be better off."

"You seem all right."

"I'm all right," she said. "Are you done?"

"What?"

"Can I pull my pants up?"

Kenny reached his hand down and touched the wound with his finger, ran the tip of his finger along the line of the cut. "Does that hurt?" he asked.

"No."

He let his hand stray up along the outside of her leg, felt her flinch when his hand touched the warmth of her thigh under the protection of her skirt. She flinched but she didn't move away. Good girl, he thought. She was no coward. He drew her closer, his head in her lap, and she folded her body over him. Skin buried deep inside, her animal heat trapped by layers and layers of cloth. Kenny closed his eyes. He rested there, wrapped in her, their two bodies together.

Then heard a ticking sound, off in the woods. Another and then another. He startled out of her embrace.

"Shit," said Junie. "Shit, shit, shit."

She clambered to her feet, wobbling on her skates, pulling her tights up around her waist again.

"What?" Kenny asked, still not understanding.

"It's starting to rain," she said. Exactly as she said it, a thin needle of cold landed on his scalp—not even wet, not at first, but absolute cold. He didn't have a hat. He tossed his cigarette into the snow next to the bench and followed her down to the frozen canal, hearing the ticking accelerate as the rain came down, individual drops and then closer together and then a steady soft hissing.

"Shit," she said again. "I'm sorry I got you all the way out here."

"Apologizing for the weather," he said. "Not bad. That's extra credit. But I don't mind."

"You will in a minute. Let's go. We don't want to be out here in the rain."

Why not? he thought, but he didn't ask it. She started back, a different stroke from before; reading her thoughts in the movements her body made, heavier now, nothing playful. Now we're married, Kenny thought; now I've touched you, remembering the raised flesh of the wound under his fingertip. *Proud* flesh, he remembered. He didn't know what she wanted from him but he knew it was something. The rain fell across his face, it soaked the stubble of his hair and dripped down the collar of his overcoat. A faint bitter aftertaste: he was needed, an actor in her own internal drama. He could be anyone: *fungible*. Inside he was all right, he was warm and mostly dry; but this time it was Kenny with his head bare to the wind and the rain. It took forever to get to the car.

Back in Junie's house, safe and warm. He was wearing her clothes: a flannel shirt and a pair of blue jeans, no underwear. They fit him fine, the jeans were even slightly too big for him, his hips loose inside the memory of hers. He wore a towel around his neck, wet hair. His own clothes rattled in the dryer downstairs. Her mother had appeared just long enough to make cocoa, then gone again; back to her cave, as Kenny thought of the sewing room downstairs. Her strength was rooted in the rock.

"Are you OK?" Junie asked him.

They sat in the booth in the corner of the kitchen, under the light. The rest of the house was dark around them: the living room just suggested by a reflection, a streetlight two blocks away shining through the branches. A dimmed-down light shone in the hallway but nobody was expected: her brother had called from a friend's house, her father from the country club. The rain had turned to black ice, all over the city, and the police were asking everybody to stay off the roads. Junie had nearly wrecked twice on the way back from the canal. Kenny tried to call his father twice, no answer, it didn't matter. He was staying anyway.

"I'm fine," he said. "I just got cold, I guess."

"I guess," she said. "When we got to the car, your lips were blue, actually blue. I've never seen that before."

"I'm glad to be educational."

"Educational, recreational," she said. "Emotional. Do you want anything to eat?"

He wouldn't have guessed that he was hungry, but he discovered that he was starving. Emotional: he filed the word away. "What have you got?" he asked.

"I don't know," she said doubtfully. "I can make something, I guess."

"Do you cook?"

"I can if I have to. I like to bake things, more than I like to cook, I don't know why."

"That doesn't make sense."

A look, one eyebrow raised: *what did you expect?*

"I'll make you something," Kenny said. He opened the wide refrigerator door, and found everything: smoked salmon, capers, special sausages, a chicken, a drawer full of different cheeses, vegetables he didn't know the names of—endive? kale? He stood bewildered in the refrigerator light, the reflection of this food in his eyes. *Cornucopia,* he thought. *Panoply.* There was Bass Ale, chardonnay. Too much of everything, too hard to decide. His own cooking was strictly on a Boy Scout/survivalist plane, a few basics, a couple of tricks.

70

"Omelettes," he said to Junie. "Does that sound good?"

"I don't eat meat," she said.

"What does that mean?"

"Omelettes are fine, but no bacon."

"I don't see any bacon anyway."

"It's in there somewhere," Junie said. "My father likes his pig meat now and then."

Well, so do I, Kenny thought; but didn't say it. Junie was off somewhere again. She shut off the light over the kitchen table and stared out the window, which was worth looking at: the telephone wires, the limbs of the bushes outlined in ice, chandeliers. The black ice was still falling. He could see it in the street lamp, hear it rattling against the driveway, like it was raining BB shot. Clear in the air, the ice turned dark and rough when it landed, like pebbled bathroom-window glass. The shapes and colors of the cars were changed, smeared. Nobody drove by.

Working by the light under the cabinets—a little spotlight, theatrical but handy—he cut green onions, sliced a little smoked salmon into slivers, broke three eggs into a cup and beat them foamy. He knew there would be an omelette pan somewhere and he was right; just as he had known there would be sour cream in the refrigerator somewhere, and a good sharp knife in the drawer. His mother had been a good cook once, a sixties gourmet, and Kenny would watch her. A prayer for you, he thought, cutting a slug of butter into the pan. Get well.

(No one thought that Kenny's mother would get well, though, not ever again. Things had happened. The chemistry inside her brain was different, that's what the doctors thought. One chemical poured through and she was happy, another made her sad, another chemical made her angry with strangers in public places. My chemicals, Kenny thought. My chemicals are telling me to eat lightly, be careful, things are moving. He stole a glance at Junie and his dick stirred in his pants.)

He set a plate in front of her with the crescent of eggs on one side, three circles of red tomato on the other, a sprig of parsley, mystery shrub. Brought her a napkin, a fork, a glass of white wine. She looked up at him, suspicious. She said, "What are you trying to do?"

"Nothing," he said. "Seduce you."

"What?"

"Nothing."

"I heard you," she said. Reached behind her, on the ledge along the window, and brought out a pair of small earthy-looking oil lamps; lit them with a paper match, small brave flames, and then she blew the match out and held it. Small things mattered, details. The butter spattering in the pan.

"Eat that," he said. "It'll get cold if you wait, and it will be disgusting. Please?"

She shrugged, pale face in the lamplight, and took the first small bite. Kenny poured the eggs into the pan, adjusted the flame, waited.

"This is good," Junie said.

"I'm glad you like it," Kenny said. A vision, then: the two of them married, in a house like this, a future. Wouldn't it be nice? Then realized that he was quoting from, reliving, a Beach Boys song. How much of this life belonged to him? Still it was a pleasant fantasy. More than that: a strange kind of certainty, as long as he didn't think about it.

Took his plate, identical to hers, and sat across from her in the booth. Glass on three sides, the rain ticking down outside. "Would you like my parsley?" she asked. "I don't think I can finish it."

"There is an example," Kenny said.

"Of what?"

"I've always wondered about parsley. I mean, it comes on your plate, you never eat it, they take it back to the kitchen and throw it away."

"Or put it on somebody else's plate."

"Well, yeah, of course. That one-head-of-parsley-per-restaurant-per-week theory. But even if they use *new* parsley for every diner, you know, it still doesn't make any sense to me. What's it there for? It's there to *not eat*."

"It's a garnish," Junie said; like the word itself was enough to make it make sense. *Garnish.*

"And now I am trying to impress you, by cooking you dinner."

"And succeeding."

"Thank you. And in order to impress you I put this *garnish* on the side of your plate, even though this has never made any sense to me, in fact seems like pretty much of a waste, you know? I mean there are farms in California where they don't grow anything but parsley, I bet."

"And children are starving in India."

"Well, they are."

"I know they are," she said. "All kinds of hellish things are going on in the world. People are getting shot, starving, they're burning the rain forest down in Brazil. I know it's not exactly news but that doesn't mean it stopped happening." She took a sip of the white wine, like she was testing it, examining. Looked at her glass. "While we sit here, smothered in comfort," she said. "Getting high, getting drunk, watching TV, picking fights with each other over nothing."

Kenny was nearly done. The food was good, rich, extravagant; he took a final bite, tasting the salt sharpness of the salmon, the rich sour cream, butter, and eggs. Top of the world, Ma; top of the food chain, anyway. I like it here on top of the food chain.

"Smothered in comfort," Kenny said. He didn't feel that way exactly. These moments of comfort, moments of quiet, did not come often for him; they were like rest stops, a place to catch a breather before he headed back into the pointless noise of his life. He didn't want this one to go away. "What are we supposed to do?" he asked. "You live the life you're given."

"My father would say, the life you make," she said. "I don't know, I don't mean to be a drag. It just doesn't seem like enough to me, to live your life for pleasure. Everything's a pleasure, right? Food and sex and movies. Everybody's happy, and when you stop being happy you move on, you get divorced, find a better restaurant."

She spoke with the true voice of depression, Kenny thought: the commonplace becoming too heavy to lift, the senselessness overtaking. The cow's life, the pig's life worth more than her own. Still, the soft light; the way that small things mattered, the two of them bound in the light of the flames, the cold world outside.

"I don't know," he said. "I don't know what else there is."

"That's why I brought you here," she said. "To tell me."

She smiled at him gravely, apologies again: for the weather, the state of the world. "This has got to stop," he said.

"What?"

"Nothing," he said. "Come here."

She looked at him, grave, skeptical. Kenny found himself not breathing again. Come on, he thought, come on, sending the thought toward her with all his power; which as near as he could tell was none. Come over here to me.

And then she did, sliding around on the coarse burlap cloth of the seat. She took her glasses off first, left them on the table. Her mouth was slick with butter but still she tasted of nothing, rainwater. Rain ticking at the glass, the ice already down. He could feel the cold at the back of his neck, the miles of cold black night pressing down at the windows; and the empty streets of the city, the canceled life.

"Come on," she said; taking the lamps, scooting out of his reach.

Kenny didn't argue. He followed her up the stairs and into her bedroom, the dim flames of the oil lamps sending crazy shadows all around her. They loomed and separated, shivered in place. Her mother was downstairs, probably asleep by now—she had a daybed in her sewing room, separate from the room she officially shared with her official husband, where she slept most nights. She had a television down there, a little dorm refrigerator. Kenny and Junie were alone as they could ever want to be.

"Wait here," she said, leaving him at the door of her bedroom, leaving the lamps with him. "I'll be back in a minute."

Again that feeling of marriage: this house belonged to them, an ordinary Wednesday night, November. Householders, housekeepers. He went in, set the lamps on the table, and sat on the edge of the bed, waiting, not wanting to jinx anything by thinking about it.

When Junie came back in, her clothes hung loose around her, unbuttoned. Quickly she stepped out of them, as easily as if she had done this a hundred times in front of him. She fussed with her bra, straightened out her blouse so it wouldn't wrinkle, just like he wasn't there; then lay down on the bed behind him, facing the wall.

"Your turn," she said.

He felt the gravity right away, knew this was something, it would have weight. He stepped out of her jeans, let them fall loose to the floor, threw the flannel shirt aside. He was hard as anything, just from seeing her. Not quite real, her body in the lamplight.

"Go easy," she said as she turned to him; and he didn't know what she meant, at first. He kissed her lips, her neck, and as he kissed her breasts he felt the trembling start inside her. He wondered. But she stayed with him, bravely, her arms just resting anywhere and then coming slowly, awkwardly to embrace him. Her hand on the back of his head, pressing his lips to her breast. Kenny thought that he might go off soon, any moment, he could feel her with his whole body.

She pushed him away, just far enough to see his face, her familiar nearsighted gaze focusing, trying to see. "I'm not using anything," she said. Up on one elbow, whispering.

"What?"

"I'm not using anything," she said again, searching his face.

Kenny flushed, not guilty of any particular offense but not exactly innocent either.

He said, "I've got a thing, downstairs. I mean it's out in the car but I can get it."

"No," Junie said. "I don't want anything. I want it to be real, all right? Consequences, take your chances."

His heart leapt toward her, this was beautiful, crazy; he was already in deeper than he knew. He closed his eyes. The way she lay there, up on one elbow, her fine long neck and her breasts offered to him. He was sure of her, even past the temptation. Too late to stop anyway but he was sure of her.

"All right," he whispered. "Consequences."

"Go easy," she said; and still he didn't know what she meant. She let herself down onto her back again and lay in front of him, open to him. *Ceremonial,* he thought; not quite a victim. Kenny would have been content to look at her for a while, enjoy the touch of her body, the places that were new to him. But there was an urgency. He didn't want to wreck it. He pressed his body against hers again, kissed her breasts one then the other and felt her hand lacing through the short hair at the base of his neck, urging him on. She opened her legs for him, he knelt between them, but before he could come inside she stopped him. She brought a small tube of K-Y jelly from under the bed, opened the top, and out came a glistening clear drop. First did herself and then him and Kenny was lucky not to go off then, the feel of it . . . And then the other thought, of Junie making preparations, of where she might have learned about K-Y jelly, but this wasn't the time. She laid the tube out of sight under the bed and pulled him down inside of her and he was partway inside her when he felt the stop.

"Come on," she said fiercely. "Don't stop."

Then he knew what she meant: *a virgin.* Kenny was frightened, excited. Her hand was resting in the small of his back and now it moved down, pulled him closer, urged him on. Eyes closed, he had a sense of falling, farther than he knew. More than you bargained for, more than you bargained for: it was his father's voice going around in his head, fear and anger mixed in with this other thing, not quite pleasure, or a pleasure that was painful too . . . He broke through, came all the way inside her and went off at the same time.

Rested on top of her with his eyes closed, quiet. Something had happened. They were each away inside, miles apart but touching. The slick, sweaty warmth of her skin. It was only, what? Eight-thirty or nine o'clock. The rain unimpeded in the trees outside. Kenny closed his eyes and rested in the warmth between them, bellies slick with come and blood, he didn't want to look. More than you bargained for, his father's voice said. Why didn't she tell you?

He drew away from her, inside himself again. She wanted things from Kenny. She had delivered herself into his care; her problems were going to be his own from now on. Entrapment: a simple fuck turned into a wedding. Really it was nothing so clear. Really it was this: Kenny had thought they were walking along on solid ground when really they were thousands of feet up in the air, walking a thin line. Now he saw how far there was to fall. It scared him. He was going to have to take care, take care of himself, of her.

She stirred beneath him and he opened his eyes, found her face, tears standing in her eyes. Shit, he thought; felt again the urge to run away. She was so much heavier than he had thought. *Consequences, take your chances.* And then the second voice inside him saying all right, I can do it, I can take the weight.

"What?" he said, and touched her cheek with his hand.

She closed her eyes, shook her head, tears streaming down the sides of her face. "Shit," she said. "I said I wasn't going to . . ."

"What's the matter?"

"It hurts," she said.

"Is that . . . ?"

"No," she said; then started to laugh, tears and laughter, come and blood all mixed up into some nameless everything. Kenny felt the same. She said, "I mean, it's almost enough. It *hurts*."

"I'm sorry," Kenny said, and meant it, and she started to laugh harder.

"Shit," she said. "This is where we started, isn't it? Apologies." Smiled and wiped the tears out of her eyes and then lay there for a moment composing her face, eyes closed, like he was about to take her picture; and Kenny thought *I love you* and almost said it.

Jesus, he thought. At the same time feeling like he had made a discovery, he had found the right name for himself and his certainty of her. He wanted to dare it, to say the word out loud, like the first words of a new language: I love you. I am your lover.

"I love you," Kenny said.

"Oh, shit," she said, and turned her face from him, trying to get away. "Don't say that."

"I'm sorry," Kenny said; but it was broken already; the exact wrong words, and he had said them. She shrugged him off and they both sat up and looked at the mess they had made, the red blood-stain—smaller than he thought—spreading into the white sheets. His own dick smeared with blood, and her thighs. She took a pillowcase, suddenly all business, and held it between her legs and went out to the bathroom again, leaving Kenny alone, cold, wondering.

Came back into the room carrying a washcloth; kissed him, then washed the blood off him, like she was erasing him. "I'm sorry," she said. "That's what people say, you know, when they want to remind you that they own you." She pitched her own voice to imitate her mother's: "I love you, Junie. That's why you've *got* to see the counselor. That's why you've *got* to get new clothes."

"I'm sorry," Kenny said, and that got them both started laughing.

"I'm sorry," she said, without meaning to, and that got them laughing harder. *Giggles*, Kenny thought; remembering a time when he had cut an artery in his foot at a remote mountain lake and driven an hour to the nearest clinic, pressing paper towels to the spurting blood—they used up nearly all the roll on the drive, got lost twice—and laughing all the way. They giggled at half jokes, roadside signs, street names. That kind of laughter, edgy.

She sat down on the edge of the bed, stroked the side of his face with her hand. He closed his eyes. Touch.

"You can say whatever you want," she said. "It just freaks me out."

"What does?"

"I don't know."

"Me, too." He drew her down to him, feeling her breasts, slightly cool now, barely brushing against his chest.

"I want to get this straightened up," she said, wriggling away.

"Come back here."

"In a minute," she said. "Get up for a second."

He stood, and lost the last of his warmth; suddenly naked, chilly. She swept the sheet off the bed in one careless motion and Kenny saw that there were towels under it, under the middle of the bed, so the mattress would not be stained. This was premeditated, then. She knew what was going to happen. This bothered him like crazy, made him feel afraid again, entrapped. The things from his pockets were lying on the table, spilled there when he changed clothes to put his in the dryer: his two-dollar pocket watch ticking like a bomb, keys change wallet pocketknife tobacco. "Can I smoke in here?" he asked.

"I guess," she said. "I never thought about that."

"What?"

"You have sex, then you have a cigarette," she said. "It's just like the cartoons."

"Do you want one?"

Junie laughed. "Not me," she said. "I'd like to miss one cliché, if I could. Just one."

Kenny settled onto the desk chair, feeling the coarse virtuous fabric of the seat on his naked butt; burlap and teak, what was so unethical about paint? He tried to arrange himself but his dick kept staring out at her, one-eyed, inquisitive. Her breasts, her legs. She was naked in the lamplight, gathering the dirty sheets into a bundle and then the towels and then for some reason the pillowcases. Maybe she knew he was watching but it didn't feel that way; he thought he was seeing the natural movements of her body. She left. He rolled a cigarette, taking pleasure in the small exact movements of his own hands. Sitting there exposed, naked. I love you, he told her; and she said nothing in return. Deal with it. He felt an excitement anyway, past the fear. Lit the cigarette and waited for her, watching the smoke curl out of the lamplight. I can spin straw into gold, the little man said. Out of the ordinary materials of his life, he had accidentally made this.

Kenny drove home around two the next day, a bright cold afternoon and a holiday feeling in the streets: nobody had gone to work that morning, nobody had gone to school with the streets glazed and treacherous with ice. Now the sun was out, though, and the ice was melting: first off the black streets, the telephone wires and power poles; more slowly off the trees and bushes, so that even now there were some that still sparkled with most of their diamonds intact. He had looked at these close-up in Junie's yard, on his way out to the car: the living twig encased in a clear sheath of ice, two or three times its own thickness. He imagined that he could feel the spring stored up in the buds, the life waiting inside the ice, but he knew he was only imagining. It wasn't even Christmas yet. The deep part of winter hadn't even started yet.

Shattered branches lay by the side of the roads, evidence of the storm. Split trees with their green hearts showing, the bark torn away with the falling branch. Something naked about the sight, something dirty, a secret he wasn't meant to see. An injury. He thought of Junie then: the taste of her mouth, the taste of cigarettes in his own. He hadn't meant to take it any farther, but his dick got hard when he was lying next to her. She didn't want to; but finally she was the one who guided him inside, little noises of pain or pleasure, or both . . . This went on for a while, half the night. They both knew they should stop. The last time she gasped, real pain, surprising, he saw it in her eyes—the mute animal fear—but she didn't stop; and the memory of this moment makes his dick stir in his pants again, driving down Nebraska Avenue. Why? The pain: she didn't stop. Kenny was raw himself, still wearing her jeans without underwear. He could have worn his own but he chose not to.

Which was it, exactly: dressing himself in girl clothes. What if Junie really was? What if Kenny was himself? Though he didn't think so, not about his own preferences, there were beautiful boys in high school that he could almost imagine but then there was the actual nakedness and kissing part, the lumpy hairy boneful body of another man that did not appeal to Kenny at all. Still, even if he was innocent, there was something else, some residue of feeling, some reason why he felt more at home in Junie's clothes than he did in his own.

There was a crazy preacher on the radio, and Kenny turned it up. The Reliant was AM only, the last car in America like that. "The Persian Gulf is *well known* to be a land run by spirits and sorcerers," the preacher said. Kenny couldn't follow the overall drift. "The *Indians* know about it," the preacher said. "They call it *ghost disease.*"

"Say it, brother," Kenny said.

"The soldiers who have come back from *Viet Nam,*" the preacher said. "The soldiers who have come back from *Korea,* and *Cambodia,* and *Ethiopia.*"

Kenny tried to think of when we had soldiers in Ethiopia, failed. Although this was the black-helicopter station, the United Nations World Government broadcast—maybe it was just another State Department conspiracy. Maybe the Club of Rome was up to tricks again, the Council on Foreign Relations, the Elders of Zion.

"*Sexual intercourse* is the medium by which this evil seed is spread from man to woman," the preacher said. "*Sexual intercourse* is the only way this can happen. We need an immediate crusade against *sexual intercourse* outside of wedlock, and the temptations of the body that we see on television and elsewhere . . ." Kenny switched the radio off, suddenly tired of the noise, plus he was 100 percent in favor of sexual intercourse at that moment and didn't want to hear it maligned. But spirit disease seemed like a possibility, a decent explanation for all that was wrong. A revolution of souls was what they needed.

Revolution of souls: take your old soul out and make it new, scour it clean, get rid of the old filth of days piled on days. So what if your new soul dressed in women's clothing? The old way was a disease, American sickness, guns and pies and Budweiser. No men and no women after the revolution of souls, no rich and no poor. The revolution of souls begins in bed and never leaves!

Meanwhile he could see the American disease working as he came down out of the suburbs and into the District, the winos with their paper cups, the junkies hawking flowers at the subway entrances, the shoppers in their bright cars. Kenny had a secret in his pants. He was alive: they were dead; they had the disease. He drove past the walkie-talkie that lived on the avenue; quiet today, he rested between garbage bags full of aluminum cans, his private fortune. Usually he was walking up and down the sidewalk, shouting, Motherfucker! Motherfucker! If I *ever* catch you fucking with my shit!

Kenny looked down on all of them from miles above, watching the wheel turning, smiling like a cherub in the corner of a bad French painting. A private joke between himself and the world. I've got a secret, Kenny thought. Ten feet tall and bulletproof. The revolution of souls had started and he was volunteering, him and Junie, he would have turned back then but her brother was already home, her father on the way. Normal life had returned. The supermarket parking lots were full of cars, the gas stations and strip malls and Hardee's. Sometimes the sound of shattering glass as the ice broke loose and shattered on the pavement; utility crews were still working the roadsides, patching up the fallen lines. The regular, waking life of the world, Kenny thought. He felt an unexpected tenderness toward it, the massive project of love and pretending. He had seen something the night before in the mess of tears and laughter and come and blood: some dirty nest of feelings, the thing that ran the world, that kept it going. He knew the name, even if she wouldn't let him use it. I am in love, he said to himself, practicing his new language. I love. I am beloved. The wheel was driving Kenny along, but now he didn't mind it. He found himself in favor of attachment, in favor of suffering, in favor of samsara. I'll take my chances, Kenny thought. After the revolution, suffering would be abolished.

Not even the sight of the row of stained yellow-brick apartments brought him down again. Home, he thought; and wondered if his father had gone to work. It didn't take much of an excuse to keep him home. On the other hand, he might not notice a simple thing like an ice storm. He parked in back, the wooden staircases climbing the houses in peeling shades of brown. A momentary darkness overcame him, a little cloud between Kenny and the sun: was it possible that he was attracted to her because of that veneer of money, good teeth and good taste? Yes, it was possible. He remembered her skating, gliding along in black, an elegant line against the gray sky. Her cut leg. Was it possible that he wanted her because he saw she was weak, wounded, because he thought he could sort her out from the crowd? This was a harder one but he finally had to answer yes, it was possible. If she was perfect, undamaged, she might be out of his reach.

But she wasn't. He had touched her. He could touch her again anytime he wanted, as far as he knew. A beautiful thing to know.

The television was going when he went inside, which was unexpected. His father didn't usually leave it on when he left the house; didn't usually leave the house if he was drunk enough to forget. A broken clock that hadn't stopped: he ran in patterns, not the same as the rest of the world but you could figure it out after a while.

Another small surprise when he went out onto the front porch to get the mail and found the morning paper there, bundled tight in its rubber band, a little turd of information, Kenny thought. This was wrong. His father loved the *Washington Post*, an ongoing thirty-year argument like a bickering marriage. He remembered the telephone, unanswered the night before. He opened the paper and read the headline: CITY PARALYZED BY ICE.

A faint copper taste rose in his mouth. Kenny was afraid. He moved gingerly through the rooms of the apartment, quiet, taking note of the evidence: a melted highball on the coffee table, an empty plate at the kitchen table, Kenny couldn't tell which meal.

Get out of here, he thought. Go back to Junie. She would take him in, turn him over to her mother's care.

He found his father in the upstairs bathroom, lying next to the tub in a pool of puke and blood. At first Kenny didn't recognize the unfamiliar shape, the maroon lump of the bathrobe against the white-and flesh-colored tiles, and then he saw his father's outstretched leg and the yellow stump of his foot and saw that he was not moving. Kenny wedged himself into the bathroom, against the sink, afraid to touch. What? The *fact* of the body, alive or not. This time the body got to say what happened next. Also there was a feeling of being filled up, welling over with feeling to where he didn't want to feel anything again. The blood came from a cut on the scalp but it had stopped. He had been lying there awhile. His face was peaceful, like he was sleeping. Kenny bent toward him, nervously touched the skin of his arm and felt the warm flesh; then saw a quick fluttering in his father's chest, saw that he was breathing and felt a quick guilty disappointment. Alive. He didn't wish any harm onto his father, that wasn't it. These funhouse turns, the way Kenny could never tell what was going to happen next. He couldn't feel any single thing, couldn't sort a line out of the tangle of feelings. It was too much. He went into the bedroom and dialed 911, counting the rings. They answered in seven.

"What is the nature of your emergency?" she asked.

"I need an ambulance," Kenny said.

"One moment," she said; a series of clicks while she transferred him and then a man's voice. Kenny gave his address, a rough description, was instructed not to move or touch his father in case of a head injury. In his imagination, his father's flesh was cold, the temperature of dirt, deep underground. He could feel the cold still on his hands, though he knew he was making it up.

He hung up the phone and didn't know what to do with his

hands, where to stand, where to wait. He went downstairs and then he came upstairs again.

He went back into the bathroom, where his father was folded, crumpled. His father wore his good maroon wool bathrobe, striped pajamas, slippers. He had been sitting on the toilet seat with the lid down. When his stomach was acting up—whatever he meant by that, anything from indigestion to cancer—Kenny's father would sit there on the toilet, waiting, Kenny didn't know for what. You and Elvis, Kenny thought. You're the King.

He went downstairs and found a pack of his father's cigarettes open on the coffee table, Merits. Kenny lit one: American tobacco, it tasted sour and strange in his mouth after the Dutch tobacco he usually smoked. Only then did he remember Junie. His heart started in his chest, as if he had betrayed her.

Junie. He paced up and down the living room, then back upstairs to stand outside the bathroom. He could see his father's blue-veined foot, callous and swollen, contorted as an old tree root. Parts of our bodies become unlovable as we get older. Kenny saw what he was bound to become, lying on the bathroom floor, drunk, passed out, and thought of the lies he had brought to Junie. This is me, he thought. This is what you need to know about me. *Escape:* he was fine for a night, for a walk in the park, but in the long run Kenny wasn't going anywhere. The good intentions and fancy houses couldn't help him. *Self-pity.* The ambulance was later and later. Maybe his father was dying. He knelt on the bathroom floor, touching his father's wrist and feeling the blood coursing through; though he couldn't tell whether it was his own pulse or his father's he was feeling. The strange gray color of his father's face, blue lips. I want this to be over, he thought.

He went into the bedroom overlooking the street and saw nothing of the ambulance. My father is dying, goddamn it! But it was all a performance, there was no real passion. Stubbed out the cigarette in the ashtray on the bedside table. His father's books: economics, policy, military history. This last was his hobby, second-guessing famous generals. If only Dad had been at Tobruk, at Stalingrad, at Guadalcanal and Waterloo . . . He looked down, and saw that he had stained the knee of Junie's borrowed jeans with his father's blood when he knelt on the bathroom floor.

The surgical waiting room at Washington General was packed, it stank of bodies and fast food, the television blared. The family of the boy who was knifed was in the corner eating fried chicken from Church's out of a big bucket. Nobody said anything, everybody looked up scared when a doctor or a nurse came into the room; the studied blankness of their faces, professional politeness. "Mrs. Grosvenor? Thank you. Could you come with me, please?".

Kenny's father had suffered a stroke. They were cutting open his head to relieve the pressure. Kenny was searching for the zero, the place where he didn't have to be anywhere at all, didn't have to think or move. His eyes rested on the television. He finally figured out who Pat Sajak was, and Vanna White. He knew the names, mostly as the punch lines for jokes, but he had never seen them before. Hurray for me, Kenny thought. I'm a good American after all. His thoughts weren't doing him any good at all.

His father might die, the doctor said. Most likely he wouldn't. The question of recovery was left hanging; something difficult. Cross that bridge when we come to it. Takes two to tango. A stitch in time saves nine. Not so much that he was tired but he couldn't keep anything straight, it was like dawn on a Greyhound bus once, coming back from New York, the gas flares and factories of New Jersey passing by in the gray light.

Kenny thought: I need to find something to think about my father.

Kenny thought: I will find a way to praise him. Religion of the body. He needs my faith in order to be healed. Kenny cast his mind back.

He has always been kind, whenever he could spare the attention. Besides, it wasn't strictly true. That wouldn't work.

He was good at his job, presumably. Kenny had no way of knowing. In this article in *Parade* magazine Kenny read once, this was listed as one of the real strengths of the career alcoholic—the ability to hold on to a job no matter what.

He had stuck with his mother for longer than anyone else could have stood it, which was true. But he had given up eventually. Anyone would have; but he *did*.

Something cold at the middle of this, like a wet stone: the wreckage, the wedding pictures of his parents, 1961. His father went to Columbia, his mother to Sarah Lawrence. Her family had money, spent by now on hospitals, on quacks and cures. The boy and girl on the wedding cake, his father in a black tuxedo, his mother in curls and lace and flourishes. This happened to everybody: they got married, they got divorced, they had the pictures to remember it by. Kenny felt a tug toward the big fake house in the suburbs, as if he belonged there.

He hadn't eaten for hours, not since breakfast, though that was almost noon. He was about to give up, head for the bank of vending machines in the basement and improvise a dinner, when he remembered the one good thing: the evening when the Clarks came to his house, to ask if they could take Ray with them to Australia. Their son was Ray's best friend, Ray was sleeping over there more and more anyway. They were planning to go by sailboat—take six or eight months from San Diego and gypsy down through the South Pacific, Fiji, Tonga, Bora Bora.

This was over dinner, Kenny had made spaghetti, Ray sat with his head bowed while the Clarks outlined their lighthearted plans to his father. Waiting for the insult, the threat; his father was drinking red wine, which was never good, it always went to his face. But that night he was pale, off inside somewhere, surfacing once every few minutes to nod at the Clarks as if he was listening. They made their pitch and then there was a pause. Nothing was said about alcohol, about breakdowns, abdications; it was all happy, all positive. Kenny and Ray knew what was going to happen next. It took their father minutes, it felt like, to drag himself up to the surface again.

"Well," he said, and put his hands down flat on the table in front of him. He looked at them, like his hands would tell him something. "I guess this sounds attractive to you. Does it, Ray?"

"I guess," Ray said.

"You'd better do more than guess," his father said. "This is halfway around the world. Do you want to go or not?"

Don't answer! Kenny wanted to say. Trick question! He's trying to get you out here in the open, trying to get you to expose yourself.

"I want to," Ray said; and they both braced themselves, waiting for it. The Clarks were like little chickens who don't know that a tornado is coming. They looked bright, expectant.

"I don't see how I can say no," Kenny's father said. They waited for the rest of it; but there wasn't any more.

"That's wonderful," said Mrs. Clark.

"I'll give you a plane ticket," his father said to Ray. "If everything's OK in a year, you can cash it in. Just so you can come back if you feel like it."

"Good idea," said Mr. Clark. The suntanned sailor, decisive. "This is the trip of a lifetime," he said. Ray was twelve then, still a little boy.

"And when you get there, then what happens?" asked Mr. Kolodny.

"We were there two years ago," Mrs. Clark said. "We're consultants."

"There isn't any problem with the work situation, as far as visas and all that."

"Do you have any plans of returning?" Kenny's father asked.

"Not *plans*, exactly," said Mr. Clark.

"We're terrible gypsies," said Mrs. Clark.

Kenny's father closed his eyes. But again it didn't come; the anger, the explosion. Kept it bottled up inside himself until the Clarks were gone, and then just drank it down. He let his son go, just like that.

He wouldn't let Kenny go as easily.

Kenny closed his eyes. That once, his father forgot himself long enough to let Ray escape; if he had escaped, if he ever would. Kenny longed for a joint, a drink, a fuck. The smell of the fried chicken, sound of the television drowning out the hospital intercom. This was what he could find to praise: my father forgot himself once.

A green-suited doctor stood in the doorway. "Mr. Kolodny?" he called out; and Kenny thought no, my father's in surgery. Then realized that the doctor was calling for *him*.

Looking back, Kenny can never make it add up; when certain things happened, how they pressed against one another. He remembers a gray screen of days, punctuated and pierced by a string of bright moments. These bright moments don't seem to have any orderly relationship to one another in time, or in consequence; they have the brilliance and solidity of dreams, they seem *exactly right* and undeniable without making sense. That first weekend at the beach, for instance: Kenny knows there were two days but he remembers it as one; he can't date his first touching Junie to the first night or the second. Someday he's going to sit down with all the evidence, look up the ice storm in a newspaper to find out the date. He's still got his father's hospital records, or somebody does. If he could only find enough real dates, he could connect the dots, separate the weeks and months into their orderly channels, little squares on the calendar . . .

Thanksgiving disappeared entirely, and Halloween. Where was he? The year before Junie, the height of his fame as a charity case, Kenny ate Thanksgiving dinner at three different houses, ate more or less continuously from noon till ten at night. The trick was to eat sparingly, to let the metabolism keep pace, and plenty of dope between meals. Pumpkin pie! Dressing! Gravy! The memory makes him queasy now, but it was a kind of feat, a triumph.

His father had his stroke in what seemed like late October. But when he went to Wentworth's house, where they had offered to keep him, the Christmas decorations were already up. He can remember this precisely: snow in the yard and a green wreath on the red door. In the living room, a small dark fir with a few ornaments, wooden angels from Mexico and a sparse string of tiny white lights that didn't blink. The cold outside and the smell of dinner, which the Wentworths had already eaten. A month was missing somewhere. And even if Kenny goes back and draws the lines, he knows that memory will sprawl across them again, bleeding like ink on a wet page.

Wentworth's mother said, "I'm so sorry. Mike told us about your father. Of course you're welcome to stay."

"Thank you," Kenny said.

"It's a terrible thing," Mr. Wentworth said; looking genuine, disturbed. It tolls for thee, Kenny thought. Any middle-aged man would think so, and Wentworth's father was no slouch in the alcohol department either, though not in a class with Kenny's father.

Wentworth himself came down the stairs yawning and looked at Kenny. "Come on up," he said, without a trace of welcome in his voice.

Kenny shrugged. Wentworth's mom gave him an apologetic half smile and Kenny toted his duffel bag upstairs. Wentworth stopped on the second floor, where his parents slept, though his own bedroom and the other spare were out of harm's way at the top of the house. "I was thinking," Wentworth said. "This would probably be OK, right?"

"What's the matter?" Kenny asked.

Wentworth wasn't giving him anything, eyes blank. "This is more convenient for the bathroom," he said. "You don't have to walk all the way downstairs."

"What the fuck is your deal?" Kenny said. "You don't want me to stay here, that's fine."

"You don't come around here," Wentworth said. "I don't see you at school, you haven't got time for me. Then when you get into trouble the phone rings. I'm sorry, man, you hurt my feelings."

All said in a sleepy monotone, like he was reciting the phone book. Kenny couldn't think of what to say. He had never heard anyone talk about feelings, not a man, anyway, or a boy, or whatever Wentworth was. Kenny was the only one with feelings. He had left Wentworth behind like a discarded toy truck, while he went charging off into Junie-world.

"Shit, man," he said. "I'm sorry."

"That's OK," Wentworth said, in the affectless monotone. "You want to stay down here or what?"

"I'd just as soon stay upstairs, if that's OK."

"That's fine," Wentworth said. "Whatever. There's sheets on the bed, I think."

Kenny dumped his duffel bag in the spare room, one dim bulb. It had once been Wentworth's sister's room, full of pink and riding trophies. All the children that were gone, all the rooms that were waiting for them to come back, but they'd never come back. They were gone to adult-world now and the rooms were left behind. Whose Abba posters were these? The teddy bears stared down from the window ledge, abandoned. Something manufactured, something fake in all these souvenirs of childhood. Childhood was a thing you bought; Kenny's parents couldn't afford one. Something like that.

Still the little girl was gone, some new adult sprung up to take her place. He twisted one up, and smoked it with Wentworth, leaning out the attic window so the smoke wouldn't leak back into the house. Then watched *Mission: Impossible.*

Lying in the darkness Kenny remembered what it was like to come inside her. My father is sick, he reminded himself, my father is in the hospital. I have neglected my friends. It didn't matter. He closed his eyes and saw her lying in her nun's cell of a room: naked on the narrow bed, waiting for him; or propped up on one elbow, like she was offering herself to him. His dick was hard just thinking about her. It was only the night before, he thought, and this was wrong again—too much had happened, she was too far away. He counted the hours again and remembered that he had spent the night before in an armchair in the waiting room, slept for some amount of time between television accidents and bawling children. An afternoon, an evening, a night, a morning, an afternoon. These measurements seemed old, archaic when they referred to hours spent inside a hospital, hours without oxygen, sunlight, or rest. His father was still there, captive. Kenny tried to remember.

But there was Junie, waiting for him in the dark behind his eyes, the pink darkness of the girl's room. *Pink:* the blood smeared on the whiteness of her thigh. What was it like to lead a girl's life? You'll never know, the ponies answered. You can't imagine, said the dolls.

Jane Mrs. Dr. Williamson was fussing with a chair, gluing a spreader back between two wobbly legs, on the floor of her basement sewing room. She also wanted to take a look at the upholstery. It was almost time to re-cover the seats, and she wanted to have a look. Curator of the house, Kenny thought; caretaker. He was being spoken to. Not that he was in trouble, just that he was getting the treatment, the professional attention.

"I spoke to Dr. Nguyen, at General?" she said. She was holding a drill bit in one corner of her mouth, like a cigarette. "He was the lead doctor in the team that operated on your father."

"I remember him," Kenny said.

"What's he like?"

"I don't know," Kenny said, trying to remember: a deadpan, indifferent face, a feeling of skepticism toward Kenny, not quite dislike. "He's a young guy," Kenny offered.

"Did he seem bright?"

"I couldn't tell," Kenny said.

"He seemed fine on the phone," Jane Mrs. Dr. Williamson said. "It seemed as if he knew what he was doing."

"They put on a white coat, they're all the same to me. I can't tell the difference between a good doctor and a bad doctor."

She took the drill bit out of her mouth and scolded him. "Your father's alive," she said. "That makes him a good doctor, maybe a very good one."

She turned back to her chair, gave him time for this to sink in. He was supposed to be thinking about peril, about gratitude to doctors and taking better care of his health. He was not supposed to be noticing her ass. But she was wearing sweatpants, a t-shirt, leaning away from him at a certain angle; she looked like Junie, but more compact, like somebody had taken Junie's length and compressed her down by about six inches. Her mother had big sex advertisements, a round ass and big breasts. *Voluptuous,* Junie would say. *Epicurean.* She had inherited this from her mother: they both distrusted the sexual aspect of their bodies, hid them in loose clothing.

"It's going to be six weeks at least," Jane Mrs. Dr. Williamson said. "Nguyen said it was touch and go, he still isn't sure how much recovery there's going to be in terms of movement."

"He said there's almost always something."

"But how is he now?"

"He can't talk," Kenny said. "He can't move much at all on the left side of his body, but that's the part that the doctor said would be most likely to improve."

"He doesn't really know," she said. "I'm not trying to say you shouldn't hope. But every stroke, every instance of paralysis, is different."

"That's what Nguyen said." And in the following silence he saw the maimed King, gray against the white of the hospital sheets, an abject thing. Sorrow: Kenny took the feeling apart, found different pieces. First was ordinary pity, the kind you feel for anyone broken, a weak, official feeling. Next was self-pity, Poor Kenny, O what will become of him? Another weak emotion. It had already happened to Kenny, most of it, whatever it was. The strong feeling at the center was this: a memory or an imagination of a memory of a time of happiness, a time when Kenny and his father and his brother and even his mother were together and doing things—a trip to the beach, maybe, a backyard barbecue. (How much of this was Kenny's own?—and how much advertising, happy-family propaganda . . .) He felt nostalgia without knowing if the place he felt homesick for had ever existed. His father was sick, would never be the same. His father was hardened into his own life, and now there was no way back. He remembered the pink bedroom: no way back to a boy's life, either, no way to understand it.

"It's weird," he said; and he wanted to shut up. He was having feelings. But that's what he was in the cave for, to show his feelings. It was *healthy*. He said, "It's hard to see him lying there," hoping this would pass inspection.

But Junie's mother wanted more. "He might be paralyzed for good," she said. "I'm not trying to rub your nose in it."

"No."

"But you need to think about it," she said. She put the chair down, turned to face him, turned the big lights of her understanding on him. "You need to feel your way into this," she said. "I mean, what's going on with you? How are you doing? What are you going to do with yourself, Kenny?"

He felt guilty, frozen, caught in the lights. She was asking him to manufacture feelings for her; asking him to counterfeit. Then anger started to rise in him. He is my father, Kenny wanted to say; seeing a picture, lit by flash, of his father lying in his own puke between toilet bowl and tub, the peach-and-white tile floor. My father, nevertheless.

"You need to get ready," Junie's mother was saying. "This could be a hard few months to get through."

And talking about it will make it easier? Talking to you? Kenny said nothing. A vision formed in his mind, his father's face on the hospital pillow: the King is dead, long live the King! The war was over, and Kenny had somehow won.

"I'm going to take care of him," Kenny said. "Take care of both of us, I guess."

"How are you going to do that? Where's the money going to come from, for one thing?"

"I don't know exactly," Kenny said. "I mean, I know he's got something coming in from work, some kind of sick leave or something besides the insurance. I'll find out."

"That's a big project, taking care of him."

"There's nobody else to do it."

She seemed to be surprised to hear this; she turned back to her work, looking for another plan, apparently. Kenny couldn't figure out what the first one was. He didn't know if there was some scheme or aim she had in mind for him, or whether this was just a ritual of concern; the queen of practical emotions, exacting her tribute. He said, "I have to live anyway."

She went on working. She said, "They have nursing homes, that kind of thing. They could take care of him. You could take care of yourself."

I have a parent in cold storage already. He didn't say it.

"I'm glad to see it, you and Junie," she said, "but my gosh, you're a glum pair! I realize, these are real problems, I'm not trying to make light." She didn't look at him; unpinned the seat cushion from the chair, and held it in the air in front of her, surveying it from different angles. She pointed it toward Kenny, a side that had been hidden from the sun for twenty years or so, that had kept its color while the rest had faded. "That's beautiful fabric, isn't it?" she asked. "That's a beautiful color."

Kenny agreed.

"The trick," she said, still looking at the seat cushion. "The trick is to not get stuck. You're seventeen, Kenny. You've got a future. You don't want to make decisions now that are going to make it harder for you. That's all I'm trying to say."

"I understand it, what you're trying to say."

"I don't think you do," she said, turning her eyes full on him, angry. Kenny was trapped in the headlights. "I don't think you've got the slightest idea, either one of you. You don't even know what it's like to be alive yet, and you're making these decisions that are going to affect every day of your lives after this. It's hard to watch, Kenny—it's like watching a drunk person trying to cross a busy street. All I can do is close my eyes and pray and hope for the best. Do you understand that?"

Kenny blinked, nodded. He felt his own anger rising up inside him, like he was supposed to live his life for her enjoyment.

"I don't have anything against you," Junie's mother said.

"Well, thanks," he said; but she missed the edge to his voice. He was dismissed, anyway. He had paid the tithe.

"Do you need anything?" she asked, as he retreated toward the door. "Money or anything?"

"I'm all right for now, but thanks."

"I'm glad to see it, you and Junie," she said. "It worries me, though. I'm just telling you that so you'll know. I don't have anything against you."

"No."

"But the two of you together, I don't know. All the long faces, I just don't know if Junie needs that right now. Don't worry about it," she said, and he was free to go.

Mixed messages, he thought, mixed feelings. Mixed drinks. That line about the glum seventeen-year-olds had been a favorite of his father's. Kenny stood in the stone hallway of the downstairs a minute, alone. The thing about this house: all of its wood and stone and careful angles connected it to the earth, made to seem to grow out of the earth; but in the process it picked up some of the earth's coldness, the underground darkness of stones and wet dirt. He thought of his father, the touch of his skin. Not physically cold—the heating was elaborate, efficient, hot-water pipes run through the concrete slab—but that underground sense of blind indifference, streams running out of sight. Down in the ground where the dead men go. He closed his eyes, remembered that his father might be dead, even then, was gone for something and he might not be back. Again that sense of hollow victory: the King is dead, long live the King! Kenny himself was the new King. Born again, King and Jesus of pain, O come let us adore him . . . His father's face, gray on the hospital pillow. Why here in particular, he wondered, why now? But there in the half-light, in the narrow hallway lined with stone, he felt his father's loss. His father had tried, once upon a time. Or maybe that whatever his father was, Kenny had grown around him, the way the apple tree in his grandmother's backyard grew around the wire clothesline she had strung from it years ago. No way to get it out without injury. He suddenly felt tired, exhausted. Was this what she wanted? To strip him of his ability to pretend, to ignore. To leave him defenseless. You want the truth, he thought, we will start with you: your daughter is a beautiful wreck, your husband missing, and yourself exiled to the land of the shades. Although you have a lovely ass. *Callipygian*, he thought; and remembered that he was here to see Junie.

Her father was alone in the kitchen, pulling a neoprene sleeve gingerly over his calf. It was a surprise to come up and find it still full daylight, an indifferent gray sky but still bright, four in the afternoon. The basement's perpetual twilight, dim skies through branches.

"I heard about your father," Junie's father said. "That's bad luck. Is he doing any better?"

"They don't know yet."

Mr. Williamson grimaced; out of sympathy, or out of pain—he pulled the brace all the way up over his knee at that moment—Kenny couldn't tell. Mr. Williamson was the odd man out, fair, freckled, and bearded while the rest of his family were dark. He was a lawyer who didn't look like one; he wore jeans to the office, big stout shirts, shoes with mountaineering soles on them. He drove a Jeep. He made a lot of money and drank too much, specialty beers and forty-dollar Scotch, and his legs were stout as baby trees, freckled and covered with an orange-blond shrubbery of leg hair. How could Junie come from this? He looked like a Celtic warrior, now in decline. Dry deltas of wrinkles converged at the corners of his eyes. "You need anything?" he asked Kenny. "Money or anything?"

"No, but thank you," Kenny said, thinking: if I took money from everybody who asked, I could go to Europe, take Junie with me. Fleeting vision of escape, gray skies over Paris. Matisse.

Mr. Williamson grunted and got up, evidently in some pain. "This feels worse every time," he said.

Then why do you do it? Mr. Williamson seemed to hear the question, though Kenny didn't ask it.

"I just think about how crappy I'd feel if I *didn't*," Mr. Williamson said, leaning against the counter, bending and stretching. A series of loud alarming sounds came out of his body as he did. This couldn't be good for you. Kenny longed for a cigarette, just watching him: the quick painful tensing of his face as he stretched his hamstrings, the wreckage in between. I'll never be you, Kenny thought.

"Unh," said Mr. Williamson. Snap, crackle, pop went his back.

"Is Junie around?" Kenny asked him.

It took Mr. Williamson a moment to surface, already deep in his runner's trance of pain and self-assertion. He would not be defeated. "Upstairs, I think," he said. "You can go up and fetch her yourself, if you want. I mean, that's fine. I'm off to the races, now— let me know if you need anything!"

All said distractedly. He was done with Kenny but Kenny wasn't gone yet. Mr. Williamson let himself out the kitchen door and chugged off up the empty street, breathing white vapor like a firetruck in a children's book, or a locomotive: The Little Engine That Could, it seemed like. Kenny puzzled over the "fetch her yourself" line until he realized it was some archaic form of courtship: the lady was to come down to the parlor to meet her gentleman friend. Or maybe some memory, fraternities and sororities . . . Junie's father was barely forty, a decade younger than Kenny's dad and even more opaque. Maybe he listened to Bob Dylan. Maybe he was in a peace march. Whatever. He didn't know the rules of his own house, didn't belong there.

A door opened, a door closed somewhere down the hallway and Kyle breezed through, casting a quick unfriendly glance at Kenny in the kitchen, going out without a word. He drove an Accord, too, a spotless black one. It started immediately, drove off quietly as an electric car. Kenny wondered where he was going: a gay bar; a martini party; an elegant reception; a shooting gallery. The kind of bruised good looks that suggested vampirism. Why not? He had the money. Again Kenny felt the faint suspicion on the back of his neck: what if she really was? What if they all were?

And then up the stairs, and into her bedroom without knocking. She was shuffling pictures on her desk again; tried to hide them away before he could see but it was too late.

"What?" he said.

"Well, you knock, when you come into somebody's room. You *announce* yourself."

"What would you be doing that you wouldn't want me to see?" he asked. He was being rude, he knew it.

"I might be otherwise engaged," she said.

"With whom?"

"My church choir," she said. "A Shetland pony. You never know."

Or Kim, he thought; and wondered where she had gone. They were inseparable, then came the hospital, now she was gone, or in some temporary exile. Which? He almost asked, though he knew he would be trespassing.

"What is that?" he asked, pointing to the half-hidden picture.

Gingerly she slid it out of the pile: it was his own face, he was suffering. His face was *troubled* in the picture. Trees in the background, a car window—it was the day on the canal, the skating trip that had ended in rain.

She said, "Kenny with blue lips."

"I don't remember you taking that."

"You weren't supposed to notice. It was when we were getting back into the car. I'd never seen you look like that, I couldn't help it."

"Very kind of you," he said.

"Don't be pissy," Junie said. "It looks like you. And thirty seconds either way wasn't going to kill you. We were back at the car by then."

He sat on the bed, drew her down toward him. They lay side by side on the narrow monastic bed, jeans against jeans. Kenny kissed her lips, and then her neck. Junie said, "What did Queen Kamehameha have to say?"

"Nothing much. I need to take care of my future."

"Jesus," Junie said. "She's pissed at you."

"For what?"

"She says it's for smoking cigarettes in here the other night. She smelled it two days later. Nose like a prize bloodhound. It's a sex thing but she can't admit it."

"She doesn't seem shy," Kenny said, and Junie laughed.

"No, shy is not the word. Retiring. Bashful."

"She *is* retiring," Kenny said. "I don't know what else you'd call the basement thing."

"She's jealous," Junie said; and Kenny couldn't tell whether she was still joking, whether this was feeling or a mockery of feeling. "My mother was born middle-aged."

"How do you know?"

"Let's argue about something else," she said. Something had come over her face, a little cloud. Her body was stiff under his hands, her shoulders bony and rigid. Language of touch: the way she could be all breasts and soft delights one minute, all elbows the next, all without meaning to. Kenny was learning her language; or they were inventing it together.

He took her hand in his own and brought it to his lips. She let him kiss the back of it; but when he tried to turn her hand, to open it, she pressed it against her body again. She said, "Don't do that."

"What?"

"It's so stupid," Junie said. "It makes me embarrassed."

He didn't know what she was talking about. "What?" he said. "I'm not teasing you."

She closed her eyes and shook her head. Let him take her hand again, and this time let him open it, passive. He could do anything he wanted with her. He kissed the palm of her open hand and felt her stir next to him, blood answering blood; kissed the inside of her wrist, and didn't notice anything until she went awkward again. When he looked, he saw the four parallel precise lines of scar tissue up the inside of her wrist. She saw him looking and drew away. "It's so stupid," she said. There was no daring now, no bragging.

A performance, Kenny thought; inspiring pity and terror. He felt an odd detachment. The scars looked deep, and serious—Kenny had learned to gauge the intentions by the scars they left: an invitation to death, a flirtation, or just a way of getting Mom's attention—but even so this was incurably junior high. She had this way of shrinking. He wanted tragedy, trombones and kettledrums; he kept on getting bubble gum. Why must I be a teenager in love?

"You're OK," he said. "That was a long time ago."

"That was last year," she said.

They lay there next to each other, each contained in each. Junie was thinking about something, miles away. Kenny was thinking about getting out. Boy-girl, boy-girl, boy-girl. He had been laid before and he would get laid again without the high hysteria and folly of suicidal virgins, self-pity, junked-up families. He had been suckered, like coming out of a bad movie and remembering that he had wept despite himself. Your self-perpetuating tragedy, he thought. The eternal flame, the temple of your self.

And where was Junie? Gone somewhere, too. One of those moments when both partners draw back into themselves, separate planets. Second thoughts; or maybe just buyer's remorse.

Shopping for love, Kenny thought. You made the bargain you could. Junie was first-class merchandise but damaged. He knew he was an asshole for thinking this but sometimes he felt like it was the only way he could see clear: people did what they wanted, they did what they could, and the other people around them were just counters, bodies. His father wanted a drink; the shortest distance between himself and a drink was his path, and if you were standing in the way, too bad. The rest was frosting, window dressing. The pornographic world. You are carrying around the hole I want to put my dick into. Bring me that hole over here.

The pornographic world: no other people, simply bodies, repositories. There was no proof that other persons existed at all. What you could see, what you could touch were bodies; bodies that existed, or didn't exist, to the extent that they could collaborate in your pleasure. Romance propaganda, religion propaganda, altruism propaganda: Mrs. Jane Dr. Williamson brings another body in and sets it down in the chair across, to perform once again the act, to gratify her own complex need to look like she was helping. After Jinx and after Kenny, she'd find another body to perform with; and there was always Junie, always handy, willing or not. Power disguised as love, power disguised as helping: the wheel kept turning, no matter what.

And in the pornographic world he was lying next to a girl, a beautiful seventeen-year-old. He raised her hand to his lips and started to kiss it again, because he knew he had to get around it; kissed the tips of her fingers, the soft mound at the base of her thumb, the lines of her palm, and finally her wrist again, feeling the blood warmth there, touching the tiny raised lines of the scar with his lips. She was frightened, then relaxed, then frightened again; and Kenny had the feeling of falling. I don't want to hurt you, I don't want to think about your feelings. A fair exchange, pussy for sympathy; but this wasn't right either, he found himself kissing the scars as if they mattered, as if she mattered to him. He told her that he loved her, he remembered that he meant it, he didn't know what to think.

And slowly she was moving with him, and nothing was decided. He moved from her wrist to her neck to her breasts, her clothes in a rumpus around them, and still he didn't know if they were making love or he was fucking her. She stood up, when they had gone a little too far.

"One minute," she said, tucking her shirt in. Don't leave me, Kenny thought, poor Kenny. Come back, I love you. Come back and do what I tell you.

She locked the door when she came back into the room, turned the light out and stood staring at him in the pale delicate gray light, the last of the afternoon. "What are you doing here?" she asked.

"I don't know," he said; but he saw that she had been as far away as he had, out in the world, wandering alone. Suddenly he wanted her close to him; wanted peace, protection from the porno-graphic world. He drew her down to him but she held back. She slipped her jeans off and folded them over the back of the chair, a moment for him to admire the long lines of her legs, the suspicion, glimpse of her dark hair under the tail of her shirt. As she was unbuttoning her shirt she reached into the pocket and took out a thing, he didn't recognize it at first, a dome of beige rubber that she set on the table and left there: Junie's diaphragm.

"What's that doing here?" he asked.

She took her shirt and her brassiere off before she answered, and lay down next to him. "In case she checks," Junie said. "I wouldn't put it past her."

Kenny stared at the thing in the half-light, a kind of fascination. He saw the mother creeping into the bathroom, gingerly opening the pink clamshell case; the family detective, the family suspect. *No pro-tection*. What harm was there to protect him from? But Kenny knew. Her clumsy hands fumbled with his belt, the buttons of his jeans. The diaphragm was watching them.

His father's face, gray on the white pillow. His father's hands gripped a rosary, as best they could. His fingers didn't work correctly. He seemed to fit here, in the pajamas Kenny brought from home, off-white with pale blue stripes and designs; flowerpots? Like everything else here, his pajamas were clean but looked like they would be dirty to the touch; like the hallways, the nurses' station, the tables in the waiting room, the magazines.

"It's hard for you to see him like this, I know," the doctor told him, outside in the hallway. "It's important for him. He needs to see familiar faces. Don't be frightened if he tries to talk."

"I'm fine," Kenny said. In fact he had seen his father like this constantly, drunk. How much damage had drinking done to him? And how much to me, he thought, me me me. Pulling the chenille bedspread slowly over his body, and over his head . . . He had seen his father like this all the time: the five-thousand-yard stare, the mouth working clumsily around some words that only Kenny understood. Here it was a Hail Mary, an easy guess. Blessed art thou amongst women, and blessed is the fruit of thy womb, Jesus. Fruit of the Womb, Kenny thought. My father is dead.

Dead: he turned the word over in the stillness of the room. The man in the next bed was dying, clearly. Mr. Lawson was grunting and crying yesterday with all the pain, but now he was just lying quietly behind the drawn curtain. Kenny's father had the window side, the best bed as always. Kenny could hear the footsteps shuffling in and out of Mr. Lawson's tent, the door opening and closing, that afternoon the monitor that was counting the heartbeats left to Mr. Lawson, one by one. November in the trees outside.

Here it was gray, quiet. The progress of the year had been suspended: Mr. Lawson wouldn't see spring; Kenny's father might not know it when he did. A sudden loud sound from Mr. Lawson's tent, a sound of surf, or a motor, a motorized pump—and then Kenny realized that he was listening to the amplified sound of Mr. Lawson's heart. It filled both sides of the room, quickening and slowing, until Kenny felt his own heart moving to the same rhythm. *Shit,* Kenny thought. Something was happening. Just yesterday Mr. Lawson had been sitting up in bed as Kenny came in, had even managed a curt nod of welcome, though he was preoccupied with pain. He looked like a retired supermarket manager, or a GS-15, one of the government's gray worker bees. Still he was determined to die courageously. Kenny could tell; in the curt military nod he gave when Kenny passed through his room; in the way he stifled his own throat when the pain overcame him. Go ahead and scream, Kenny thought, let some of it out. You won't bother anyone here. In some ways the grunting was worse.

That was yesterday, though. Today Kenny hadn't seen anything of Mr. Lawson, except as he was reflected in the faces of the nurses and technicians as they came and went. A knot of relatives, sheepish, embarrassed, in the way. Kenny saw everything in glimpses, on his way to the bathroom, to the waiting area for a smoke. When he came back, the relatives were gone, and the sound of the heart had quickened. Did you get used to it? Kenny wondered, feeling his own heart accelerate, the autonomic, sympathetic . . . The technicians learned not to hear it, not to respond, they had to. Kenny felt the sweat start in his scalp, felt his hands go damp and clammy. He stared at his father, who didn't hear, or didn't seem to. His fingers clicked from one bead of the rosary to the next, skipping two or three, or staying on the same one. His lips were muttering, a prayer, an incantation, Kenny couldn't tell. Maybe it was nothing.

He closed his eyes and tried to calm himself. The heart beat faster and faster and then, all at once, seemed to stop. It reasserted itself slowly, unsteadily; a swirling, liquid sound instead of the piston beat of before. Kenny heard footsteps, voices through the curtain. Mr. Lawson was going. Kenny kept his eyes closed and heard the sound of the ocean surf in the heartbeat: the crash, the flood, the outflow, the water gathering itself for another movement, poised . . . Thought of Junie on the beach, the salt taste of her cunt, a complicated elsewhere. Kenny wasn't only here. Another life was waiting for him, outside. Life and death, drink and drama. Maybe this was the last of it. Maybe he was done with his father. *My future,* Kenny thought; he saw nothing clearly, except that she would be in it; then remembered the teenaged drama of her cut wrists, and then all the rest of it seemed like tinsel, too, the walk on the beach and the unprotected fuck.

The heart beat slowly, oceanically. Kenny wanted to believe but she kept shrinking on him; another dramatist, like the gray face on the pillow. Kenny didn't have enough sense to keep himself out of trouble.

Except Kenny wasn't done with her, he knew it. The comfort of thinking about her. She brought him solace. In that moment, he wanted to see her. It was simple, like hunger, thirst. He wanted to see her. He closed his eyes, and in the darkness he imagined her face.

"Shit," somebody said next door. The heartbeat stumbled, galloped. A stream of orders, footsteps rushing, the door was opened and stayed open. Kenny unclosed his eyes but there was nothing to see—just the heartbeat filling the room, the drunken stumbling of its pace. Faster, slower, inconclusive; it seemed like it had lost its way.

"Come on," said the same voice, and another echoed it, "Come on!"

The heartbeat stumbled again, and then stopped. Started again strongly, a brave sound, beat for a minute or more and then it stopped and it didn't start again. There must have been ten or twelve people on the other side of the curtain. Kenny could hear them all not saying anything.

His father opened his mouth and tried to speak.

"What?" Kenny asked.

"Thanga," his father said.

"What?"

"Thangga," his father said.

"Thank God," Kenny said.

His father blinked his eyes, yes. "Fuggin noise," he said.

And Kenny saw that his father was coming back after all.

They sat through the first half of the concert tentatively, restlessly, like children at a recital. Kenny folded his hands in his lap. Junie twisted her program into origami knots, into constituent fibers. Kenny started to itch and sweat in his good wool sweater, the one he got from his mother for Christmas two years before. The secret language of clothes: this present was sane, it didn't require explanation, she had shopped for it herself and mailed it herself and it arrived from Baltimore with two days to spare. It was the last time he had let himself hope for her. This feeling of good-bye was at odds with the music—a string quartet—at least at first. It seemed determined to be spry, to make the music leap and shimmer. An Appalachian brook in spring sunshine, clattering over boulders. Outside was four inches of snow on the ground, more predicted on the way that night.

They were in the east court of the museum, a colonnaded square that rose forty or fifty feet to a glass dome. Rubber trees and elephant-ears surrounded a fountain in the center of the court, usually playful, shut off for the concert. They sat on industrial metal folding chairs in concentric semicircles, no more than thirty in the audience. The threat of snow must have kept them home; there were twice as many empty chairs as people.

The tickets were a gift from Junie's father, of course. He subscribed to everything and never went. A man of unpredictable generosity. He gave Kenny a bottle of wine once, for helping to rake the leaves in the yard, that turned out—after he and Junie had drank it—to be worth forty or fifty dollars. It was good wine, Kenny thought, maybe not great, a little too much like iodine. Further proof that he didn't know anything.

Something offhand, indifferent about the feeling in the courtyard; like the quartet was playing to the empty chairs, and not to the few bodies scattered between them. Fuck Vivaldi, Kenny thought. He thought of a record that Wentworth had called *Sounds of the Dragstrip,* about forty-five minutes of burnouts, blowups, and wrecks. And what was Junie thinking? Maybe she *liked* Vivaldi, maybe this frantic paper-shredding was just her way of listening. (Later, looking back, he keeps trying to talk to himself, like he could break through the glass of ten years between them and shout to his younger self *be kind, be kind . . .*) And then they started the last piece before the intermission, something by Bach, and Junie sat still and paid attention. This told Kenny to listen, and he did, and this matched the feeling of the place exactly: the island of warmth and intelligence and all the coldblack night pressing down against the dome. Human intelligence, he thought, concentrated . . . There

109

was no sense of making pictures, of Moorish castles. Kenny liked the mathematics of it; the music chimed with his own sadness. The empty seats confirmed the feeling: intelligence, beauty laid out for anyone who chose to come and listen. And almost nobody came.

Then the quartet was finished, and there was a break. The audience was free to roam the galleries until the music started again, in twenty minutes or so. They left their coats draped over the chairs. Kenny wanted to take his sweater off, it was too thick, a ski sweater, and the air inside the courtyard was thick, fertile, fecund; life and leaf rot mixed, and damp earth, and heat. Trails of sweat went dripping down his back, like raindrops, but the shirt he had on underneath his sweater was old and frayed. He didn't think it was actually torn but he remembered clearly that the collar was frayed so you could see the white lining under the plaid fabric. And Kenny already didn't belong. Junie, all in black, looked wrong for the museum, too; but she was *trying* to be wrong, succeeding, while Kenny was born wrong. Poor-boy blues; except he wasn't exactly poor. He left his sweater on anyway, and followed her down the darkened hall.

"Aren't you hot?" she asked.

"I'm all right," he said. "Cold-blooded."

"Me, too, but I'm still hot in here. What do you want to see?"

"You," he said, "without any clothes on."

"Gee, I mean, that's just *so* immature," she said; a complex game of mockery, hard to say who was the object. A roomful of Picassos, they passed without comment. The other concertgoers were gathered around the Impressionists, talking and laughing in muted voices, church voices. Water lilies! Cathedrals! Art! They made him lonely; the disappointment of the painting itself, after seeing the images on raincoats, calendars, posters. Even the first time through these galleries, he'd had the feeling that these paintings were worn-out. Kenny thought sometimes that the world was shrinking on him. This made him lonely, without knowing exactly why. He took Junie's hand and she let him.

They wandered away from the others, they fled. The galleries were lit as usual but the corridors between seemed much darker than usual; or maybe Kenny had only been in here in the daytime. Whatever. The gloom, the dusty potted plants and the Roman statuary that emerged from the shadows—again, it was hard to hold in mind that they were real, and not rigged up from fiberglass—reminded Kenny of a funeral home in California, the one his grandmother was buried from. He pictured the letters above the door in Roman capitals: FUNERAL HOME OF WORLD ART. A bronze Rodin lurked in the gloom, a man in a strange hat. He glowered at the two of them. They passed a gallery of Matisse, brilliant colors in the light, like displays of fresh fruit.

He followed her downstairs into the saints-and-angels section. St. Sebastian was the one with the arrows; after that he forgot. The sacred bleeding heart of Jesus. He let his eyes blur: the dominant colors were brown, red, and gold, an occasional washed-out sky blue. He could see these paintings better if they hung them upside down. As it was, they took him to church and left him there.

"Are we supposed to be down here?" he asked Junie. His voice whispered after him on the marble floor, the hard walls, sibilant *s*'s and *t*'s; church, again. *Et cum spiritu tuo . . .*

"I didn't see a sign," she said. "I mean, I don't see why not."

Trespassing, Kenny thought. You had to be born rich, white, confidant. Kenny thought they might go to jail but it never occurred to her. He asked her, "What are you looking for, anyway?"

"I can never find it," she said. "I have to get lost first and then I always end up in front of it, but I can never just come in and find it."

"What?" he asked; but she was gone again, and he was following. They hadn't seen anyone, guard nor guest, since they left the Impressionists. The paintings sat on the wall, official, self-satisfied, like a lecture on citizenship, a short course in history. Common sense. Empty words in a loud voice: A stitch in time saves nine. A penny saved is a penny earned.

"Here it is," said Junie. "I told you, I can only find it by accident."

She stopped in front of a gigantic Salvador Dalí painting, the Last Supper rising out of the clouds with some sort of geometric structure evanescing behind Jesus. Some kind of parody of church art going on, along with a commentary on art-art, then the Buckminster Fuller aspect . . . Kenny couldn't quite make it add up. Plus it was butt-ugly.

Junie said, "I don't know why, but I really like this."

He said, "This is like a test or something, right?"

"You don't like it?"

"I don't know," he said; then realized that he was lying to her, and corrected himself. "Actually, no, I don't like it."

"This isn't a test," she said; a warning.

"What are we fighting about?"

"You're such a fucking perfectionist, Kenny." She was close to tears. "This is supposed to be nice, right? It's romantic. Violins and art and so on, right? But I'm afraid to *like* anything, Kenny. I'm always afraid you're going to make fun of me."

"I'm sorry," Kenny said; and was. The true asshole spirit; thinking of his father, judging the universe from the standpoint of nothing at all. A lover's prayer. Dear Jesus don't let me fuck this one up.

"I mean, I guess it's stupid and everything but I *like* this painting," she said, "and I brought you down here because I wanted you to see it and now I feel like about a nine-year-old."

"It isn't stupid," Kenny said. "I mean, I don't think you're stupid at all. It's just, I don't know."

"You still think I'm stupid for liking this."

"No, I don't," he said; trying to still the voice that did distrust her. She was drawing away, almost gone. He had to hold on to her and couldn't think of how. "I just don't like this painting, is all."

"I got that message."

"Actually, it makes my eyes want to vomit."

She stared at him, wide-eyed, like he had slapped her; then against herself she laughed, and shook her head, and they embraced each other; and Kenny noticed once again that she was exactly his height. They rested, heads on shoulders, for a minute, then slid to the floor. Kenny leaned against the wall, under the Dalí, and Junie leaned against him.

"I can't stand this," Junie said.

"I know," he said. "It isn't you."

"Well."

"Don't make me say it."

"What?"

"I am *fervently fond* of you. I am *avid*. I am *ardent*."

"I am somewhat avid myself," she said. Leaned back against his chest and closed her eyes, left Kenny to puzzle out what exactly she meant. Resting. His hand inside her dress, lost in the loose folds of black cloth. The two of them were literal, always. Nothing between them that was not expressed in bodies. He had just slipped aside her underwear to touch her when the guard came in, to tell them that the concert had started ten minutes before. The guard was polite but firm.

They didn't dare enter the courtyard, either, since the music had started. They listened from the doorway, watched the musicians through the foliage. If anything the music sounded better from the doorway; at least when he could concentrate. Kenny leaned against the cool marble and Junie leaned against him, shifting and twitching her beautiful ass against him. She was turning into a wicked girl, a very wicked girl. Their empty overcoats sat slumped in the folding chairs, side by side, listening.

This was the saddest story Kenny heard: the girl's little brother, the one who was puking in the bushes, he read the side of the nonalcoholic beer can and saw it said less than one half of one percent alcohol by volume. He was ten. He figured that half a percent was better than nothing and probably plenty for him and so he went in with his other little buddy and bought a case and drank it. Now they were puking, undrunk, miserable while the party raged around them.

"Somebody's bound to call the cops," Wentworth said.

"You think so?" Boy asked. He looked around. "The windows are closed, mostly. The band's in the basement. I mean, some asshole could always call the cops."

"There's always an asshole," Kenny said.

"Dude!" said Wentworth.

"Mister Bitter!" said Boy. "I'm not attached, though."

"Me neither," Wentworth said. "This is just so . . . *seventies.*"

"And that's the good part," Kenny said. There was a keg of beer in the kitchen, a band sawing away in the basement. The Cringers went to Kenny's high school. Their specialty—in fact, their whole act—was dredging up the worst songs of all time and then playing them, mostly in suicide-tempo thrash versions but sometimes at length. The high or low point of their act was a nine-minute dirge version of "Honey," by Bobby Goldsboro. Everybody hated them. They played at every party. "Billy, Don't Be a Hero," "Hooked on a Feeling," "Born to Run."

"It makes me feel like sniffing glue," Boy said.

"I was reading that in the paper the other day," Kenny said. "The ten warning signs. If your child comes home with gold or silver paint on his face . . ."

They all three cracked up laughing and Kenny didn't finish. Then they went out to the car and smoked another joint while they were driving around. They went downtown without even knowing what they were looking for but there was nothing: scrap paper blowing around in the cold wind, an occasional wino. Kenny was alone in the backseat of Wentworth's car, a teal Suzuki, a kicky, college-student car. Wentworth had a future. He had his applications out. Boy had his applications out. Junie got her SAT scores back the week before and they sucked just as bad as the first time she took them but she'd get in somewhere. She didn't test well; or maybe, Kenny thought, maybe she was just plain fucking dumb. She was out with Kim that night and Kenny was not feeling kindly disposed toward anyone or anything. He said, "A kicky, college-student car."

"Dude!" said Boy.

"My parents picked it out," said Wentworth. "You want to walk?"

"I'm just noticing," Kenny said. "I bet it gets terrific gas mileage, too. You checked it lately?"

"He's walking," Wentworth said. "What do you think?"

"Fine with me," said Boy.

"OK, I take it back," Kenny said. "I love this car!"

"Shut up," Wentworth said.

"Teal!" Kenny said. "Potpourri! Avocado!"

"Shut *up!*" Wentworth said.

"I'm hungry," Kenny said.

They wound up at the Awful Shoppe, where the cops all ate between shifts and the cooks had prison tattoos. The air inside was saturated with grease and cigarette smoke and something else; it took him a minute to figure out that it was hair spray and perfume, wafting over from the next booth. Kenny snuck a peek and it turned out to be a man in drag. A quick obscure feeling, guilt, or something like it. He didn't dare look too long and hard or the man in drag would recognize him, would see what they had in common and give them both away somehow. The hands gave him away, the way he flipped his cigarette around. Kenny was denying himself, he felt the betrayal. Somewhere he had joined up with Junie's party, the party of sex, the revolution of souls, but he couldn't show himself yet. Kim Nichols in her nonexistent brother's clothes. And what was Junie doing with her? It was just mentioned, between Junie and her mother. Nothing direct between her and Kenny. Maybe there was nothing to say; maybe there was no way to say it, maybe Kenny would never know. *Jealous,* he thought; and quickly admitted it. You're mine now.

"I want to go to Mexico," Boy was saying. "Copper Canyon, I've been reading about it. They say you could put the Grand Canyon into it four times over. And the Terahummerasomethingorother Indians, what's their name?"

"Who?" asked Wentworth.

"The ones who always win the marathon," Boy said, which didn't ring a bell with anybody.

"A swinging senorita in a Mexican bordello," Wentworth said. "You ever heard of Boy's Town?"

"Fucking donkeys," Kenny said. "That was the hot rumor in the seventh grade, anyway, girls fucking donkeys. Various common household pets as well."

"What?" Boy said, irritated.

"German shepherd," Wentworth said.

"Then why didn't he say German shepherd?"

"I don't know," Wentworth said. "We could ask him—he's right here, more or less. Mr. Kolodny, why did you give us that fancy bullshit about pets instead of just saying it was German shepherd?"

"It slipped my mind," Kenny said. "I remembered it was a dog, but I couldn't remember which kind."

"Newfoundland," said Wentworth. "Irish wolfhound. Great Dane."

"No, Pekingese," said Boy.

"A brain fart," Kenny said. "I believe that's the technical term for it."

"Or maybe he's in love," said Boy.

Kenny scowled at both of them. Like sharks, he thought; they like their water with a little taste of blood.

The food came then and they all tucked in: french fries, milk shakes, chocolate pie. Wentworth didn't eat any more or less than

Kenny and Boy did but he was fat and they were skinny. There was something pornographic about watching him wolf down his Key lime pie, coffee, *and* a Coke on the side; about watching him pour the real cream into his coffee, the patterns it left, like cigarette smoke, in the dark coffee before he stirred the sugar in. Wentworth was hungry. What was Boy's vice? Apart from snakes and reptiles, of course. A basement full of penises according to Tom Harris, the English teacher who liked to psychoanalyze his characters. And who will psychoanalyze Tom Harris? He lifted weights, had a fire hydrant for a neck.

"Food and sex," Boy said.

"And tobacco," Kenny said, rolling himself a postprandial cigarette, lighting it, staring out the window. Sometimes when he was stoned the words just wandered through—*postprandial*—or formed themselves into pairs and trios, and performed the Lobster Quadrille: navigate, vegetate, investigate knave evaginate.

"Speaking of which," Wentworth said, "are you really nailing the lesbian?" He was one of those boys who didn't have any power in himself but when he was around Boy he drew on Boy's power: they were together, he could say anything he wanted.

"None of your business," Kenny said.

"I know it's not," Wentworth said. "The thing is, I'm curious. *We're* curious."

"Youth wants to know," Boy said.

"Still none of your business," Kenny said. He was feeling the discomfort they intended to produce; boys in threes and fours, rotating from victim to victim. Not even Boy was exempt. But they didn't know what Kenny didn't know: what Junie was doing with Kim, somewhere out in the night.

"That's the other thing," Wentworth said. "How come it's always two girls together in those magazines? It's always one girl, two girls, hardly ever a guy and a girl."

"That's easy," Boy said. "Dicks are disgusting!"

He said this a bit too loudly, and exactly at the same time as one of those unpredictable moments of general quiet came over the diner. Everybody heard. Everybody quit talking, and the drag queen at the table behind Kenny cleared her throat.

"Well, they are," Boy said defensively, quieter.

"Ask the man that owns one," Kenny said. A quick uneasy memory of his father's apparatus, seen from the perspective of a seven-year-old, glimpsed under the bathrobe or his father getting into the shower. The hairy wrecking ball, back and forth.

"I'm fond of mine," Wentworth said quietly. "Mr. Lucky and I get along fine."

"Have you seen him lately?" Kenny asked; gesturing toward Wentworth's gut, attempting his revenge.

But Wentworth was undaunted. "In the mirror, just today," he said. "At Boy's house, as a matter of fact."

"Don't start," Boy said.

Wentworth ignored him. He said, "The thing is, I've seen this before, and it's always been a mystery. This is in the guest bathroom upstairs at Boy's house, you know, the one with the little seashell soaps? And on the shelf behind the toilet she's got a little basket of—"

"Potpourri!" Kenny chimed in. They said it together. Boy scowled.

Wentworth went on: "Anyway, there's a new decor item in the bathroom these days. She's put a mirror up in a little nest of dried flowers, on the back of the toilet tank, sort of leaning against the wall at the *exact right angle* for you to see yourself when you are pissing. I mean, is this unintentional? It seems like you could guess, you know?"

"On the other hand," Kenny said.

"Exactly. I mean, do you like to look at that part of yourself while it's committing that particular act? Does anybody?"

"Well," Boy started, but didn't go on.

"It isn't Mr. Lucky's good side," Wentworth said.

Kenny stubbed his cigarette out. A sudden wounding loneliness, a true knowledge that he was in the wrong place; there was nothing for him here. His two-dollar pocket watch said one-fifteen.

"I'm done," he said. "I'm fried."

"What are you talking about?" Boy said. "We're going to Ellen Hunnicutt's tonight."

"Not I," said Kenny. Ellen Hunnicutt was a junkie, everybody knew it, all her friends were junkies. Her family was unbelievably rich and never in town. Her mother didn't seem to exist. Her father was a big-game hunter who kept a trophy room full of souvenirs: the mounted heads of eland, buffalo, elk, a dozen others; a table made of a silver platter, set on four real zebra legs; an umbrella stand made from an elephant's foot; the fetus of a hippopotamus, standing on all fours. He had shot the mother but there wasn't room for her. This was where Ellen gathered her friends, in the trophy room. They watched television, listened to English rock, snorted heroin off engraved silver cigarette-cases. Sometimes they shot each other up in the bathroom. The scene with Ellen's friends was to look straight but act bent. Kenny went there once in a while, he was never exactly sure why; maybe because he tended to find a girl when he was there. Twenty empty bedrooms in Ellen's house, at least; standing orders to turn the covers back, so as not to leave stains on the comforters. And Kenny was welcome, a member of the club for some reason he didn't want to think about. They recognized him for one of their own at Ellen's house; while Boy and Wentworth didn't quite fit. He would have felt uncomfortable going with them, even if he felt like it in the first place. "Not tonight," he said. "What do you want to go there for?"

Boy glanced significantly at the cops in the opposite booth, who were laughing loudly; probably over a really *decent* beating they had given somebody, Kenny thought.

"I don't know," Boy said elaborately.

"Nod, nod, wink, wink, say no more," Kenny said. "Drop me at Wentworth's house, OK?"

Now Boy was pissed. He wanted Kenny to provide a social cover for him at Ellen Hunnicutt's, that was Kenny's guess. Or something, or something else. A spy, Kenny thought, avoiding the eyes of the beautiful drag queen: I'm not what I appear to be. I'm on your side. The eagle flies at midnight. They paid the check and went out into the cold night again and drove around aimlessly. *Time:* looking back, the most different thing is how much time he used to have: expanses, vistas of unbroken time . . . They drove back to Wentworth's house by way of anywhere else, driving by the party again where things were now quiet, stopping off so Wentworth could buy a quart of beer with his beautiful fake ID. No hurry, as much time as anyone wanted, more; time to kill in two-day parties, three-day marathons of Risk, that Kenny passed, stoned, holed up in Sumatra, waiting to finally lose. Time to spend the afternoon at Junie's house, looking at art books off her mother's bookshelves and talking about nothing. He could piss off Wentworth, or Boy, and not really worry about it; because there was always enough time to patch things up, sooner or later they'd be all right again, because there was really nobody else worth hanging around with. It was only later on that these days seemed golden; and only then because he had run out of them.

Frustration: a game they used to play with each other, with lips and tongues and fingers, or more than a game. Kenny didn't have a name for what it was. The rules were simple: to bring the other to the point of coming but not quite, and then just stay there, holding it off. Both of them played at the same time; if one of them flagged, or got too far away, the other one brought them back with lips and fingers and tongue. His whole body would ache. He couldn't decide if this was cruelty or kindness. It didn't seem to matter; didn't seem like there was any difference. After an hour or two—their record, in February, was three and a half hours—Kenny's blood would be pumping hard through his whole body, *engorged*. No part of him she couldn't touch and get him going, get him started. After an hour or two they had to ration their touches, even their looks. That was the beautiful part: when she would touch him with the tip of her breast, just the tip, the nipple barely brushing his chest, and Kenny felt it with his whole body, and shuddered at the feeling . . . The game was Junie's idea, at first, and he wondered where she learned it. And then he didn't care, not just out of his own pleasure but out of finding hers, where she would bend to him: the inside of her wrists, always, and some-times her breasts but not always. Her neck, especially the little hollow at the base, the peaceful valley sleeping there, and if she was lying with her back to him he could kiss the soft small hairs at the back of her neck with amazing results. This was new to Kenny: he had always been a visitor to girls' bodies before, quick to come and quick to go. Now he owned one girl's body, for as long as they played. She didn't mind if he looked, not after a while; didn't mind if he traced the lines with the tip of his finger, if he kissed her and held on. Kenny learned how far to go, and how to take it farther. Cruelty was never far away; teasing, aching. He woke up sore himself, in Wentworth's sister's bedroom, pink and frilly; pink and frilly. *Frustration.* He tried not to end up inside her but sometimes he couldn't help it.

The same night he went out with Boy and Wentworth, Kenny saw something else. They let him off and he went around into Wentworth's backyard and rolled one last cigarette for himself and lit it, sitting at the picnic table. It was too cold, really, but he wasn't allowed to smoke in Wentworth's house. He sat there breathing smoke and vapor into the air and feeling his hands freeze, watching the sky.

Then something happened. One minute he was sitting there watching the sky, where a heavy layer of clouds was breaking up into scraps with the moon behind it. The moon was almost full and the clouds were edged with moonlight as they broke up; scraps and tatters, cities and continents of clouds. Then he was driving out toward Junie's house.

It was almost two and he didn't expect to see her. He just wanted to see her house, for reasons unknown. He analyzed himself as he drove along but came up blank. He rolled another cigarette and lit it as he drove along, no small feat. When he got to her street he cut off the engine and the lights and sat there in what was left of the heat, smoking. Her house was dark, shuttered. Junie's car was in the driveway. Kenny didn't even know what he was looking for. The house just sat there.

He was ready to leave when he saw the headlights coming toward him down the street, a cul-de-sac. He slouched down in the seat. Suddenly Kenny didn't want to be seen. The car—anonymous American junk—slid up into Junie's driveway, behind the line of bushes; but they were bare, no protection at all. The door opened and he saw the two of them, Kim and Junie, in the interior light. Junie's head ducked over—he saw it clearly—and she kissed Kim on the lips, quickly, and then got out of the door and shut it and the car went dark. She went up her own steps quickly, fumbled with her key, let herself in and shut the door, all in a rush, as if she were upset. Kim Nichols waited a decent minute after the door shut, then heaved the giant car into drive (Kenny saw the backup lights flash on as she shifted) and down the driveway and out into the street. As she passed Kenny she waved hello, like it was noon or something. Kenny waved back, because he couldn't think of what else to do.

Then she was gone and the street was dark and empty again, the bare branches making witchy shadows in the streetlights. A kiss; but what kind of kiss? Good friends, good-bye, regrets, passion. *Spent* passion. Kenny felt like the one who had been caught. Maybe it was meant for him, to teach him a lesson. Maybe it would have been worse if they hadn't seen him, *worse* or better, he didn't have a useful definition. He sat there, anyway, while his car cooled toward freezing, making little ticking sounds. A kiss. Two girls could kiss, but not these two. It wasn't safe, it was illegitimate. Maybe they didn't care about gossip but still. Then Kenny took himself down off his high horse. Really he was jealous.

Jealous of what, though? It wasn't Kim, not exactly or at least not only. It was more like whatever person, man or woman, that was going to take Junie away from him. He knew it would be somebody, sometime. She was his for a while. Maybe it would be better if it *was* Kim; she would be loved, anyway. That was the feeling that he had for Junie: he wanted her to be loved, tended, taken care of; he wanted husbandry. *Marry me,* he thought.

He wasn't surprised to see her come outside again, already in her nightgown. She wore a heavy sweater over it, black sneakers. She came over to the passenger side of the car. Kenny unlocked it, and she sat down with her arms crossed in front of her. "What are you doing here, Kenny?" she asked.

"I don't know," he said.

"Are you spying on me?"

"No."

"Then what are you doing here?"

Marry me, he thought again. What if he had said it? (Nothing: but in memory these things stick and grow, epiphytic tendrils of regret, *sentimental* . . .)

"I didn't expect to see you," Kenny said. "I wish I could tell you that I knew exactly what I was doing."

"What?"

"I don't know." He buried his hands under his arms and slumped down behind the wheel, mummified. Looking at the visor as he spoke. "I guess, I don't know. I just wanted to see if you were still here."

"It's complicated," Junie said.

Their breath hung in vapor in the air of the car, along with her words: *it's complicated.* The words concealed some other reality that Kenny didn't want to think about. Kenny wanted it simple, I need you, I love you, I can't live without you, like the words to the songs that his father loved.

"I don't know what you mean, still here," she said.

Kenny tried to think of a way to explain himself. "I just drove all the way out here to look at your house," he said. "I don't know."

"You don't own me," Junie said.

"I never thought I did."

"Where I go, or what I do, or who I do it with, OK?"

"OK," Kenny said; but full of misgivings. So *typical.* She was shrinking on him again, a teenager in love, or not.

"I love you," Junie said. It caught him crossways, with his heart leaning away from her, he wasn't ready. At first they were just words, more words in the cold air. Then he heard what she meant and a big wave of plain happiness went through it. Goddamn, he thought. Look what I got.

"I thought I wasn't allowed to use that word," he said.

"Don't laugh at me," she said, and Kenny saw that she was

crying; didn't know why, they didn't seem exactly like tears of joy. Put his arm around her but she shied away, stiffshouldered and bony. "I went out with Kimmy tonight, I went out just to tell her," she said, snuffling. She still wasn't talking to him. "I came back and you're in the driveway spying on me, Kenny, keeping an eye on me."

"I didn't mean to."

"I don't want to live like that," she said. "I don't want to be under anyone."

"I didn't mean it like that," Kenny said. "I didn't mean that at all. I just, I don't know. I couldn't sleep. I love you."

"Ssshhh," she said, and pressed a finger to his lips.

"I thought . . ."

"I get to say so," Junie said. "You don't."

She laughed; that same giggly loss-of-blood laughter, not quite sane, and Kenny joined her.

Kenny said, "How about a hearty 'me, too'—is that permissible?"

"That's disgusting," she said, and leaned over and kissed him. "Don't be cute, please."

"I'm sorry," Kenny said.

"Don't be sorry," she said. "Don't start apologizing or we'll never stop." She kissed him again. "Now go," she said. "I'll see you."

He watched her up the stairs, the door closing, the wind in the branches. He watched the closed face of the door for a minute, two minutes. Nothing else was going to happen. He couldn't feel his hands much anymore. With clumsy fingers he started the car, turned the heater up to high, started off slowly toward Wentworth's house, *happy*.

Kenny went to see his father after school, the day they let out for Christmas vacation, or maybe another day, or another. The days won't sort themselves out for him. It was always afternoon, or night;

125

maybe because he got up late. This one was indeterminate gray, a bucket for the day to empty itself into. It was threatening to snow in an offhand way; maybe a few light flakes already drifting down, between the Kool billboards and the fortified-wine groceries. Down and dirty, Kenny thought. I'd die here, probably. Realistically.

"I'ssa news," his father said. "I'm a nome."

I'm going home: he didn't seem to care one way or the other as he said it but Kenny felt a shock. He saw himself lashed to the wreckage, sinking. His father had settled into his new manner, passive, indifferent, gray; he could speak—though it was only Kenny's hours of practice that let him decipher it; his father spoke with thick lips and his tongue swollen to fill his mouth. He didn't care. His eyes were elsewhere, thinking or not thinking, Kenny could never finally tell. Just then he was nodding to himself, silently agreeing, with something or somebody that Kenny couldn't see.

His father said, "Negst ee,"

"What?"

"Next *week,*" he said.

"That's great," Kenny said; though he didn't see how it was possible. He hadn't seen his father out of bed yet, and his father's hands—once enormous, fearful instruments—wouldn't work to hold a knife and fork. But who will help me bake the bread? Not I, said the little red hen. Who will wipe the spilled egg yolk from his face?

You will, you will.

Trapped: he looked around the tiny, orderly hospital room as if there were a hidden door there, some means of escape.

The devils: One for the wheelchair, and one for the tank; one for insurance, and one for the bank; one lived in the TV, bitching and whining; one slept in the hall light, constantly shining; one for the alcohol, one for the rag; one for the sag-sprung hole in the sofa where Dad sat gaping at Peter Jennings.

Kenny can't remember who built the wheelchair ramp; who wrote the checks, for rent, etc., when his father was in the hospital; whether Junie or his father came first. One minute he was ten feet tall and bulletproof with love, and then his father was home again. It's possible, maybe even likely, that his father's homecoming came first, and Junie's declaration came after—except for the clouds, the fat dark clouds breaking up in the moonlight that he watched from Wentworth's backyard; and there was no reason for him to be in Wentworth's backyard, not if his father was already home.

There's a note, a souvenir. He found it on the driver's seat of the Reliant, parked in the high school lot, after school the next day— and here's another thing that won't add up: how could he be out till three and back at school in the morning? Wasn't anyone watching? But Kenny's still got the note. It says this:

> Last night I saw you driving out of our street and I wondered
> if you were gone for good. What if there was an accident?
> What if you just left? Not that you would. But then I thought
> that it wouldn't matter, we're a part of each other now. It
> scares me, Kenny. It makes me happy.
>
> June Williamson

Baby steps, Kenny thinks, reading it now. Those first, tentative . . . but this is wrong, an underestimation, he knows it. Nobody knows what to do with love. Sometimes he believes, as he did when he was seventeen, that all adult life is a fiction: that the settled or sedate quality of adult life is only due to insulation, emotional distance. The familiar house, the familiar wife, the familiar children. Coloring inside the lines, staying there. Adults: when love strikes them, it's like an illness. Kenny has seen this in men he knows. Experience doesn't make them any better at it. Love makes them blind, love makes them strange to themselves. *Adult:* twisted around old injuries, like the apple tree in his grandmother's backyard, growing around the wire clothesline . . .

But he was seventeen, he was clumsy, because he didn't know what to do. He would get older, he would get better at love. He thought that what he felt for Junie was a kind of practice love, a first attempt that would lead to something better later; later, when he acquired the bitter wisdom that characters always seemed to have at the ends of novels. Tempered by the fires of life, etc. That *careless-ness*—it bothers him now, looking back, that casual devaluation. Kenny has learned nothing in the meantime that would have helped him, *nothing.*

He hasn't even learned to stop himself. He's always on the way to somewhere else, always becoming, always leaving; so that things become real only at the moment he leaves them. The present is a formless fog, a blur of bright lights noises and a few concrete certain-ties: I'm afraid, I'm hungry, I want to see you, I'm lonely. Then he departs, and through the rearview mirror he can see the outlines snap into shape: I should have, I could have, I *didn't.* Junie, he thinks. She was alive inside him, sleeping, taking shape through every waking and sleeping hour. He could feel the memory of her anytime on the surface of his skin; he still can. Junie, he thinks. He was in love; she loved him. It should have been enough.

They went out to dinner and then to Kim's house. The bones of the event. And it felt like it was after Christmas, although he's never been able to exactly place where Christmas went that year. He got nothing memorable: a book from Junie's mother, a book from Junie—what? He can't remember. He has two books of hers still, but he stole both of them: *Letters to a Young Poet,* by Rainer Maria Rilke, and an illustrated version of *The Walrus and the Carpenter.*

They went to a French place in Georgetown, anyway, name

forgotten. Junie was known there as her father's daughter; certainly a fuss was made over her, and Kenny, too, though he wished for less. He was wearing a green sport jacket that he found at Value Village and Junie's mother altered to fit him—dark green, almost black, but a green sport jacket nevertheless. His black shoes, shined, were worn-down at the heel, and his necktie wasn't fooling anybody. Fake! Imposter! He could feel them, the people who belonged here, staring at him around the corners of their menus.

"Relax!" Junie whispered when they were seated.

"Yeah, right," he said.

"You look like you're going for a probation hearing or something."

"Dentist's office," Kenny said. "Assistant principal."

"Ssshhh," Junie said. "Not so loud."

The captain came around and poured them each a half glass of wine. Now this was criminal. He fidgeted in his seat until they were alone again.

"It comes with the meal," Junie whispered. "You get these different courses, and a different wine comes with each one."

The captain returned, and set between them a plate with a dozen oysters resting on ice, a pattern of lemons around the edge of the plate, two tiny forks and the inevitable parsley. "Read what it says," June told him, picking up the card next to her forks. Kenny saw that he had one too; a menu of some kind.

"Belon and Kumamoto oysters on the half shell," he read. "You can't even read that?"

"Not without my glasses. I left them in the car."

"Why?"

"I wanted to concentrate," Junie said; selecting one of the darker, smaller oysters from the plate. The other kind were a bit fatter and pearl gray throughout, without the black lips of the small ones. She tipped her head back and slid the oyster into her mouth; Kenny watching the fine workings of her throat. She kept her eyes

129

closed for a moment, then opened them and said, "A Kumamoto, I believe."

"What's the difference?"

"Taste them, it isn't hard to tell one from the other. I can't remember which is which, is all."

He stared down at the glistening, pearly oyster flesh, each arrayed for sea-burial in the little boat of its shell. They looked immaculate, chilly, sanitary, but Kenny had to work up his nerve. "You left your glasses in the car on purpose?" he asked.

"Quit stalling," Junie said. "You've never eaten an oyster before?"

"Never a naked one."

"Naked oysters are the best," she said. "Go ahead."

For his first oyster, Kenny picked out one of the plumper, all-gray jobs; it looked safer, friendlier. He held it in midair, staring at it. Was this alive? He couldn't remember.

"Go for it," Junie said.

She had her teasing face on; wolfish, grinning. Her hair had started to grow out by then, just past a crew cut. Kenny was suddenly angry with her: for bringing him here, for teasing him, a public joke in a public place. They were all staring at him, trying to eat this ridiculous food. It wasn't meant for him; but he had to eat it anyway, like it or not. Do or die or both.

Then slipped it into his mouth and tasted—nothing. Not at first. Then gradually some delicate, concentrated essence of cold seawater, a faint something else. Not sweet exactly but balanced.

"That's not so bad, is it?" Junie asked.

He felt like a fool for feeling like a fool. Before he tried to answer, he took a sip of wine, some stone-flavored aftertaste that went exactly with the oysters. A table full of surprises. A science of taste, unsuspected.

"You didn't bring your glasses," Kenny said.

"Didn't you ever notice, when you're driving at night and it starts to rain or something, you turn the radio off?"

"I do," he admitted.

"I don't want any interference," Junie said; and he felt her own knee pressed against his, under the tablecloth. He drew away, looking half-frantically around to see who was watching; but nobody was watching. Junie knew already. They were public, anonymous lovers.

"I thought you were anti-pleasure," Kenny said.

"These are the *domestic arts,*" she said. "There's a difference."

Just then he saw her mother reflected in Junie's face; her severity, pride of distinction. Despite the glasses, Junie caught him.

"What?" she asked him.

"Nothing."

"Try the other oysters," Junie said; and Kenny did, letting the small, dark oyster slide into his mouth, holding it there for a moment. This one had a coppery, metallic edge that the other one lacked; a little stranger, a little more dangerous taste. Kenny liked it all right but he was glad he had started with the other.

"What's next?" Junie asked.

Kenny envied her blindness; though the other diners were starting to recede into the background, the blurred faces in the grandstand behind home plate. He looked at her face in the candlelight and saw that she was wearing a little lipstick, something with her eyes, some small trickery that he approved of totally. He said, "We aren't done with the appetizers yet."

"I want to know what comes next," she said.

He picked up the card, thinking lipstick, perfume, at last I understand; thinking of his mother, who wore dime-store cologne by the tablespoon, who missed her mouth with lipstick. Kenny read the card for her: "Sweetbreads."

"Oh, Jesus."

"What?"

"That's like, *lymph node* or something. I can't eat that."

"Maybe you could ask for something else," he said. "A substitute."

Now it was her turn to look nervously around the restaurant, like the Fraud Police were on their way to send them back to the nursery section. "That's all right," she said.

"I don't see why they'd mind," Kenny said. "I assume they've got some food back there somewhere. Maybe they could make you a soft-boiled egg."

"I just won't eat it," Junie said.

"Have an oyster," Kenny said.

"No, thanks."

"What?"

She was twisting the corner of her napkin into a hard little cord; pressing hard enough to turn the skin behind her fingernails white.

"What is it?" Kenny asked.

"My *anti-pleasure* instincts, as you call it."

"I'm sorry," Kenny said. "I didn't mean . . ."

"No, you're right. I mean, it bothers me that so much time and energy and money are going into one dinner. People are sleeping on the streets outside. And then I think about how much film and paper I could buy with the money that this dinner is going to cost."

"You already have all the film and paper you need," Kenny said.

"What do you mean?"

It's self-indulgence, he wanted to say; you belong here; it's stupidity to pretend you don't. It isn't like you. He picked up an oyster and examined it, a Belon, pearly flesh in the candlelight. Some part of this was its mouth and some part its asshole, presumably. Organs. He slid the oyster down his throat, undifferentiated.

"Don't make speeches," Kenny said.

"What do you mean?" she said; a warning.

"We're having a good time."

"Thank you, Dad." She wouldn't look at him; the waiter came, and took away the plate of ice, the empty shells and two or three remaining oysters that they were suddenly too busy fighting to eat. In front of each of them, the waiter sat a small earthenware dish (a *ramekin,* he remembered; the word came to him like a gift) in which three or four small bland-looking objects were simmering in some kind of dark brown sauce. The way the sauce smelled was amazing; and Kenny thought maybe she was right, maybe there was an art to this. He tore off a corner of a roll and sampled the sauce with it and it was amazing. What—butter and garlic and something else, dark brown. Quickly, while he was still hungry, he tried one of the sweetbreads, and it tasted like what? Not too much. Mostly it tasted like the sauce, which was fine with Kenny. "I like lymph node," he announced.

"Don't," she said.

The waiter brought tiny lamb chops in a complicated mustard sauce; the smallest carrots that Kenny had ever seen; a salad of Dr. Seuss greenery, tendrils and petals; a Roquefort soufflé; a fresh half-glass of wine with every change in the food. A kiwi sorbet. A poached peach. A demitasse of espresso apiece, to speed them home.

The alchemy of food and wine, comfort on a winter night and lulled conversation from the tables around them—intelligent, profound, as long as you couldn't make out the words—eventually brought Junie around again, though the ghost of her bad mood lingered in the air over the table. You should start a magazine, Kenny thought: *Bad Mood.* Who would subscribe? (I would, he thought, I just did.) She ate about half, all the vegetables and none of the meat. Kenny finished the baby lamb chops for her, naturally, a big hungry boy (exactly her size). He felt delicate and gross all at once, sucking the meat from the tiny bones. What next? Eel pie, mackerel, a plate of robins . . . Junie was staring, off in the distance somewhere.

"What?" he asked.

She shook her head. "I'm just sad," she said, "a little."

"Why?"

"A year from now . . . ," she said. "I don't know. I got into college today, Kenny, the one I want to go to anyway. Out in Oregon."

"That's great," he said, not trusting himself to look at her. They were both almost whispering; somewhere near dessert, they were enjoying themselves in adult-world; neither of them wanted to be thrown back down to the nursery for talking about college. At the same time Kenny felt the news. He was losing her. He had known it all along but he forgot most times. They could live without remembering it, they could fight and fuck and go for walks, but the basic idea was always there: Junie was leaving, Kenny was staying behind.

"Oregon," Kenny said. "I hear it rains."

"It actually rains less there than it does here," she said. "It rains less *inches* but more *days.*"

Kenny tried to figure if this was a good deal or not and then gave up; it didn't matter to him, one way or the other. He let himself look at her and there she was in the candlelight, going, gone. A sadness overtook him, not at this specifically, just in general. The part that nobody talks about: it's not bad being depressed, the blue tinge around the world. If there's nothing you can do anyway, nothing that will help. She was going, off into adult-world for good, and Kenny was going where? Somewhere else. Little humans. He wondered if this was part of the secret world of adults, that somewhere between the dessert and the last sip of coffee they all looked up and saw that it was no use, the cold world waiting for them outside despite this temporary comfort. He smiled for Junie, resignation, a performance. She shook her head. She was *helpless.* Kenny was *blue.*

He lifted the last sip of the last glass of wine toward Junie and said, "The future."

"The future," she said, and raised her glass and touched his with it and they both drank. Others were watching them, Kenny could sense it: two beautiful young people, sentimental. Everybody saw themselves reflected in them. Kenny wanted to tell them: you were never like this.

After dinner, because they were supposed to, some prior arrangement that was opaque to Kenny, they went to Kim's house. He can't remember why. His own mood had been thrown into confusion by Junie's college news, and by the excesses of the dinner; he felt loose-limbed, heavy, passive, ready to be taken downstream.

A cold clear winter night outside, more stars than Kenny could remember once they got out onto the parkway. He slouched down in the passenger seat of the Accord, staring up at them. "Life is good here in the suburbs," he said. "You've even got extra stars out here."

"Don't start," she said. "And sit up."

"Why?"

"The seat belt would cut your head off if I had a wreck."

Kenny lolled sideways in the seat, so his head came to rest in her lap.

"Don't," she said, but he ignored her. I could sleep, he thought. *The firm yet supple outlines of her thighs,* he thought, quoting what?— old blue-cover pornography. Found in his father's sock drawer, or passed around in junior high. *She turkey-trotted to another grunting, gasping orgasm.* Kenny slipped his hand under the hem of her skirt, to feel the bare skin underneath. "I'll have a wreck," she said.

He sat up but he didn't take his hand away; instead, he let it wander up her leg, into the privacy of her lap. He glanced at the speedometer: sixty, sixty-five, somewhere between. "Don't," she said; and Kenny heard her but it was like he didn't hear her. He felt like he was dreaming. He let his hand stray higher, and he felt the dense, springy mat of her pubic hair under the cotton. She was already wet, he could feel it through the cloth.

"I mean it," Junie said. "I'll have a wreck." But there was no particular force behind her words, and she didn't make any move to stop or to move away. What? Neither of them had permission for this. He slipped the panties aside and stuck two fingers inside her and she said, Oh! and kept driving. Kenny didn't touch her anywhere else. She sat up straight, in case anyone was watching: ten or ten-thirty, a sprinkling of cars but nothing much. She was as wet as he had ever felt her. He started to stroke her, softly at first and then harder, and then she was moving with him, small movements of her hips. Kenny turned to look at the road and almost wrecked it; she stopped, he felt her back away. He had to trust her. He turned back to watch her face, her eyes fixed forward on the road, and after a few seconds she started again, gently rocking, small sounds bubbling in the back of her throat. She was seeing less and less, Kenny knew that. It didn't matter. He closed his own eyes and felt her rocking against his hand, the small movements getting ruder, harder, he felt himself reduced to the touch of her. His own dick was straining against the cloth of his jeans. The cage of her pelvic bone, the weight of her, harder and harder. "Oh, shit," she said, "oh Jesus, Kenny," and then he knew she wasn't far. Almost opened his own eyes but he didn't want to stop it; wanted to be inside her, suddenly more than anything, but it was impossible; and then it was too late. She started to come, a shudder that started as a trembling deep inside and spread, and he could feel it and wondered if they were going to die from it and saw that maybe that was the plan; maybe that was always the plan.

When he opened his eyes they were driving normally at about fifty-five down the parkway and Junie was fine, a deep red flush on her chest, her cheeks. "How did you do that?" Kenny asked.

"I didn't mean to."

He drew her hand over to his dick and she let it rest there for a second or two; then took it back and placed it on the steering wheel. She said, "That's your problem, buddy."

"I'll whine," Kenny said.

"What?"

"I don't know."

"Well, I don't know either," she said, "and I don't I want to think about it. You started this."

"There's a rest stop or a turnout, something," Kenny said.

"We could get arrested."

"We could figure something out," he said. "You missed your turnoff anyway."

"Jesus, Kenny," she said, and she was angry again. "Why is this always such a fucking bargain? I come and then you have to come, except it isn't the other way around. Why can't you just leave it alone for now?"

She was scared: scared of what they were doing, what they might do. Maybe she was right to be.

But it was too late to stop. "It's OK," he said softly. "There's a place to pull off a little ways up."

"You're not even listening to me."

"Please," he said; and it was nothing in the words but the way he said it that moved her. She glanced at him, suspicious. Then *against her better judgment* pulled the red car off into the turnout. This was going to be all Kenny's fault. He didn't mind. There were parking places, a mysterious building, always locked. Kenny had been here before, or another place that was identical. A path down to the river? They locked the car and left it and in the moonlight—a little less than half a moon, not quite enough to see by—Kenny found the path, where it led into the woods. The leaves of the bushes were bright in the moonlight, the path a dark opening between them, leading nowhere. "Where are we going?" Junie asked.

"I don't know," Kenny said; leading her by the hand, stumbling over rocks and roots in his black city shoes, rundown. It was cold. The ground was clear of snow, but the mud was frozen into ruts and humps and old footprints; other people had been this way before; the thought caused a sadness in Kenny that he couldn't explain. That stale, used-up . . . she leaned against the trunk of an oak tree, at the edge of a little clearing in the moonlight, he could see her against the rough bark, and she stepped out of her panties and then he was inside, under her skirt, the unbelievable fact of her warm pussy under all those clothes and all that cold night and Kenny shot off almost as soon as he was inside her and they stood there resting against the tree, her legs around him, her back pressed into the bark of the tree. He was still inside her. The feeling came back over him again, of all the others who had been there before, who had littered these woods with their used rubbers; but this was different, a sacrament, skin to skin. No protection. Kenny's knees started to tremble from the weight of both of them and she slipped away from him, back into herself; back onto the ground, supporting herself, away inside her clothes.

"Steady there, soldier," Junie said. "You're shaking."

"I'm cold," he said; although he wasn't cold. What? Angelic visitation, something. He was *lit up* with love for her; he was the burning bush itself, the flaming sword, the tongue of fire. He looked around the small moonlit clearing, the river flowing somewhere close by the sound of it, the intermittent cars on the parkway; and Kenny thought that she had come with him; she had been afraid but went along anyway, that if he said go, she would go with him. Love he could touch, love that had weight and consequence. Holding her against him. Leaning against the tree himself, now, with his coat open and Junie wrapped in it, her back to him. He tasted the short hair on the back of her head, felt the warm belly under the layers of cloth.

"You're crazy," Junie said. And the fact that she could say this, the idea that she trusted him . . .

A cop was waiting in the parking lot when they got back, a park policeman shining his searchlight into the empty driver's seat of the Accord. He got out of his car as Junie unlocked the door of theirs. "This your car?" asked the cop.

No, thought Kenny, don't get sarcastic. The temptation was almost more than she could resist, either of them: we were just walking down the parkway, trying these keys in every car we saw . . . At the same time, he was scared. What if he had caught them, come looking for them?

"Did we do something wrong?" Junie asked.

"You're not supposed to park in here after ten," the cop said. "There's a sign on the way in and another one right there." He shined the flashlight on a brown enamel sign ten feet in front of Junie's car, NO PARKING 10 P.M.—6 A.M.

"Shit," Kenny said. "I mean, shoot." He tried to think if he was drunk, what the rules were. The cop scowled at him.

"Can I ask what you were doing in here?" the cop said.

"We were looking at the moonlight," Junie said. Kenny wanted to kiss her for it: she was so calm and clear, so matter-of-fact, like anyone with half a brain would be out looking at moonlight tonight.

"You went down to the river?" the cop said.

"Not all the way," Junie said.

"You should go down to the river sometime. I mean, before ten o'clock." He shut off his searchlight and the three of them stood around in the dark for a minute, their eyes adjusting to the moonlight again. The cop said, "Why don't you go ahead on, then. Next time, I'm going to have to give you a ticket, though."

"Thank you, officer," Junie said.

"Don't mention it," he said, and let himself back into his patrol car. "You drive careful."

Junie let herself into the car and then Kenny, the cop waiting for them; and Kenny saw how lightly she was getting off, and something started in him. Something that he hated, it was Junie but it was in her, she was part of it: the life of ease, of privilege. While everything stuck to Kenny. If he had been the driver, he would be on his way to jail by then. And Oregon: a clean place, like Sweden or something. Junie would lose herself in the smell of the leaves, the good clean white Christian smell of the mountains. She would hike, she would ski. She would have a high grade point average and good teeth and Kenny would be doing something else, he didn't know what. Poor boy, Kenny thought. Although he wasn't poor, not exactly. Poor boy in wornout shoes and a green coat; imposter in the adult world, in the city of happiness, the place where early *promise* was fulfilled, where *potential* became *kinetic*. She put her hand on his leg as they drove away and Kenny covered it with his own; like he was trying to hold her near, when really he wanted, at that moment, to push her away.

His father came home in a big white ambulance, they lit the flashing lights on top as they disembarked him, as if to alert the neighborhood: Elvis is back. Kenny did the honor of pushing him up the new ramp, into the living room, where a rented hospital bed took pride of place in front of the color Sony. (His father always bought for durability: Sony, Maytag, the last slant-6 from Dodge.)

Kenny didn't understand until the ambulance drove away and he was alone with his father. "Could you get me some ice cream?" his father asked.

Kenny went to the kitchen to spoon it out for him. His father always had a terrific sweet tooth when he wasn't drinking; Kenny supposed the two were connected. The noise of the TV pursued him into the kitchen, back talk and laughter. Let's get sarcastic. It was about four or four-thirty in the afternoon and Kenny thought, you'll ruin your appetite for dinner. He caught himself thinking this. Then realized that he was alone, that there was absolutely nobody else who was going to take care of his father. A shivering ran down his neck; a quick desire to run away, though he knew it was already too late.

"I've got some schoolwork to do," he told his father; true enough, though he hadn't kept up in anything but English for a couple of months, not since his father's accident. Let's see, Kenny thought, about eight weeks worth of reading, a couple of math quizzes, I'll be caught right up. He said, "I'll be upstairs."

"Can you hear me up there?" his father asked in his new voice, tremulous and blurry.

"Sure. Turn the TV down and I can hear you."

"I can hear it perfectly well," his father said, "but I have a hard time making it out, you know? What they're saying and so on. I can't follow it."

"Well, just give a yell if you need anything."

"I'm going to have to use the bathroom in a minute. I'm OK for now but I'm going to need a hand."

And Kenny saw that he was not exaggerating or making a statement or putting over something on Kenny. His father needed help to go to the bathroom and there was nobody else. Kenny left him propped upright in the hospital bed and went up to his room, where the afternoon sun was walking slowly across the walls, casting a shadow of the window casement. The sound of the TV followed him even up here. If Kenny left, his father would be helpless, alone. He *knew* this before the ambulance left but he didn't *realize* it. Kenny sat on the bed and rolled a cigarette. He wasn't supposed to smoke but there was nobody to tell him not to; Kenny ran the house now. It didn't matter if he got caught. There was nobody to catch him. They weren't even sure if his father had a sense of smell anymore.

He let his eyes rest on the book he was supposed to be reading for English, *Slaughterhouse-Five*. Billy Pilgrim, poo-tee-weet. Maybe if he smoked a little more dope. As it was the book seemed to be constantly agreeing with itself. It wasn't long or dense but still he couldn't seem to finish it, or even start. A sense of futility.

"Ken?" his father called to him. "Kenny?"

Another victory like this, he thought, and we are done for.

It's another thing he can't remember, can't figure out either, why they went to Kim's house that same night; the night of the dinner, of Junie's high-speed sex experience, moonlight, and policemen. They must have had enough, both of them. But for some reason they couldn't break the appointment; and in fact it wasn't all that late when they got there, not even eleven o'clock.

Kenny had a bad feeling, like something was going to happen, although he was almost sure it wasn't. If Junie was ever going to talk about Kim, about what did or didn't happen with her, about the feelings that Junie may or may not have had, she would have taken her chance before then. Maybe when they were married, Kenny thought; then wondered where the marriage part had come from. He saw them, twenty years later, looking placidly back from their bland suburban living room . . . a made-to-order life, straight out of the Sears catalog.

They parked on a street of ordinary houses, somewhere close to the river. Junie led him down the driveway of the one house that was different, an old farmhouse set back from the road, in a little scrap of woods. It was hard to see in the dark but Kenny got the impression of windows, and of shutters, of porches and ells, a house that had grown organically in small disorganized projects. She led him up to the door like this was nothing strange; maybe it wasn't. She knocked but she didn't wait, just led him in. A set of parents were displayed in the living room, Kim's presumably: a round, gray-headed woman with a monk's bowl haircut, and a drawn-looking thin man with an oxygen pipe going into his nose. Liberals, Kenny thought; a roomful of books and magazines, no TV, natural fibers. They leapt up when Junie came into the room, or the mother did; the father straggled upright, tangled in the hoses.

"June!" the mother said. "Jesus, Mary, and Joseph, it is so good to see you." She was beaming, holding her arms out; and Junie raced toward her, and into her embrace, with an ease and speed that Kenny found surprising. She went from one to the other, embracing them both. There might have been tears starting in the mother's eyes; an open heart anyway, to look at her, but Kenny was surprised at the force of this reunion.

"Lyle," Junie said, "Celine, this is Kenny. Kenny, this is Lyle and Celine."

"It's very good to meet you," Kenny said; and they repeated the words, or something like them, but they were cool toward him, appraising. Stealing a daughter's girlfriend, Kenny thought; you'd have to be pretty advanced to think of it as a crime.

"I think Kim went to bed already," Lyle said. "Not to sleep, of course."

"I'll get her," Celine said.

"I can find it," Junie said.

"No, I'll get her," Celine said. "She won't mind. If you disappear back there, we won't have a chance to visit with you. Sit."

She waved her hand as she left the room, like a dog trainer; which she might have been, she had that hearty, no-nonsense . . . The kind of person people liked, she was used to being liked, Kenny could see that. Lyle eased himself back into his recliner. "Where did Junie drag you up?" he asked.

"We know each other from high school," Kenny said; but this sounded inadequate, a partial truth. "We sort of ran into each other on a beach trip."

"At a Girl Scout camp, actually," Junie said.

"Like Kim met you," Lyle said, and worked his bushy eyebrows up and down. In his blue jeans, sneakers, and blue work shirt, he looked like a retired farmer, gaunt, a picture out of the Great Depression. His hands were long and liver-spotted and scarred. Kenny had that sense of walking into another family's life, into their history, the smell of other people's cooking, other people's books. It was intimate, more than Kenny wanted.

"I don't know if I told you or not," Junie said. "I met Kim when we were both at camp, in what?" She appealed to Lyle. "The fifth grade? The sixth?"

This was disingenuous, Kenny thought; she never talked about Kim around him, and now they were all best friends.

"The summer between fifth and sixth grade, I think," Lyle said, after a minute's consideration. "I could be wrong. You had already been there a year before, hadn't you?" Junie nodded. "And then there was some requirement about how old you had to be. I can't remember. Maybe it was sixth and seventh grade."

Kenny heard regret in the hesitancy of his voice. That and the oxygen tank made him seem old. Kenny could hear him breathing, through the tubes. They must be wondering where they stood with her now, and what Kenny was doing with her. The father's big hands settled on his own knees.

Just then the mother came back from upstairs, and Kim behind her; Kim in jeans and a buttondown shirt as usual, as always.

"It's Ken, right?" Celine asked him; he nodded, she turned to her daughter. "You and Kenny are friends from school?"

"Fellow sufferers," Kim said. She looked unhappy to be part of this. Kenny tried to figure out what he was doing there. An announcement, maybe. A reconciliation. Kim said, "We had Tom Harris together last year."

"That awful man," Celine said, and they all sat down. Then Celine leapt up again. "Can I get you, what? We have juice, or I could make some coffee?"

"I'd like a glass of wine, if you've got any," Junie said.

Celine and Kim looked nervously at Kenny; apparently it was all right for Junie to have wine in this house but they were afraid he would inform on them. Like me, like me, like me, Kenny thought, suddenly tired of himself. This *performance*. Just tell me what to say and I'll say it. "I wouldn't mind a glass of wine myself," he said experimentally.

"I'll open a bottle," Celine said, disappearing into the kitchen and then returning with five real wineglasses and an expensive-looking bottle. She lined the glasses up on the coffee table while she opened the cork. This had the feeling of a ritual, a ceremony of gracious living; Kenny remembered the trip to Verona, the rained-out opera in the Roman amphitheater. Joie de vivre, Kenny thought. Hard to argue with it, but Kenny resisted. The glasses were dusty and they didn't quite match. A blue plate in the dining room with a bright yellow sunflower glazed on it. He was a criticizing bastard, he knew it, but he was the one being judged; closed his eyes and thought of his own mother, stranded for life in Baltimore.

"How was dinner?" Kim asked Junie.

"It was unbelievable," she said.

"Where did you go?" Lyle asked; and Junie told them, and they bobbed their heads in approval; at the same time skeptical, like they didn't think it was quite right for children like them to be allowed into such a palace of luxury. A Puritan streak could be seen in her cotton clothes and simple gray hair; *one* glass of wine, but good wine. They raised their glasses and drank to nothing. They stopped just short of clinking the glasses together.

Celine held the wine on her tongue, closed her eyes, like she was smoking a joint. "Very nice," she said.

"I can never tell the difference," Lyle said. "You might as well give me the cheap stuff."

"That isn't true," Kim said.

"Not like your mother," Lyle said; and the silence descended again. Kenny sipped his wine and it was complicated and, he supposed, good. Really he had had enough of the food-and-wine experience and in fact of the whole sensual world at that point. Tired and mazy and he wanted to be alone, somewhere in a dark room by himself with a book to read and the light of one lamp coming over his shoulder, the only waking soul in a dark house. Kenny looked around at the others: whole histories of experience, sacred moments and hard times, that he would never be a part of.

Kenny excused himself and went to the bathroom, which was on the second floor, inconvenient. The stairs were lined with photographs: ski holidays, the Italian trip, different people's weddings, small children who were maybe Kim and maybe cousins, dressed in the toddler clothes of the seventies. In the bathroom, Kenny ran water over his face but his face still felt greasy and hot. More pictures in the bathroom, elaborate frames that held a dozen snapshots each. One of them was camp: Junie and Kim on horseback, swimming, posing for the camera sitting on a diving board, flatchested, awkward, twelve. Kim playing the guitar while Junie sang in front of a wall of peeled logs, apparently some kind of talent show. All that happy family, happy childhood. Kenny shut off the bathroom light and closed the door behind him but he didn't go back downstairs right away. In his absence, the four of them had found their voices, and he could hear them talking and laughing, hearing only the general melody of conversation, the ebb and flow. *She was a virgin when I met her,* Kenny thought; making a story out of himself, out of her life. But there was something there. Her childhood had lasted a lot longer than Kenny's had, the same with everybody else; but the troublesome thing with Junie was that she had been able to *make* it last herself. When her own parents wouldn't cooperate she found Kim's. Secrets, the love of horses, the gradual introduction of the elements of adult life one by one—art, culture, food, sex—Kenny had the feeling that she had been able to go through more of the stations; while Kenny had been thrown out of his childhood all at once, into a bare place where nothing was prepared. The night the cops called about his mother, the first time.

The photographs: picnics, reunions, Christmases. Junie in ski clothes, grinning against a backdrop of brilliant blue sky. Junie reaching up to a cat in a tree, already tall but thin, in her girl clothes.

He sat in the dark at the top of the stairs and listened, as he had listened to his own parents, listened to parties, to their elaborate polite arguments—Kenny's mother had a master's degree and read the paper as religiously as his father—and to their fights, which were quieter but sometimes boiled over. Sometimes things broke. But the sorrowful thing that Kenny was thinking about was not his parents but the child that he himself had once been: the child alone at the top of the stairs, listening to the mysteries of the adult life below him, listening for clues, eager, never dreaming—not then, not later, not for a long time after—that his parents were only improvising. They didn't have any idea themselves. Junie in shorts, in a lawn chair with a goat licking her arm. Smiling for the camera.

Kenny dipped the washcloth into the soapy bucket and wrung it out. His father lay facedown on the plastic sheet, eyes closed, naked. The tub and the shower were both upstairs—the downstairs bath was just a half. The *sacrifice*. He started with his father's feet, washing carefully between the toes, the toenails that were thick and tobacco yellow; the yellowing horns of callus on his heels and the pink, wrinkled elephant skin under his arch, strangely delicate. His legs were white, his body was universally white except his arms, his hands, and his neck. Kenny washed the backs of the calves, the thighs. He moved his father's legs apart and washed his father's anus clean, which was one of the things that he had been frightened to do but turned out to be just another motion with his hands, rinsing carefully afterward. This was the physical world, the wreckage of the body. Decades of fat, architectural. The arms were getting strong again with the work of carrying the body, rolling the wheelchair. The unloved body, not by its master, not by anybody else. And I will look like this someday, Kenny thought. He didn't plan to but his father didn't plan to either. Strange the way the body lapsed back to vegetable shapes at some point, the ruined skin around his father's elbows, puckered and sagging, dried apricots. His arms were at his side like a diver's. When they were clean Kenny raised them over his father's head, so that it looked like he was sunbathing. Kenny scrubbed at his father's sides, his armpits. I will not be disgusted, Kenny told himself; I will not fail in charity. Birth, suffering, death, rebirth. This body is mine, all suffering bodies are mine, all bodies are suffering (remembering Junie moving over him, lips and tongues, the feel of being inside her on that night in the park). He scrubbed at his father's back but it wouldn't quite come all the way clean, a tinge of gray . . . Another change in form at his father's neck, where the shirt gave out: the skin had gathered in the sun, making rivulets and deltas of deep permanent wrinkles. The vegetable body. There was nobody else to do this, there was no point in complaining. Kenny knew, it was just samsara, suffering and pleasure were two sides of the same coin but he couldn't muster the detachment he needed. It's not all suffering, Kenny thought, helping his father to turn his torso over and then setting the legs straight. It's not all suffering. It's not all suffering. It's not all suffering.

The Taming Power of the Small: This hexagram means the force of the small—the power of the shadowy—that restrains, tames, impedes. A weak line in the fourth place, that of the minister, holds the five strong lines in check. In the Image it is the wind blowing across the sky. The wind restrains the clouds, the rising breath of the Creative, and makes them grow dense, but as yet is not strong enough to turn them to rain. The hexagram presents a configuration of circumstances in which a strong element is temporarily held in leash by a weak element. It is only through gentleness that this can have a successful outcome.

In this dream, Kenny is a whore but it's basically OK. The women come to him, three a night. They give him a gold coin with a rolled rubber inside it, and some other small token that his waking self can't quite remember. *Silky*, Kenny thinks, remembering the soft clean sheets and the perfumed women who come to him. Something feminine, receptive. Somebody else is running him, a vague presence, neither male nor female; the presence doesn't have Kenny's best interests at heart, he knows that, but the life is his to enjoy for now. A deal with the devil. The women who pay for him are clean and beautiful. He never leaves the room. He isn't man enough to escape; not that he wants to.

The middle one on this particular night is Asian, a small compact woman with long black hair, older than Kenny, a woman he could love (he knows this without knowing why). She says nothing, which happens often. Other times they tell him stories, fantastic and dirty; other times they want him to curse in their ears. Kenny is always glad to see them when they arrive, always tired of them by the time they go, but not this woman. They make love—no, they *fuck;* Kenny is paid, disposable—they fuck slowly, decorously. She comes, she weeps. No talking. When she leaves, Kenny feels the restraint for the first time. He wants to leave but he can't. He wants to follow her.

The next evening she comes back. She talks: she tells him that she is a violinist, that she suffers from stage fright always, but the evening before, after she and Kenny fucked, she was able to make an important debut without fear. The crowd, the lights. She was a success. She is grateful, she wants to tell him; the gold coin and the other token, the one he can't remember; she tips him, and then she leaves, the way she is supposed to with a whore. The bitterness persists through two days of his waking life; that and a different feeling, homesick, wanting to go back to a place where she could find him (though he knows, in waking and in dreams, that she's never coming back). Perfume, skin.

It was February for months, for as long as Kenny could remember. Then one day it was March. Nothing changed, but it seemed like something might. A possibility, a restlessness. Kenny didn't want to think about it; movement, migration, these things were only taking her away from him.

This happened in English class, the only one that he was bothering with at all. They were talking about Toni Morrison or Alice Walker or somebody, a book that Kenny hadn't read. Normally he would have but he had been busy, shopping, cleaning, running all the little errands . . . Really it was a difficulty of faith. Lately he couldn't believe in anything but what he could touch. The life of the body. Because this other, this elaborate pretending, wasn't going to lead to anything. Kenny knew that the others, the bright-eyed boys and girls in his class, had read the Cliff Notes or the Monarch Notes or "skimmed" it and made an educated guess about the second half; he had done it himself, flipping through the pages to see if all the characters were still alive, reading the last paragraph. The bright-eyed boys and girls didn't have to learn anything at all. They were there to pass the test, and when they did, they could go on to the next step. While Kenny knew: he could pass as many tests as he wanted and he still wasn't going anywhere.

Mrs. Connolly was droning on and Kenny was watching, listening from his seat in the far back of the class, deep into a sex dream (the memory of his life as a whore still clinging to his waking self, like wisps of cobweb, half-remembered). She was the body he was putting his dream on: smaller than Junie, nimble, monkeylike; he could imagine her tight thighs, her nipples big and dark and hard, shrinking into tight points when she was excited. Sex with a teacher. Sometimes he looked at her and it seemed like they both knew. And something had changed over the year, too—something that he learned from Junie, that women were full of secrets, that sometimes you could get at them. Before, with Mrs. Connolly, the fantasy was strictly out of *Penthouse*: the teacher's lounge, deserted, or the old unused equipment room at the edge of the athletic field, Why Kenny what are you doing here . . . Now he could almost imagine it, not just the place to put his fantasy but Mrs. Connolly herself.

A spring day, anyway, or just before spring: flat gray skies and the promise of rain for once, instead of snow. The classroom idle, overheated; the boredom hung like a faint foul odor. The ground was damp outside and the air smelled faintly like the damp dirt, that first mineral clue, or what? An *intimation*, Kenny remembered, and looked to Mrs. Connolly for approval; but she was public, preoccupied. Look at me, he thought, love me, admire me.

Like spiders or bear cubs, the students were restless with the coming change of season. Mrs. Connolly talked and talked and her words ran off, down the gutters between the chairs, out the door, unimpeded. She seemed distracted herself. Her face was a performance of teaching, a mask that was growing thinner and thinner. A person in there, Kenny thought. Tell me your secrets. I want you: I want you to come here, to tell me how you got here, how you ended up in this classroom, what you were hoping for and what you want now. He sent the message like a radio beam, one planet to the other: this isn't just about sex, although sex may be involved—*will be* involved—but I desire you . . .

Mrs. Connolly stopped, like she had heard him. "You're not paying attention to me, are you?" she asked, in her flat colorless voice.

Nobody seemed to notice, nobody but Kenny. They saw each other over the heads of the others.

"Maybe I should just give it up," she said. A murmur of confusion arose in the front of the class, where the asskissers sat. Mrs. Connolly closed the book she was reading from and laid it on the desk, looking meanwhile out the window, like there was a message for her there. Even then, it seemed like she knew what she was doing. She stayed inside herself, unlike Junie; maybe it was just something about being older but Kenny didn't think so. I'll get you off, he thought, get you out of your head. She turned and looked at Kenny, like she heard him.

"I'll make you a deal," she said. "I'll put this off till tomorrow, OK? Either it's boring or I'm boring or I don't know what. But you have to do one favor for me in return." She paused for dramatic effect; Kenny thought that maybe she had seen a movie about a teacher somewhere. She said, "I want you to listen to a poem I'm going to read, and really listen to it, OK? I just want you to get one poem out of this class. That's enough."

More mumbling, butt-shuffling. This would go down in a small way as a memorable day; nothing to compare to the time Mrs. Englehart threw the glass ashtray at a student or the time that Brian Faircloth played the bugle in class, but still. Kenny sat back, enjoying the show, while Mrs. Connolly leafed through a little paperback. "What do you want to hear?" she asked, without looking up.

"Robert Frost," said one of the asskissers.

"Sylvia Plath," said a girl in black.

"Eddie Van Halen," said one of the resident idiots.

She looked up brightly at this latest insult, ready to rumble. "I'm sorry," she said. "I don't see Van Halen in the anthology. Maybe you could bring a poem next time to read yourself?" She turned to the class at large. "Maybe all of you could, next time— bring your favorite poem in and read it to the class. I'm sure we'd have quite an array. What am I even doing here?"

She had their attention. They weren't used to hearing a teacher be sarcastic but Mrs. Connolly didn't care. She leafed furiously through the anthology, stopped twice but neither suited her. Finally composed herself and read:

> The white chocolate jar full of petals
> swills odds and ends around in a dizzying eye
> of four o'clocks now and to come. The tiger
> marvellously striped and irritable, leaps
> onto the table and without disturbing a hair
> of the flowers' breathless attention, pisses
> into the pot, right down its delicate spout.
> [giggling, butt-shuffling, nervousness]
> A whisper of steam goes up from that porcelain
> eurythra. "Saint-Saens!" it seems to be whispering,
> curling unerringly around the furry nuts
> of the terrible puss, who is mentally flexing.
> Ah, forget it . . .

She snapped the book shut at this point and put it into her large leather handbag, along with her glasses and her fountain pen, which had been lying on the desk. What else? She searched around for a minute, opening and closing the drawers of her desk. More fidgeting, laughter from the children, who were apparently forgotten. When she had everything she took a final look around and said, "I have nothing further to say to you."

Then she left. She just opened the door and walked out of it and then there was no teacher at the front of the classroom. A long confusing minute, thinking it over, then the room exploded in nervous talk and laughter. This was better than the day that Mrs. Englehart threw the glass ashtray at a student after all. They had driven another teacher from the classroom, maybe from the profession. Their ignorance, which they were proud of, which they fought for every day, had won again, driving its enemies before it . . . Kenny left in the confusion.

He thought he had lost her, thought she might have gone back into a teacher's bathroom or lounge—those mysterious forbidden rooms—to have a nervous collapse, or whatever. Then he spotted her in the parking lot, walking between the cars; spotted her raincoat actually, and then figured out it was Mrs. Connolly. It was a black vinyl raincoat with large yellow polka dots, actively wrong. Mrs. Connolly had a past, presumably. He had to walk the long axis of the school before he could get to a door that led outside, down the rows of closed lockers, past the classrooms and the drone of teachers' voices, on and on, the endless perky question: Class?

She was still there when he escaped; she was walking across the battered grass, a gray carpeting of pull-tabs, cigarette butts, and pigeon feathers. Kenny ran to catch her but it wasn't hard. She was proceeding languidly in her black unpractical shoes. She was thinking.

"Where are you going?" Kenny asked.

She didn't seem surprised to see him at all. "I was just wondering that myself," she said. "Either San Francisco or back to graduate school, I think."

"You're not going back, are you?"

"Why, are you?"

She looked up at his face, skeptical, slightly playful, the hint of a smile.

"I don't know," Kenny said.

"Whatever you say," she said. "I'm going to buy myself a cup of coffee, I think."

Kenny couldn't decide if this was an invitation or not but walked along beside her anyway. She was shorter than he thought, and more opaque. Her plastic raincoat rustled with the movement of her hips, and Kenny remembered that only a few minutes ago he had been speculating about her nipples. Something had happened to make that seem wrong. What?—the pornographic world, he thought; where sex and power ran together. When she was still a teacher he could do whatever he wanted with her, the whole sex rodeo in his daydreams. Now she had taken off the uniform, become a small quick woman with brown hair, something birdlike . . . and Kenny liked the company of women, he had learned this from Junie. He was curious about their lives, their girlhoods. A fascination; learning to slow down, learning to listen.

"What's your name, anyway?" Kenny asked.

"Candy," she said; without further explanation. She had disappeared inside herself, walking toward the avenue but talking to somebody else, in another room somewhere. Kenny felt useless; and then he realized that he had also walked out of the school, that he was in trouble, too. He tried to summon a sense of gravity about this but he could only find fake, official emotions. There was no real surprise or freshness; he had already made this decision in small increments, months of not deciding, not doing his homework.

She led him into Bennigan's, where it was dark and quiet; the permanent airless quiet of the shopping mall. It was ten-forty-five in the morning and they were the only ones, except for the bright blond college girl who greeted them in a green smock. "Sit anywhere!" she said.

They took a booth together and sat opposite; Mrs. Connolly (Candy?) looking out the stained-glass window next to them, out at the distorted cars in the parking lot, red and yellow, red skies. A second college girl took their order for coffee.

"I've never been in here before," Kenny said. "It's like McDonald's with drinks."

"It's worse than that," Mrs. Connolly said. "I will now perform my last official act."

"What's that?"

"I wanted to tell you," she said, "that you could do this standing on your head, any of this."

"What do you mean?" Kenny asked.

"I mean that you can read, and you can write, and you can think, which is not as usual as you might think. You can see that, looking around the classroom. You know what I mean. I used to look at you and go, *there's one*."

"Well, thanks, I guess."

"But you never even did the reading, you never spent more than forty-five minutes writing a paper. I don't mean to lecture you, I mean, I'm glad you're here. There's no good way to say it. I was curious about you, is all."

Kenny noticed that she had moved into the past tense. "That poem," he said, trying to change the subject.

"I just wanted to talk about cat balls, to see if anyone would wake up. Did you like it?" Kenny nodded. "I thought you would. It's Frank O'Hara. Are you gay?"

Kenny looked up sharply, surprised and angry, like she had slapped him out of nowhere. "What do you mean?" he asked.

"I'm sorry," she said. "I mean, there's nothing wrong with it, one way or the other."

"No, you're right," he said; and the awkwardness between them started to thicken and harden. Why were people, why were *women*, always apologizing to Kenny? What did he do to make them wrong all the time? She was staring out the window now, and the coffee was never coming. Most people only have one left hand, Kenny thought. Plus there was this little core of difference inside him, and he was afraid of being found out: the drag queen in the coffee shop had recognized it, maybe, and so had Mrs. Connolly. He didn't even have a name for it, didn't know why he had to keep it hidden, but this was where the panic started. His dark secret love. His dark secret: love.

"I'm not trying to accuse you of anything," she said. "It's just sometimes, you seemed to understand things, I don't know."

"I mean, I have friends that are gay," he said. "It's just not me, not exactly."

"I wonder if it's as black-and-white as that," she said, rummaging in her bag for something, not finding it. "I'm not talking about you in particular. There are a couple of different schools of thought, you know—one says that it's a whole continuum of feelings and expressions and so on, that there's no clear line. Then there's the sort of genetic school that says that either you are or you aren't. Which do you think?"

A *third* college blond—aggressively heterosexual, teeth and hair and bulgy breasts, though in other circumstances Kenny wouldn't have noticed—brought their coffee, which Mrs. Connolly drank black. Kenny spooned sugar into his.

"I don't know," he said; then decided to gamble, to show her a little bit and see what she would do with it. "I guess I think it's the first way," he said. "I guess it's just a question of where you are on the line, where you are on the spectrum, and then what circumstances, you know, come up." (Faltering here, but it was too late to back down.) "I mean, I guess most people, if they met the right person . . . Maybe not most people, but a lot."

"You think so?"

Kenny came up lame. "I don't know," he said.

"That seems romantic to me," Mrs. Connolly said. "You know? That kind of like straight, white, middle-class thing that wants to include all the other experiences, too, you know, I could be gay if I wanted to. I don't know. Other people's territory." She went back to rummaging, finally coming up with the poetry anthology, which she laid on the table like a priest with a Bible: *The Modern American Poets*.

Mrs. Connolly tapped the cover and said, "You read the biographies of the people in here, men and women, and they were all so sexually *various*, you know? Not very successful, is the main impression, but various. I mean, Bishop and Lowell and Ginsberg, for

Christ sake. Sometimes I feel like poetry is a thing for *them*, and not for us—I'm straight myself, I guess you don't know that. So I guess I admire it, as much as anything else."

Her face was stained red and yellow in the funhouse light of the window. Hands cupped around her coffee, the nails unpainted, small dark hairs on the skin of her arms; she stared at her hands.

She said, "Sometimes I feel like one of those awful French teachers, the ones from Indiana or somewhere who were always going on about the glories of *la belle Français!* I had about seven of them. They turn them out in a factory in Terre Haute. You know, just never quite getting it and then always telling everybody how great it is. That kind of half-assed translation."

Kenny must have been looking blank because she stopped when she looked at his face; then returned to her hands, sipped her coffee. "I don't know," she said to the table; then nothing, for a minute, and then: "I sort of hoped you *were* gay," she said. "I was hoping you could explain it to me. I mean, partly because you seem to get it, and partly because of the way you looked when you started the school year, I mean that lifeguard thing with the bleached-out hair and the tank tops. You looked like a member of the Village People or something. I had the biggest crush on you."

Kenny looked up sharply but she was keeping her eyes to herself. You *had* a crush or you *have* one? A crowd of talkative assholes, all men, came in for an early lunch. Kenny put it together. She was *available,* or she wasn't far. The silence lengthened between them. Her hands were cupped around her coffee still; the next step was for Kenny to take one of her hands in his, to make the connection. He thought that it was better to regret the things you did instead of regretting the things you didn't do; but in the end he kept his hands to himself.

Finally she said, "I'm sorry. I didn't mean to, I'm just sort of— I tend to blurt things out. Which is another beautiful word, isn't it? *Blurt.*"

"It's good," he said. "Right up there with *sycamore.*"

"Which Annie Dillard—never mind, I told you that in class, didn't I?" She colored when she saw Kenny's little joke he was playing.

He said, "I know what you mean, though," trying to apologize. "Sometimes a word will come along and you'll just notice it, like finding a dollar in the street. You wander around trying it out for the rest of the day. That is an *indefensible* hat."

"See, I knew," she said. "That's all I wanted to say: you understand this stuff, you have a knack for it. A way with words."

"Well, thank you."

"I can't imagine what good it's going to do you. I mean, look at me. Seduced by language, and the next thing you know you're dumped in some English classroom, reading Shakespeare to the sheep. Present company, of course, excepted from that description, but wouldn't you agree?"

"I don't know."

"Yes you do," she said. "That's why you left. I'm going to go get a drink, now, Kenny. It's probably better if you didn't come along. I'd probably be in plenty of trouble anyway if somebody came in and saw us here. On the other hand, maybe not. You want this?" She pushed the anthology across the table toward him, saying, "I don't need it anymore."

Kenny opened the fat paperback to her place mark, a paperclip over the page. There was the O'Hara poem. "Do you mind?" he asked. "I didn't get a chance to finish it."

"Read it out loud," she said. "You'll never hear it otherwise. Besides, I'd like to hear it. Loudly, slowly, and clearly."

Kenny looked to the left and to the right before he started, afraid of what? Maybe he was gay after all. Reading poetry out loud in Bennigan's was certainly suspicious. He read it to her, loudly, slowly, and clearly, trying to imitate the colorlessness of her voice: *Chez Jane,* he said.

The white chocolate jar full of petals
swills odds and ends around in a dizzying eye
of four o'clocks now and to come. The tiger
marvellously striped and irritable, leaps
onto the table and without disturbing a hair
of the flowers' breathless attention, pisses
into the pot, right down its delicate spout.
A whisper of steam goes up from that porcelain
eurythra. "Saint-Saens!" it seems to be whispering,
curling unerringly around the furry nuts
of the terrible puss, who is mentally flexing.
Ah, be with me always, spirit of noisy
contemplation in the studio, the Garden
of Zoos, the eternally fixed afternoons!
There, while music scratches its scrofulous
stomach, the brute beast emerges and stands,
clear and careful, knowing always the exact peril
at this moment caressing his fangs with
a tongue given wholly to luxurious usages;
which only a moment before dropped aspirin
in this sunset of roses, and now throws a chair
in the air to aggravate the truly menacing.

She listened with her eyes closed; and afterward, said "That's so nice" to Kenny, like he had written it himself, still with her eyes closed. Kenny closed the book on the poem and opened the front cover. *Kathryn Ann Connolly* it said, in a careful colorless hand, and below it was written her telephone number: 555-3519. The pages were dogeared, worn with reading. What was she giving him?

"I'll take the book," Kenny said, "if you're done with it."

"OK," she said, "it's yours. Now go. I'm just going to move over into the bar over there."

"Well . . . ," he said, standing up awkwardly.

"Two things," she said. "First: thanks for following me out. That was the one thing I was afraid of, that we wouldn't get a chance to talk. I mean, I wish we'd started months ago, talking."

She held her hand for him to shake, official once again, a teacher, if only for a moment; and Kenny took it, and felt how small the bones of her hand were, how delicate.

"And what's the other?" he asked.

"Oh, God," she said, and dropped his hand. "Today is my day to say anything and everything. Just that lifeguard thing, Kenny— that bleached-out hair and the good tan, it's dangerous, Kenny. I mean, you have no idea. A word to the wise."

"Not me," said Kenny.

"Not me, either," Mrs. Connolly said. "I'll see you."

Kenny left. The last glimpse of her, looking back, she set her big leather bag next to one of the barstools, all alone. Full cold daylight out. He stood there blinking; thought of going back but his own fake ID was bad and she would throw him out anyway. Today was not the day, whatever she meant. He had her phone number, hot in his pocket, sleeping between the covers of her book.

Unfaithful, Kenny thought, remembering Junie for the first time in hours. He was blue, disconsolate. He was not taking care the way he should; she was already going, almost gone, there was no point to it. A vista of parking lots, gas stations under a gray sky promising rain. The cars scuttling forward in ragged rows; crabs on some blind seafloor, moving against the hard bodies of the others. My fault, he thought. My fault, my fault, my most grievous fault. He moved off blindly toward her, forgetting she was still in class.

He went looking for Junie at the art school later that evening. Her class was going to have an exhibit of their photographs and she was trying to get ready; if Kenny wanted to see her, he would have to find her in the darkroom. He felt himself drifting, needed to touch her. Downtown the streets were dark, windblown, but there was still that first note of spring he had noticed earlier. The air felt unnaturally warm, and he drove with the windows down. Twice he heard laughter.

The institute was around the back of the art museum, growing out of a little courtyard; the doors opening inward to a blank white wall, a set of stairs, the faceless facade of a spy headquarters. The smell of turpentine was immediate. He climbed the stairs, watched by a series of security cameras, and went looking for her on the third floor, where he thought the darkroom was. Paint was dripped and splattered everywhere, sawdust, plaster, chips of limestone. A boom box played the Talking Heads (of course) from one of the side rooms. It was easy to get lost: no two of the rooms were the same shape, and in fact it didn't seem like there were two of anything here: a row of regular metal school lockers—once blue, now various colors averaging to gray—stood next to a set of retired bus-station coin-op lockers, stood next to a pile of ductwork and heating machinery, stood next to an almost complete front end from a '52 Studebaker, the kind that looked almost the same coming or going.

Kenny thought he knew where the darkroom door was but he was wrong; by the time he discovered this, he'd lost the stairway, too, and drifted derelict for a while, taking in the assortment: bad paintings of every description, sculptures made from auto-body parts and ambiguous rusting piles of junk, a flat-black water fountain, the smell of welding in the air. It was pleasant to imagine that he belonged here, if only by proxy. What was it? A feeling of play, of nonsense; also the enterprise, the serious work of manufacturing. Kenny liked the two things at once, light/dark, serious/play.

Deciding that he needed directions, he followed a radio back into one of the studios, where he discovered Junie and somebody else.

She was half-sitting, half-leaning against a heavy worktable, looking long and tall and dark black in her outline. She was resting back on the palms of her hands, offering her body like a display; or that's how it felt to Kenny. Junie was in a discussion with a man who was cleaning brushes in a metal industrial sink; a painter, apparently, and an ironical one—the worst kind, Kenny thought. The canvas on the wall was twelve or fifteen feet long, a filthy gray fog like the smoke from an oil fire, out of which loomed the individual body parts of five or six clowns and a sinister gridwork in darker black, like the pipes of a refinery. More geometry, Kenny thought; she has a weakness for it. The painter himself was somewhere in his twenties or early thirties, sneakers and paint-stained khakis, a black t-shirt, curly brown hair that flopped down over his shoulders in a seventies style, like he had escaped from a Peter Frampton album. He was listening intently to her, paying no attention to the brushes in his hand. Brown hair, brown eyes: he looked like an intelligent spaniel.

Junie was talking loudly over the sound of the water, and when he shut it off her voice boomed in the empty room: "It just seems like THE BOARD OF DIRECTORS . . ."

Then she saw Kenny, and she didn't know what to do with herself for a moment. She shut up, and then she folded her body into a more modest shape. She put her body away. "Hello," she said eventually. "What are you doing here?"

She was unfriendly; he was unwelcome. He was high school, and she was trying to impress this Older Guy, and even that was the best he could make out of it. Worse possibilities suggested themselves.

"I was downtown," he said, tonguetied, lame. "I was, um— thought I'd say hello, I don't know, if you're busy."

"I've got to meet Roland anyway," the painter said. "I was supposed to be there twenty minutes ago. It's good to see you."

"Thanks," Junie said; and the painter turned back toward the sink and both of them disappeared, the children. She had been dismissed, which could only make things worse. It might have been better if he had just gone home, but he had come all the way downtown to see her . . . He followed her out, across the maze of hallways and through the inconspicuous door of the darkroom.

"Who was that?" he asked.

"None of your business," she said. She stood with her back to him, stirring a tray full of pictures of herself with a pair of long-handled tongs. It was a big darkroom, well ventilated and bright with orange safelights. The pictures were the nakeds, the ones with the sleeper's mask over her face. Kenny saw with a little lurch of the heart that she meant to exhibit them; *my* body, he thought, *my* secret, *my* love. Possession; but it was hers to give away as she wanted.

"Don't spy on me," she said.

"I wasn't."

"You've done it before, sneaking up on Kim and me. I can't stand it, Kenny, I *won't*."

All without looking at him, without giving him her face, which he could see clearly in the orange moonlight of the room: a sleep-walker's face, betraying nothing. She went to the enlarging stand, stepping around him, not touching, and focused the negative—the same image, or some small variant. Then she drew a sheet of paper from the safe and burned the exposure, her hands dancing in the faint light of the enlarger, holding the light back from the edges of the page. *Dodging and burning,* he remembered.

"Excuse me," Junie said, on her way to the developing trays, holding the blank exposed photograph (the magic hidden, latent in the white gloss of the surface).

"I didn't come to spy on you," he said again. "I just wanted to see you. Sometimes I just do."

"It's just like *every corner* of my life," she said, and dipped the print into the tray, gently rocking it under. "I'm just not used to it. I don't know if I want to *get* used to it. You're at school, and then at my house, and then you're down here all of a sudden."

"I thought you didn't mind it."

"I'm not trying to break up with you," Junie said. "It's just, I don't know. There are some parts of my life that are just *mine*."

The image swam into focus, faint at first and then more definite; an everyday miracle, Kenny thought, let us praise St. Kodak. He saw the outlines of her body and then fill in with a cold gray texture, a translation of her flesh, and Kenny saw her body like it was something he was leaving behind, the last lights of a familiar city disappearing in the rearview mirror; and for the first time he saw that they could fuck this up. Until then he assumed that love would make them bulletproof.

"I love you," Kenny said, trying to call her back to him.

She held the dripping print over the developer, examined it, then plunged it into the stop bath and then the fix, setting the stopwatch that dangled from a string around her neck before she answered him.

"I wasn't talking about that," she said. "I'm not talking about whether I love you or not, or whether you love me"—a good long ways from a ringing declaration, Kenny noticed right away. She said, "I just want to have a life, Kenny, a regular life like everybody else. Mike Stack, the one you saw me talking to? He was my *teacher* from last year, Kenny, from before I even met you."

"I didn't say you shouldn't talk to him."

"No," she said. "You just walked in there. I could tell how much you liked it."

"I don't have to like it," he said.

"But there's nothing to be jealous of," she said. "If I'm not around you all the time, it doesn't mean I'm off fucking somebody else, do you get that, Kenny?"

"I never thought so," Kenny said.

"You should have seen your face," she said. "I mean you walked in there and it was like we were both naked on the table or something, Kenny."

"I'm sorry."

"Well, I know," she said; her anger spent, dullness creeping back into her voice. Kenny knew the feeling: this was complicated. This was puzzling. She said, "I just want to have a life, is all."

"I don't want to put up walls between us," Kenny said.

"That's such a lie!" she said. Now she was staring at him, her print forgotten. She said, "That's complete bullshit, Kenny, you're the one. You never let me anywhere near you, I've never even seen your house or seen your family. I mean, you practically live in my family's house."

"I never thought you wanted to," he said.

"You never invited me," she said; and then there was nothing at all to say for a while. He had meant to spare her, that's what he told himself; now he saw that it was shame that drove him. He kept her away, that much was undeniable, although he hadn't noticed up till then. One of those uneasy silences in the middle of an argument, a temporary loss for words but nothing settled, like the greasy, electric feel of the air when a lightning storm is about to break. Kenny didn't see how they got to where they were, or how they were going to get back safely: he had hurt her without meaning to, without even knowing. "I'm sorry," he said again.

"It's all right," she said. "Watch your eyes."

She laid the print on a tilted board and switched on a viewing light; and the safelights, which had been as bright as day the moment before, were drowned in the bright white light. Give me my darkness back, Kenny thought, the red-lit warmth. She peered at the print, her face inches away.

"I hate this picture," Junie said, without looking up.

"Then why are you showing it?"

"Because everybody else likes it." She turned to him then, severe in her wire-rimmed glasses. "You were the first one but everybody else thinks the same thing. That other stuff is boring, this isn't boring. That's what people say."

"This has a naked girl in it."

"Maybe," she said. "I don't know, I tend to *underestimate* when it comes to sex."

"Not me," Kenny said.

She looked at him; prepared to like him again, prepared to smile, but there was no way back across the gap; not now, at least.

"You know what it is?" she asked. "That was the only picture where I didn't have any idea what I was doing. All the rest of them I thought about it and *then* I did it but this one I just did it. It's my crazy-woman picture I guess."

"You're not crazy," Kenny said.

She looked at him sharply and Kenny panicked.

"You're a little fucked-up is all," he said, "like everybody else. Like me."

"Well, I'm glad to hear that I'm normal."

"Don't."

"Don't what?"

"Don't make something out of nothing," Kenny said.

"But I'm just like everybody else," she said. "I'm fucked-up, everybody's fucked-up."

He opened his mouth to say something back but he had run out of words again. Just the plain fact: they could screw things up to where it didn't matter if they loved each other or not. The idea scared him.

"I love you," Kenny said again; but it was just words.

Fucking after fights was best, the edge of anger pushing them hard against each other so a little of the fight spilled over: you're mine now, you're mine now, you're mine now . . . She thrust against him, she dared him to make her come. The loving touch, and then the other kind. His teeth on her nipple. Junie bites. Nothing either of them wants to know: how close they've always been to violence, fuck you, no fuck you.

And afterward it's good to have the body of the other to harbor in. A stranger's body, maybe; lying in the dark of her narrow bed, Junie with her back to him, touching along the length of their bodies. It's quiet, a candle on the table with its small flame rising straight up in the air. Breathing, both of them in time. A truce. A moment that is attached to neither the past nor the future but suspended in between; that's the beautiful thing about coming, Kenny thinks, it's being sideways out of time. If death is like this give me more. The hardest thing is to stop, to be where you are and just ride the wheel, not caring where it's taking you. She stirs against him, restless. The skin between them is warm, blood temperature, the air has a slight cool edge. Good bones; he touches the primitive cage of her pelvis. The animal body. A couple of big cats fucking, then lying in the sun. Their bodies want each other, their bodies fit, their brains can go fuck themselves. Junie shivers, not from cold. He remembers the fear, down at the beach, the way her body shook and racked. His dick stirs against the warm curve of her ass, the velvet softness, it doesn't care. Junie is weeping, for some reason unknown to him.

He holds her body close, but the rest of her is gone.

She cries quietly, and after the first trembling there's no more. He wants to ask what's wrong but the words have already failed them. They have gone past words, they would only be entangled. Before she has quite stopped crying—he can feel the hot childish tears against his palm—she takes his hand and presses it to her face, like she was hiding herself in it. Presses herself against it, holds there for a minute; then kisses the palm of his hand, his wrist. His body takes immediate notice. She's kissing him with her tongue, a feeling that travels directly to a hot place at the base of his spine, don't stop.

Kenny is hard instantly. A moment of fumbling then he sees what she means to do: face down, she lifts her hips toward him and pulls him inside her. She's miles away, her face mashed into the pillow. She wants to get fucked. Body to body, there's more here than Kenny wants to think about and then he isn't thinking at all anymore, that passive . . . the *victim*. And then his own hips driving hard.

Afterward she closes her eyes and sleeps or pretends to sleep.

He pulls her black jeans on himself—he wants to wear her clothes—and goes downstairs. It's perfectly safe, they're all asleep. He takes one of her father's fancy beers out of the refrigerator, which he is perfectly welcome to; sits in the living room under the one light but there isn't anything to read. Then shuts the one light off and sits alone in the dark. Junie, alone in the dark upstairs. This paradise where they were going to be girls together, not literally but something has been broken. Something has been lost. For a minute he thought that he had found a way out of his father's life. He didn't have to be a man. He could be what?—an amateur lesbian, a lover of women's bodies. But she wanted him to fuck her. He sees that now. Something has been broken. He sits alone until the beer is gone, blank, waiting for whatever is going to happen next. Then it's time to go home to take care of his father.

In his bad dream it's the counselor, the one from the beach, McHenry: Junie's screwing him behind some kind of glass. Kenny can't touch them but they know he's watching. Junie stops and looks him in the face and says, How do you like me now? Because he's such a selfish bastard. She laughs, she means to hurt him. The things that he is told in dreams are true.

———

His father had the television off for once when Kenny got home that afternoon. He was staring out the living room window at the church across the street. A wedding rehearsal was starting up, people coming and going in shiny bright-colored cars. Weddings and funerals made it hard to park.

"Can I talk to you?" his father asked, in his new twisted voice. Kenny was about the only one who could understand him.

"Let me get squared away," Kenny said. "You need a hand?"

This was code for going to the bathroom; his father shook his head no. "There's some business down there, though," he said, angling his head toward the bedpan.

Kenny emptied it for him and then returned it and then went to the bathroom again to wash his hands with the yellow antibacterial soap. Anti-life, he thought. I'm anti-life and I vote. Remembering the curious distaste in his father's face, as if some other body had filled the bedpan. He could use it by himself now; he could get to the bathroom in his walker, for that matter he could mount himself into the wheelchair and roll out onto the sidewalk to terrorize the neighborhood, if only he felt like it. He didn't seem to. GODZILLA RETIRES. ELVIS IN THE BATHROOM.

"I got a letter," his father called out. "We both did. It's from Ray."

Kenny was cooking hamburgers, peas, sordid American food. Tomorrow: canned chili and dog food. The range hood was blasting out the grease and smoke and he couldn't really hear his father. "Hold on," he said; gave the burgers a last experimental pat with the spatula and went out to the living room, where his father was looking grave. Kenny asked, "What's Ray got to say for himself?"

"He's tired of it," his father said. "He wants to come back, I guess."

"Has he still got the ticket?"

His father glared at him, like this was a rude question, and impertinence. "I suppose he does," he said. "I don't have any reason to think he wouldn't. Anyway, they can afford to ship him back one way or the other."

"Who?"

"What's their names. You know. I can't remember things sometimes, you know that"—again, like it was Kenny's fault. "The people he went away with."

"The Clarks."

"I guess they're driving him crazy, I don't know. You can read it if you want to."

He aimed one of his big numb hands at a note on the bedside table, like he was throwing it away; and Kenny picked it up and put his eyes on it, glad for the interruption. Some voice of warning started up inside him when he heard Ray was coming back. Keep away from the wreckage. That feeling of the whirlpool, the downward spiral with nothing but blank water at the bottom . . . Viking funeral, Kenny thought. Chinese fire drill. He read the note as he walked into the kitchen again, as he flipped the hamburgers:

Hello from Down Under:

We're fine here and it's been an adventurous year. I'm looking forward to telling you all about it. Right now it's fall here and we're eating oranges off the tree in the yard. Go figure. Plus we're about fifteen minutes from the beach.

I think that I'm going to come home, though, if this is all right. [And here Kenny stopped, and flipped the hamburgers, and thought about the fact that Ray thought he needed permission.] *It turns out Mrs. Clark is going to have a baby, which I guess is good news. It seems like it was unexpected, anyway. Also I was very bothered by the news of your accident and I want to see you. All in all, it seems like the best thing. If this is OK with you let me know and I can start to make the arrangements. The school year here is the same as there (plus about five times harder, which I'll fill you in on*

when I get there). (Ask me anything about Gallipoli.) Anyway,
hope you're doing better. Tell Kenny I saw Midnight Oil. Let
me know if this is all right.

Raymond

Shit, thought Kenny. Let me know if this is all right. But how much anger is enough? He already had stores of it, stockpiles; enough anger for his father's lifetime and his own.

He set the table, put the ketchup on, helped his father into the wheelchair and wheeled him to the kitchen table. The range hood drew the night air in, cold air, faint messengers of spring.

"What do you think of that?" his father asked. "You think it was a mistake, letting him go like that?"

Letting him *escape.* Kenny didn't say it.

"You can't tell about these things," his father said. "You do the best thing, the way it seems to you at the time. You can't know everything."

"That's right," Kenny said.

"I had a feeling, though." His father lapsed into contemplation, silence. They dug in, the loud clattering of knife on plate as Kenny's father buttered his peas. Kenny couldn't watch him while he ate, not exactly gross, but the presence of disease, disfigurement, he couldn't quite get used to it. His hands, his mouth, the muscles he used to express himself with his face, none of them worked the way they had before. He was taking his death in installments, a little part at a time: 10 percent dead, or 8 percent, or 15. And it was tremendously hard work for him to go about the normal business of life; it required all his concentration to keep from dropping his fork, to raise it level to his mouth and bring it in. He ate his peas with a tablespoon and still spilled. His *will,* Kenny thought; it was his father's will that was driving him, down in the lizard brain, I want, I want, I *will* . . . Also this: Kenny didn't need to think kindly of him, didn't need to be charitable, because he was taking care of him.

His father laid his fork and spoon on the table beside his plate, a third of his hamburger eaten, finished.

"You do what you can," his father said. "You do what you think is right at the time, that's all you can do. You know?"

"I guess," said Kenny, unwillingly.

"I know that things were not the way they should have been around here." Suddenly his father turned his eyes on Kenny, his big dark headlights, wounded worse than ever and full of the sadness that he loved above all else. Kenny froze in the lights. "I know that things were getting out of hand," he said. "I guess one of the things was, I just wanted to tell you I'm sorry."

Beware! Beware! The alarms were ringing loudly in Kenny's head. Something was coming, something bad.

"All that drinking," his father said. "I've been trying to think about it."

"What?" Kenny asked.

"They talk about self-medication, I've been reading about it— where you try to make something better with drugs or alcohol. You know, I think the real problem is *depression*. I think it's wrong to just focus on the drinking part by itself. It's just a symptom, in my case. You know, it's a sickness, Kenny."

"I know that."

"It's not something that you choose to do. It's not like ordinary sadness. It's a disease."

Not just that he had to support his father's life; but that he had to support his father's *version* of his father's life. Kenny had to admire the nerve. There is only one King, he thought, and Elvis is his prophet.

"I guess it's complicated," Kenny said, hoping to end this.

"I know it's been hard for you," his father said, wiping away months of work with a sentence, a simple breath. "I appreciate everything that you've done, standing by me. It seems like we're going to have to make a choice here, especially with Ray coming back. I mean,

I don't know if I can use the word *family*. I don't know if I've got a right."

"It's OK," Kenny said.

"We just have to hang together," his father said. "We have to take care of each other."

A little late to start now. Kenny didn't say it. He saw himself bound to the hospital bed with thousands, tens of thousands of tiny invisible threads, like Gulliver. On the other hand, he didn't have anywhere else to go, not in particular. He had not been back to high school since the day he followed Mrs. Connolly out; he didn't have a job, or any plans, or even any particularly vivid dreams. There was a kind of guilty pleasure in drifting, in not-knowing. He had gotten to the ending point somehow, painted himself all the way into the corner, and now he was waiting for things to start again. Or not: he thought of male nurses, lives unstarted. Then there was Junie, the one good thing. Sometimes he thought she would rescue him; but just then, it felt like she was already gone.

"Would you do me a favor?" his father asked.

"Sure, I guess."

"Would you run up to the avenue and get me a pack of cigarettes? There's money in the drawer of the hall table."

"You're not supposed to," Kenny said.

"I'm not going to die from it. I mean, look at me."

He held his big weak hands toward Kenny again, demonstrating his weakness, his wreckage; and again the alarms went off, a trick! Beware! The green shoot down deep inside his father, like the blade of grass, the blind dark root that breaks upward through the sidewalk, crumbling it. It was masquerading as weakness. Something Kenny didn't have: the *will*.

"What will Dr. Nguyen say?"

"That little zip? He won't say anything, not unless you tell him. Come on, Kenny, be a good guy."

"I don't think so," Kenny said.

"What do you mean?"

"I don't want to see you back in the hospital again. You're doing all right. Why don't you leave it alone?"

"I know you smoke up there. I can smell it."

"What does that have to do with anything?"

"Damn it, Kenny, one goddamn pack of cigarettes. It's not going to kill me and it's not going to kill you."

"I don't think so," Kenny said.

"Why don't you get the hell out, then?" his father said, in the low solid voice he used when he meant business. "If you don't want to pitch in around here," he said, "I'm sure there's somewhere you can go."

Pure Kabuki, Kenny thought, the empty sleeve, the empty gesture. He didn't want to follow his father but he couldn't seem to stop himself. "Who's going to wipe your ass if I'm gone?" he asked.

"You can hire people for that. The Blue Cross will pay for it. You hire them and they do what you ask them to and they don't give you a lot of crap about it."

"Go ahead," Kenny said; full teenage now, blabbermouth. "See if you can find somebody who cares what happens to you. See if you can hire somebody to take care of that."

A mistake, he knew it as he said it, and in the lull before his father's reply he heard the first fat drops of a spring rain falling down outside the open kitchen window. He wished for a cigarette, an airplane, a magnetohydroscope to whirl him away from here, down into the submarine world, the blue light, anywhere.

"I'm surprised to hear you say that," his father said softly; and just then the doorbell rang. Escape! He ran to answer it.

Junie stood in the entry light. He saw right away that something was wrong. Her face was blotched with tears; her hair was wet, although it wasn't raining hard, was barely raining at all.

"Can I come in?" she said.

"Of course you can," he said, and held the door open for her, and prayed that his father wouldn't fuck this up. He sent the message: now is not the time, now is not the time, now is not the time.

Not that it mattered, the house was bad enough, without any extra ugliness: the hospital bed unmade in the living room, the bedpan in plain sight, the TV going with the sound off. His father wheeled himself in from the kitchen in his striped pajamas and his maroon wool robe, the good one, with the cigarette burns in it. The remains of their dinner were visible on the table behind him; the smell of hamburger grease hung in the air, and the smell of his father's body.

"This is June," he said to his father. "My father," he said to her.

"Very good to meet you, June," his father said, pumping her hand gravely. She struggled to understand his words but his face was reassuring—his good-father act, distinguished gentleman, his at-home-in-the-world look. Sometimes it was easy to see how he managed to hold on to his job so long.

"You're a friend of Ken's from school?" his father asked her; and she cast a sideways look at Kenny, who translated for her.

"A friend of mine from school," he said.

"More or less," she told his father.

I am not ashamed of you—he sent the thought in her direction, hoping she could hear it. I didn't tell him about you because I didn't want him to poison it (knowing at the same time that he *had* betrayed her, he *had* denied her).

"We're a little better friends than that," Kenny said.

"She's beautiful," his father said; as if she had left the room somehow. "I don't know why you didn't bring her earlier. He's secretive, don't you think?"

"What's he saying?" Junie asked.

His father went on talking, oblivious: "He had a little box un-

178

derneath his bed, a cigar box. Heaven help you if you opened it. But I mean, it didn't have a lock or even a latch that worked right. I was in there one day, I don't know what I was looking for but I picked it up and it fell open and you know what fell out? A few seashells and a shark's tooth, that was all. That was his big secret.''

"I don't think she can understand you," Kenny said; and it was true, she was listening with the blank politeness of the foreigner who has not been able to get it across, *no hablo inglés* . . .

"Come on," he said, taking Junie's hand.

"Where are you taking her?" his father asked.

"Upstairs, where we can talk. Is that all right?"

He pretended to ask his father; really he was asking Junie. She looked from one face to the other, panicky. I told you it was bad, he thought. Told you, you wouldn't like it.

"Let's go," Kenny said.

"Don't forget those cigarettes," his father said. "You were going to go and get me cigarettes, remember?"

"We're going *upstairs*," Kenny said, and led her away. The yellowing wallpaper, the open bathroom door. Kenny never saw the point of living like others could see you but now he did: she took it all in, the piles of decaying laundry, the soapstain (permanent) on the bathroom sink.

His room was worse: the unmade bed, the cigarette butts stubbed out in an old beer can by the window; and then the undiscarded refuse of his childhood, not so many years ago, the basketball posters and the Farrah Fawcett picture and the terrarium where the lizard lived that Boy had given him. Junie lived like a little adult, with prints of real art on the walls, folk fabrics, good furniture. Her clothes were folded neatly into their drawers, a room he knew as well as his own, a world he thought he belonged in for a minute.

"This is picturesque," she said; trying to be brave.

"But squalid," he said, trying to play along.

Junie shrugged; she couldn't disagree; then Kenny saw that it was worse than he thought, and he put his arm around her and lowered her to the bed while she began to weep. Don't say anything, he thought. Don't say *anything*. Just hold on here, and we'll be fine. He shut off the bedside light and they sat in the dark, the angle of light coming out of the hall, and the cars of the wedding party casting their headlights through the window, making moving patterns along the walls. Let us be children together, Kenny thought. Let somebody else take care of us. Then her tears were gone, and she caught her breath again, and it was time for Kenny to know.

"I need to tell you something," Junie said. "I just found out today."

There's the official version: the history of a year in which the events are set out, more or less in order, in which people are driving the same cars from scene to scene, in which they wear the clothes appropriate to their age and station.

Then there's the rest of it, intangible, fleeting. The feeling was there for as long as it took to feel it and then it was gone, changed into something else: complex as a perfume, orchestral music, grace notes and bottom notes. *Love,* for instance: he always had some feeling for her that could be called by that name, maybe still, maybe ten years later, maybe always (as he had promised her once, the only time she would listen). But somewhere it shifted, from *I can't wait to see you* to *Baby please don't go* to *Please take your clothes off* to *When will I see you again?* Not that he stopped feeling any one of these things: Kenny was pure and impure all at once, hopeful, regretful, blind, and psychic. The exact feeling at any moment was beyond any one word, complex and shifting, changing itself into something else and gone before it could be defined.

Something was left, though, some dry powdery residue of feeling like pine pollen. *Evanescence:* like the faces in a dream. Somewhere Kenny is still feeling every moment of this, not even memory but still feeling it. A sight of spring leaves, a turn of the wrist can open him back up, and suddenly he is feeling it again in all its confusions. Yesterday it was a woman in a department store—he had gone in to buy socks—who was wearing the perfume that Junie's mother used to wear. He didn't recognize the logical connection until later; it was the perfume itself, the smell that brought the feeling back over him. He stood in the Men's Furnishings section, burning with love and fear, the beginnings of tears in his eyes. Ridiculous, he knew it. It didn't stop.

"You think biology is going to be abolished, just for you," Mrs. Williamson said. "I'm sorry, I shouldn't get angry."

Kenny didn't see why not. They were in the lair, Mrs. Williamson behind the desk, Kenny in the punishment seat out front, Junie looking pale by the window.

"I don't know," he said, for the hundredth time that day.

"What are you going to do?" Mrs. Williamson asked her daughter, for the hundredth time that day.

"I don't know," Junie said.

"It's your life," her mother said. "That's what I want you to remember: it's your own life and it's worth something. It's not something you can just throw away lightly."

"I'm not doing any of this *lightly*," Junie said.

They ran out of words again—each of them apart, magnetized in opposite poles, Junie as distant as any of them. Alone, the broken nun with her closecropped hair, a wooden slat chair, a stone wall, medieval light. The witch, he thought, brought in for burning. The witch's betrayer, the inquisitor. He watched her body, as if the life inside her would suddenly reveal itself, a little fetal light; but her body was outwardly unchanged. Kenny wanted to go to her, to touch her; but he knew it was forbidden. Things had been broken. The beautiful curve of her face in the dim light.

Junie's mother caught him. "That's another thing," she said. "I thought I could trust you. You're not stupid, either of you. I could pinch myself."

There was no apparent reply to this, either. Nothing presented itself. Kenny understood that he was there to take his punishment and he would just as soon get it over with; because beyond that was a world of complication that he had barely glimpsed. A marriage, Kenny thought. A catastrophe. He couldn't tell.

"I know you don't want to hear this," Junie said. She was speaking straight to her mother, Kenny had gone. "This thing is alive inside of me, I can feel it. Do you understand?"

"I know there are a lot of difficult feelings," Mrs. Williamson said; a mistake, to show her professional side to Junie.

"This isn't a *feeling,*" Junie said. "This is a baby and it's alive inside me. You talk like I was making this up or something."

"I wish you were," Mrs. Williamson said. "A *baby!* Jesus. You talk like it was a puppy. I know I sound unsympathetic."

"Well, yes, you do."

"But somebody's got to do the thinking for you. You can do all the feeling you want, if you'll let me do the thinking, all right?"

"No thank you," Junie said. "I'll figure this out."

"How do you think you got here?" Mrs. Williamson asked.

They weren't allowed to see each other in private; they could talk on the phone; they could see each other with a third party; Junie needed to rest, and think; Kenny was a disappointment.

He went to Boy's house afterward, in the hopes of getting high. He drove through the end of an afternoon, the crowded cars invisible, disappearing in the half-light. You could put your hand through it. And none of them, not one of them, knew what was inside Kenny: none of them suspected the size of his feelings, the tragedy. In a Reliant, stuck in traffic.

Even in front of her mother, in the middle of anger and tears, Junie had said that she loved him.

His own child was growing in her belly.

This terror of the future, the wreckage, the weight.

This end of things: though the narrows, the birth, beginning. He had no business being out in public. He kept reminding himself that this was a mistake, a misdemeanor, but a primitive joy kept breaking through: you're mine now, you're mine for life. Not to possess her but just to have it settled: to be constant in love, to be loved in return. The things that only fools hope for. The high-priced wisdom that came at the ends of novels: everything fails, everything changes. He thought of Mrs. Connolly and wondered what she would tell him. Told himself that he had given his heart, and now it was up to Junie, because his heart was all that he had; thought it sounded fine. Then remembered that he had kept his life to himself, that he was selfish. Too many ideas at one time; and most of them wrong, this primitive joy, the hunter at the kill. He looked down at the dull lives in the cars surrounding him and he felt sorry for them. Kenny had the pure flame, even if it was burning him.

Wentworth's car was out in front of Boy's house, and Kenny sat in the car for a minute, wondering if he should go in. He had no business being out in public, he knew it; and there was this joy in his chest, he was afraid to kill it, even if it was the wrong thing to be feeling. You're mine now.

Finally there was nowhere else to go, and he didn't want to be alone; didn't above all else want to have to talk to his father about it: ASK ELVIS!

"Jesus," Boy said. "I thought we'd never see you again."

"First the school lesbian and now the English teacher," Wentworth said.

"What?"

"Rumor has it," Wentworth said.

"You were seen," Boy said. "We have witnesses."

It had been a mistake to come here but Kenny didn't see any way to gracefully leave. The boys were being cruel; he had hurt them by not coming around, by neglecting them, he saw that. Not that either of them would admit it. Meanwhile his own heart was doing tricks inside his chest like a circus pet. I'm a man, he thought; looking at the other two. Not that it was anything to be proud of necessarily but he had crossed the divide. He was past the baby steps. This was real trouble.

"How did you pull that one off?" Boy asked, grinning. "I mean, a teacher. Home run. Touchdown. Three-pointer."

"It wasn't anything," Kenny said.

"We have witnesses," Boy repeated. "You were seen to accompany Mrs. Connolly off the campus and spotted later on coming out of a bar."

"It was *Bennigan's*," Kenny said. "Like a shopping mall."

"A place where alcoholic beverages are sold and consumed," Wentworth said. "A bar. We have a question for you."

"We've been wondering all year but we thought we'd never find out: is there a *Mr*. Connolly?"

"I didn't ask," Kenny said. "She didn't say."

Impolite disbelief. Boy rolled a joint and lit it and passed it to Wentworth and Kenny came third and last; a reversal of the natural order in which Boy came first, at least in his own house, Kenny came second, and Wentworth third. Wentworth was fat, after all. His parents were liable to intervene at any moment, though they were mostly indifferent. While Kenny and Boy could do what they wanted, most of the time. Kenny saw that he was losing his place here without finding a place for himself anywhere else.

"She's been spotted before," Wentworth said. "She was at a concert, no evidence of the husband."

"Which one?" Kenny asked.

"Stray Cats," Boy said. "Dave Edmunds. One of the English vermin."

"She was *dancing*," Wentworth said.

He couldn't think of Mrs. Connolly now; she was part of a different archaeology, a future that would never happen now. Men and women, Kenny thought, boys and girls. He said, "She hasn't been back?"

"You ought to know," Boy said.

"She's gone," Wentworth said. "Are you coming back?"

"I don't think so."

"What are you going to do?"

The question hung in the air while the joint came around to Kenny again. He took a hit and listened to the bubbling sound of the aerators around him, the spicy green smell of Boy's bud—always the best bud, never less—mixing with the dirt smell and the lizard shit. *Fecund*, Kenny thought. You could grow shit on the air alone in here. And what did he plan to do next? He thought about it as he exhaled and saw illegal dreams, things he could never tell: true love and children, a small respectable life. A *man's* life.

"Beats the hell out of me," Kenny said.

"It's a shame," Boy said. "The undisputed pussy champion of the whole school and he retires at the moment of his greatest glory. Somebody ought to call the sports pages about it."

Kenny looked from him to Wentworth, spring sadness on him, the dead brown husks of the winter left behind, everything that came before, *already gone* . . .

"I hate it when that happens," Wentworth said.

Coming back from Boy's house, Kenny had a vision: they would go to Oregon anyway, they would make a way through it. He saw them living in some shingled cabin, the two of them and their unimaginable baby, Aaron or Art or Cyril or Charles. Ray could come visit them, could stay with them while their father came around—to where?—but Kenny knew it was a common fantasy all along. *A cunning cottage we can share.* And why were his fantasies so regular, so American? What did he want for her, for them, what did he want out of this life? A voice answered: *get through it, that's enough.* But now he had to ask for more. The tall pine forests and coastal mists of Oregon. He knew he was making it up.

When he did get home, his father was gone.

The empty bed was the first thing he saw, and the dark living room. A sense of panic and of guilt; he was supposed to be here hours ago, was supposed to be taking care. Now his father was lying somewhere, bleeding . . . Kenny searched the kitchen, the bathroom, calling out to him: "Dad? Dad!"

He wasn't there. He wasn't anywhere. The bed was rumpled but cool. The second floor was empty, it had to be, but Kenny checked it anyway. The closets were full of the usual clothes and there was no dead body in the garbage area, no wheelchair tipped over the porch. Nothing was missing: his father kept hundreds of dollars between the pages of a particular book, his household stash, and it looked like it was all still there.

The phone rang and Kenny jumped to get it but it was nobody, a real estate agent trying to find out if their house was for sale. "We rent," Kenny told him; and then hung up when the agent tried to hassle him for the landlord's number.

"Fuck all of you," he said to the empty, lit-up house—including the agent, the landlord, his father, others. The masculine apparatus of assistant principals and cops. Kenny was roped-in, stuck. He saw that he was going on a ride whether he wanted to or not. He sat down in the easy chair, rolled himself a cigarette, and lit it, trying to think of a good possibility and failing. Junie: he wished for her, longed for her. He wanted to turn the lights out again and sit there in the dark and give himself over to the longing. Desire, the dark ride: the subway at night, the lights flashing by in the darkness, gone and then nothing. Deeper and deeper.

When his cigarette was done Kenny got up and stubbed it out in the ashtray on the hall table, ammunition for his father, for a later argument, but in that moment Kenny didn't care. He had the feeling of somebody watching, a camera in the corner of the room. He had the feeling of his life being played out in a big bare room, fluorescent lights and linoleum floors, like the dayroom at the last hospital his mother was in—but empty, Kenny alone . . . Hard lights, hard places, echoing bare walls. A room that was made for the convenience of the keepers.

Should he call the cops?—but they had better things to do, no sign of violence, or theft. The hospital would have forgotten his name by then, except for the physical therapist. No obvious next step.

Finally he went out searching, because the waiting was too hard. Old posters fluttered from the telephone poles: REWARD! 300 LB. POLISH-AMERICAN LOST NEEDS MEDICATION! HAVE YOU SEEN ME? Kenny zipped his jacket against the damp chill—a raw-edged night, pneumonia, early spring—and walked in widening circles around the house, through the alley, then a block out and another block. Ten o'clock or ten-thirty, the ordinary comings and goings of a Saturday night, the blue light of the TV flickering out of every window.

The lights came to him around a corner, the shadows and reflections of a cop or ambulance strobe, alternating red and blue. Kenny knew he was home. He didn't hurry.

Grand slam, he thought: a police car, an ambulance, and two fire trucks. His father's wheelchair was spilled on its side, in the strip of grass between the sidewalk and the street. His father was lying on his side with his head up on the curb, apparently asleep. They were halfway between the apartment and the avenue and Kenny knew right away that his father was drunk.

"Nothing much to see here," the cop said, as Kenny approached the body.

"That's my father," Kenny said.

The cop was surprised, as if this couldn't possibly be true.

"How did he get here?" the cop asked. "He's still wearing his bathrobe."

"Is he OK?" Kenny asked.

"They're checking him now."

The drama unfolding in a pool of bright white light, the EMTs and the fallen body. Kenny stopped at the edge of the light and felt the eyes on him. Neighbors watched from their porches in their television-watching clothes, bathrobes and sweatpants. They stood immobile with their arms folded over their chests, like Indian extras in an old Western. *I'm innocent,* Kenny wanted to tell them; but it wasn't true. He had not been taking care.

"He's stable," the medic said. "He have a stroke or something?"

"A few months ago."

"That's about right," the medic said; and Kenny had the crazy feeling of pride, passing the test, coming up with the right answer. "This looks like it might be alcohol related," the medic said.

"No shit," Kenny said to himself.

"What?"

"I said it wouldn't surprise me," Kenny said, and turned and walked away.

Out of the lights, down the sidewalk, the eyes of the neighbors on him and the eyes of the firemen, big helpful men with mustaches, they looked like baseball players, beer drinkers, churchgoers. Kenny kept expecting somebody to come after him, haul him back, but none of them did. At the corner he stopped and allowed himself a quick look back and they were staring at him, all of them but the EMT, and his father of course, who was still asleep in the pool of light; the maroon bathrobe pulled over his bulk, a potato lying in the road, a cow. Kenny knew that he wasn't leaving anything behind; this was still his life, it would always be. He just had other things to do.

Unpremeditated: for the first time Kenny knew what the word meant, the way that a fully formed idea can suddenly spring into a blank mind. He was 100 percent certain while a minute before he didn't have a plan at all. Back at the house he piled his cleanest clothes into a duffel bag, raided his father's housekeeping stash for five hundred dollars, looked at Farrah Fawcett for the last time. He took *On the Road* with him, Mrs. Connolly's poetry anthology, and the copy of Rilke's *Letters to a Young Poet* that he had stolen from Junie.

He was seventeen for another month, a difficulty. His fake ID was bad and said he was twenty-four; which would work once in a great while on a stupid 7-Eleven clerk but never on a cop. AN OBSTA-CLE IS JUST AN OPPORTUNITY IN DISGUISE (plaque above the desk in Ralph J. Briscoe's office). Onward.

Kenny drove out toward the suburbs, out of the diesel and stink of the city, out of the yellow sodium-vapor lights to the new leaves and shady darknesses of Bethesda. It was what?—eleven-thirty by his pocket watch, Saturday night, the party-crowded streets near the popular bars. *Ginful,* Kenny thought. See where it gets you. But his heart wasn't in it, he had gone beyond judgment. He had obligations. Then into Sherwood, down Maid Marian, and onto her dark street.

Junie's house was sleeping, silent. Kenny cut the engine and let the Reliant drift the last thirty yards; then sat in the car and waited, to see if anyone heard him. The usual dog, two blocks away, barking at what? The clouds in front of the moon. A passing molecule. He saw his father's shape again in the circle of lights: a photograph, a thing that Kenny will carry with him. Usually Kenny had to wait to find out what mattered, it came slowly, like the image materializing out of the developer; but this night was instantly fixed. Whatever happened from here, every minute was important. Junie was waiting for him, whether she knew it or not.

When he was sure the house was quiet, he eased the car door open and slipped out: a raw night, smell of wet dirt. He thought of the Mexican figurine: springtime was coming but not born yet, caught between the thick vaginal lips. *Stillborn*, Kenny thought; then chased the word from his mind. He didn't need complication that night, didn't need pessimism. He wanted vim, zip, *Reader's Digest*, Ralph J. Briscoe, American get-up-and-go.

Tiptoeing around the side of the house in the dark he tripped over the cat and sent her screaming into the surrounding darkness. Stopped, stock-still, and waited for the inevitable light—you idiot!— but none came on. It was strange to be stealing his way into a house where he had been welcome, where he had been taken in; but at the same time it was exciting. My turn, Kenny thought. We'll do it my way for once.

He slipped in by the side door, which he knew was never locked, and felt his way along the dark hallway in the downstairs, past the door where Junie's mother was sleeping, the rock walls rough and cool under his hands. He was nervous; something would happen if he were caught, it was hard to say what. Dad with a revolver. Mr. Mustard in the Library with a Candlestick. The wild card was the brother, who was unpredictable in his comings and goings. Kenny sat in the dark of her living room, listening for tires, disturbances. The darkness was alive around him, dark feet and dark wings; and Kenny was a part of it. I am the dangerous one, he thought. I am not going to be done to any longer. I am going to do some doing of my own.

She was soundly asleep in her prim, high-collared nightgown (she slept in the nude when Kenny was with her). My victim, Kenny thought. Suitably high-powered moonlight drifted in through the window, across her face, her one hand pressed to her cheek in alarm, Oh, no! He studied her face, her fine long neck, and remembered how he had wanted to kiss her neck when he first saw it.

But how to wake her? The old-movie standby, the hand over the mouth—but she was pregnant, delicate, he didn't want to alarm her. *Pregnant:* he let the word linger on his tongue, silently tasting it. Fecund, fertile, gravid. Kenny felt a rude indelicate pride: *my* woman, *my* child, *my* life. He pressed his lips to her beautiful ear and whispered, his hand standing ready in case she cried out after all. "I love you," he whispered; softly, not trying to wake her up at first, but trying to plant himself in her mind. "I love you, Junie."

She muttered something to her companions in sleep, it sounded like "The bridge!"

"I love you," he whispered again.

"Oh!" she said, and turned onto her side. Kenny felt her breath on him, the hot breath of deep sleep, and as always her breath was colorless.

He kissed her neck, the place behind her ear, and heard her breathing quicken under him. You are in my power, Kenny thought, you are getting sleepy. You will cluck like a chicken when you wake up. Touched her breast, softly as he could; kissed her neck again and was surprised to feel her nipple harden instantly through the soft flannel of the stupid nightgown.

"Oh!" she said again, softly.

Kenny whispered her name, said that he loved her. She stirred again, but not toward waking. It felt to Kenny that he was sending her back into sleep, toward some dream of sexual possibility or impossibility . . . She rolled onto her back again, lay with her arms at her sides, lay with one leg up, half-bent, and the other loosely out, open to him. His hand strayed down the flannel of her belly and he thought *pregnant*. Something was living in Junie's belly, the secret place below her navel. A chakra, he had read and believed it, a secret energy center, bigtime kundalini. He let his hand stray south from there, didn't mean to but things were taking on a life of their own. Found the lip of her nightgown and under it and discovered, to his surprise, that she wasn't wearing underwear.

"Kenny!" she whispered hotly. She stiffened under him, scuffed his hand away like a stray fly. "Kenny, what are you doing here?"

He backed away, undignified.

"I came to ask you a question," he said.

"What?"

"I can wait till you wake up."

"What is it?"

"It's important. I want you to be awake to think about it."

"I'm fine," she said, rubbing her hands against her elbows, arms crossed, and looking around her small room like it was strange to her. Wisps and cobwebs of dreams still in her eyes.

"How did you get in here, anyway?" she asked.

"I let myself in."

"You're not supposed to be here," she said, remembering.

"I know I'm not," he said. "That's why I had to let myself in. Are you all right?"

"I'm not," she said. "You know. It took me forever to get to sleep, and now you wake me up."

"I'm sorry."

"It's all right," she said. "I'm glad to see you. Things have been so strange." She took his head and cradled it to her chest and they rested there; or Junie did, while Kenny's body was contorted into an awkward shape. He was supposed to be having elevated thoughts but mainly he was thinking about the shape of her breasts, a single thickness of cloth away.

"What are you doing here?" Junie asked; and the sadness of her voice called Kenny back. He moved away from her, composed himself. She sat primly on the edge of the bed, the last of the Waltons, sleep-tousled.

"This is going to seem weird," he said.

"What?"

"I don't know what you're going to say."

"What are you trying to say?"

Kenny in short pants, stammering schoolboy.

"Will you marry me?" he asked.

She looked away quickly, disappointed then angry. "Don't fuck with me, Kenny," she said. "Not now."

"I'm not," he said. "I mean it."

"Don't!"

"Don't what?"

"Don't tease me, Kenny, I'm confused enough."

She sat slumped at the edge of the bed, resting on her elbows, staring down at the carpet, disconsolate, distant, gone. Kenny racked his brain for the words that would make everything fine and sunny. You aren't pregnant anymore. We're twenty-one now. Love conquers all.

"I don't know what I'm supposed to do," she said. "She wants me to get rid of it, they both do. I mean, she doesn't say so but she keeps talking about my future, my beautiful future. Do you like my future, Kenny?"

"I don't know anything about your future," he said, measuring his own words; everything depended on this particular moment and what he did in it. He said, "Every time somebody talks about your future, it's like, your life after me. I don't want to think about that. It's just another script that somebody's written for you."

"So I should do what *you* tell me, instead."

"I don't know," he said; but this wasn't the answer, it wasn't the time to go passive, let things happen. There was no place ready for him in her future. If he wanted a place he would have to make one for himself.

"You didn't answer my question," he said.

"What?"

"Will you marry me?—or put it this way"—here he knelt, a joke, a parody, but it wasn't. He said, "I love you, I will be faithful to you, I'll do whatever I can. I know that it might not be enough. But I want to try."

"I can't answer that," she said.

"I know. But you have to."

"Get up off your knees," she said. "I mean, it's so stupid, Kenny, I don't mean you, just everything. It's not the answer. It's like I said, What's two plus two, and you said, Ice cream."

Defeated: they sat together side by side, two sad sacks, slumped into uncertainty. Then Kenny saw that she was weeping. He saw a chance in her weakness, an opening.

"What?"

She shook her head, unable to speak. (And if she hadn't been weak, hadn't been wounded, would Kenny have stood a chance?)

"It's just so stupid," she said, when the tears had passed enough to let her. "I don't know what the fuck to do, Kenny, I really don't. And you come in here confusing me."

"I don't mean to," Kenny said. "I know what I want, though— I want you, there's no big mystery about it. I mean, I don't know. I don't know what's going to happen next week, or whatever."

He stopped, tonguetied. The search for the magic words had failed again.

"I can't make anything better," he said. "I can't make anything different."

"What do you want to do?" she asked.

"I want to get out of here," Kenny said.

"Where?"

"Oregon, I was thinking," he said. It sounded desperate and silly in his ears. "I don't want to wreck everything," he said. "You could still go to school."

"How would we live?"

"I don't know," he said. "I mean, I'll get a job. I've got to do something, anyway."

A silence; and in the quiet he saw that he was stupid, seventeen and stupid, and she had outgrown him. Without her there was nothing in front of him, a blank buzzing screen, white, indefinite. There was *nothing*.

"I never told you this," she said. "I always thought it would sound like a mother or something, you know, I love you *but*. But you scare me sometimes, Kenny, the way you let your life slip away from you. You don't know what you're doing."

"No."

"But you make these decisions anyway, you just *go*."

"I don't know any other way."

"It makes me angry, the mess you make," she said. Then, in a new voice, like she was arguing with herself, she said, "You never know enough, though, do you? You never know exactly what's right and what's the wrong thing to do."

"I never seem to."

"So you let somebody else run things for you, you drift. I don't know."

She was saying something. The light slowly came over him: she was agreeing with him. He said, "What do you mean?"

"Let's *go*, Kenny."

His heart started to do tricks again. He thought she must have misspoken but her face was grinning, wolfish: I dare you. I double-dare you, Kenny thought. He said, "Where to?"

"Wherever. Oregon sounds good to me. Let's just get out of here. Do you have any money?"

Kenny kissed her before they went on but she turned away; and he saw that this was neither fun nor games. Run for your life, he thought.

"Five hundred dollars," Kenny said.

"I've got a credit card," she said. "We'll take the Honda, it'll never break down. What else?"

"Get some clothes," he said. "A lot of clothes, I'll help you carry them. Whatever else you need to take."

She stared at him, a figure from her dream; annunciation. I bring you tidings. She didn't move any closer to him. Kenny didn't take her hand. He didn't want to seem to capture her; she had to ease herself into the net, by her own volition. Later this would seem hard-hearted but he wanted her more than anything, before or since. When she turned to him again it was decided.

"Where are your clothes?" Junie asked.

"They're in the car, out front."

"What were you going to do, if I said no?"

"I don't know."

"Did you know I'd go along the whole time?" she asked. "Did you have me figured out?"

"I never doubted you."

"What does that mean?"

"I don't know," he said. "The one real thing. I knew there was something real between us and that would work itself out. I know that sounds stupid."

The magic words: she looked at him, she kissed his hand. They were all right, for the next five minutes, the foreseeable future. She said, "Marriage, I don't know, it's complicated. Not the feeling but the logistics. And I guess I don't know about marriage."

"What?"

"I don't particularly want to be owned," she said. "But I'll go for a ride with you, all the way to Oregon. How far is that?"

"Beats me," Kenny said. "The other side of the country."

"We'd better get going."

———

The neon sign said WELCOME TO BREEZEWOOD, PENNSYLVANIA, CITY OF 10,000 MOTEL ROOMS. It was raining, three in the morning. Kenny circled the strip, looking for suitably cheap. He couldn't tell; he was inexperienced with motels, with everything. They were both beginners.

The Motel 6 was SORRY as was the Super 8 and the Motel 3 looked dubious. Junie hadn't spoken in an hour, lost inside. She was actually leaving something behind. He wasn't going to tell her about his father for a couple of days; not that he was trying to fool her, not exactly. But it pressed on him like a guilty conscience. He was leaving anyway. He probably should have told her.

The rain was occasional, dispassionate. The neon signs of the restaurants and motels refracted in the raindrops on the windshield, emeralds and rubies. "Any guesses?" Kenny asked.

She roused herself, like she was sleeping, and asked, "What am I guessing at?"

"Motels," he said, "unless you feel like driving."

"No." Her voice was flat, remote, and Kenny wondered if she was still good to go. Good clothes, good shoes, somebody to take care of her when she broke—and now it would fall to Kenny, everything, and she had to know how little he could do. "I don't care about motels," she said. "Cheap is better, I guess."

"It looks like a choice between cheap but funky and expensive but nice. I mean 1953 Motor Court."

"I'll take the Holiday Inn then," she said. "I have a morbid fear of bugs."

"Expensive."

"We're going to put it on the credit card anyway."

She was still in her parents' orbit, still in the control of their gravity. "Won't they know where we are then?" he asked. "They can just follow the trail of receipts."

"It's three in the morning," Junie said. "We can stay in the Roach Motel if you want to."

"Whatever, whatever, whatever," Kenny said, and drove them to the Holiday Inn.

Checking in, he was nervous: the clerk was going to call the cops, runaways. Kenny knew a friend of Boy's who was legally an emancipated minor. He carried both their duffel bags in, ostentatiously—look! We have *lots* of luggage!—then stood uncomfortably while Junie handled the actual negotiations with the bored, pimply clerk. If anything the night clerk was younger than they were, and he was running a Holiday Inn, while they were just trying to get control of two tiny lives; the music sweet and stupid, beaming down from hidden speakers with their hidden load of propaganda: you will love McDonald's. TV is great. More baseball, more frozen dinners. What was the word? *Subliminal:* maybe it was true, maybe not. It seemed like bad luck, though, to go around believing in a high school rumor when you were trying to escape from high school, saltpeter in the cafeteria food.

Adults: now they were carrying the weight of their own lives, the weight of one another's, the weight of the tiny efflorescence in Junie's uterus. Even the words seemed wrong in his mouth, now that they were no longer jokes but descriptions: uterus, cervix, fetus. He carried her duffel bag from the elevator to the room in deference to her uterus. *I'll take the weight,* he told himself.

Junie flopped onto one of the gigantic beds, sighing. "I'm so tired," she said. "What's on TV?"

"I thought you didn't like TV?"

"I don't want to think," she said. "I've been thinking and thinking. I want to watch like *Charlie's Angels.*"

"Don't say it."

"Farrah Fawcett," she said. "Farrah Fawcett-*Majors!*" and clicked the remote.

The big eye of the TV bloomed to life and the chatterbox laughter: *M*A*S*H*. Kenny paced the room trying to avoid it. All the motel-room totems, the complimentary matches and Kleenex, the tiny soaps, the rigid synthetic material of the brocade bedspread, a faint chemical smell in the air . . . Potpourri! Suddenly he missed Wentworth, wondered if he would ever see him again. Good-bye, good-bye. Sometimes the size of the jump they were taking got too big to ignore, and then it scared him.

Down the perfumed hallway with its brocade wallpaper and wallpaper music and back with a Coke and a bucket of ice. She was standing wide-eyed at the window, staring out at the parking lot. Something had changed while he was gone. He could feel it in the air, like the aftertaste of a telephone call, words still ringing in the corners of the room . . . She was going back, he knew it. She wouldn't look at him.

"Junie," he said, from across the room. (Sudden vision of them in a house, their own house: *this* was the television and *this* was the sink . . .)

"Nothing," she said.

"We're all right," Kenny said, and went to her and stood behind her, embraced her, looked over her shoulder at the rainy night outside. What was she looking for? The cars and trucks passed by on the Pennsylvania Turnpike, a hundred yards away, a night full of purpose and movement, loneliness, Kenny thought, all of them going away. Here in our house. He said, "I love you. It's all right."

"Don't talk," she said. "Not right now."

She was going home, he knew it then. It was amazing that she had come this far with him.

He let his hand drop to her side, her hip; slipped it under the cotton of her skirt and she let him. The cruel line where the strap of her underwear bit into her hip. She was beautiful, she was going, gone. She let him do anything he wanted. They stood at the window with Kenny's hand touching inside her panties. Panties, cunties, titties, dickies, Kenny thought. The sadness was inches behind him, racing to catch up.

She moved with him from the window to the bed, sat on the

edge of the bed unbuttoning her dress while he moved from switch to switch, shutting off the lights. The marital half-light. He brushed his teeth and then she brushed hers and they met on the cool clean sheets.

"We're not going to hurt the baby," Junie whispered. "The doctor told me. Just nothing unusual."

Still he almost lost his nerve: the language itself was discouraging—uterus, fetus—and Junie was nowhere to be found. She was letting but she wasn't *with* him; and he remembered the angry fuck, the one after the fight, and the little unmentionable discovery they had made, the animal self. That's not right, either, Kenny thought; don't blame it on the animals . . . then felt her shift, and then she was with him. Mysterious but he could feel it, there in their little house, the only house—he knew it by then—the only house they were ever going to have. No kissing, that was one of the rules. Kenny went along but he didn't understand. Some sense of urgency. He touched her and she was wet and then he was inside her, more quickly than he wanted to be. His loneliness, he wanted so much; wanted to touch her deep enough so they would never come apart again, a little scar tissue, a place to call his own. *You're mine* but she had never been, would never be; *of her own free will* she guided him into the place where she needed him, rocked against him with her eyes closed, blind, and then they were both blind and then they were coming, both of them, at the same time and Kenny thought *now* and nothing happened. They fell short.

Junie started to weep.

"What's the matter?" he asked; knowing at the same time something was wrong, or everything.

"What?"

She shook her head, turned her back to him and gathered her shoulders against him.

"Junie!"

But yelling didn't help. Suddenly he was angry, she had abandoned him, led him here to abandon him. Back and forth and back and forth. He didn't want to be angry with her, he didn't care, something was wrong; something made him slip the sheet back carefully, where he saw the dark red stain seeping out from between her legs; the miscarriage. Kenny knew the word. Junie had known, all the time they were fucking, she had to. Junie's secret.

"Jesus," he said; and pulled the cover back over both of them, and lay naked next to her until she had finished weeping; near dawn.

Kenny ten years later: twenty-seven. He leans against the side of his rental car on an October afternoon and watches the leaves, reflected in the windows of the house in Sherwood Forest. Somebody else lives here now. The winter after Junie finally went to college, her parents divorced. Her mother is dead now, and her father remarried, and Junie still living out West. The house looks *exactly the same*. He expects her to walk out the door any minute, tall and dark and seventeen; or maybe her father, jogging along in his knee brace. Things end and don't end but they certainly stop.

Kenny stands there like his own ghost, both of him, twenty-seven and seventeen all mixed up. The freedom that he was enjoying a minute ago—a rental car, a town he doesn't live in anymore, a wallet full of credit cards, and a sunny afternoon to kill—is gone, and in its place is pain. He can feel it physically, an emptiness in his chest. She's gone, she is still gone. He didn't bargain for this.

The house looks beautiful still, kept-up, expensive. The gardens are a little more formal, a little out of place against the insistent naturalness of the house; and Kenny finds himself thinking of Jane Mrs. Dr. Williamson and the fact that she is dead, and Kenny never went to the funeral, he never said good-bye to her. What was the name for what he felt for her? He liked her and disliked her both but it was beyond that. Times when he would be doing things in his life, making decisions, and he would stop and ask himself what Junie's mother would think, what she might say. He thought of her all the time but never wrote her a letter. A *connection*. An anger at himself, at the world: she belonged to him, there should have been a place for him. And yes he was living his own life and yes he was busy but still. Some part of him continues to believe that if he could find the right word, the right gesture or sign, if he could write a perfect letter or a poem that they would begin again and the years apart would turn out to be a mistake. Part of him is still waiting.

This is fucked, he thinks, and gets in the car to drive back into the city. He can't quite leave, though. He can't quite bring himself. Memory: *this* is the bush that always scraped the side of her car when we drove in. *There* is the door where she appeared in her nightgown and sneakers. The reason country people have different souls: they grow up surrounded by the same things all their lives, the same trees, houses, wells, so all their memories are embedded around them. While Kenny has been uprooted. Part of him will always be left behind here, there, anywhere. Scraps and flutters of Kenny scattered around the landscape.

"Can I help you?" the woman asks.

Kenny blinks, composes himself. She has come from out of the house without his noticing. His eyes are open but he didn't see her come out, stand at the edge of the yard like the rail of a ship, protected. Kenny gets out of the car, to show that he means no harm.

"I used to know somebody who lived here," he says. "I didn't mean to bother you."

"Mrs. Williamson," says the woman—white-haired, pink-cheeked, dressed in aqua senior-citizen uniform, some sort of satiny tracksuit. She looks like the Dog Lady on educational TV, hale and practical.

"Actually, I was a friend of her daughter's," Kenny says.

"People come by here, all the time," the woman says. "She must have been a remarkable woman. I wish I could have met her."

"She liked to help people," Kenny says.

"I'm sure," the Dog Lady says. "But it must be more than that. It seems like people are looking for something when they come here. What are you looking for?"

Kenny stands tongue-tied. He doesn't want to translate what he's feeling into her words, and it's none of her business anyway.

"Whatever you're looking for, it isn't here," the Dog Lady says. "It's just a house. Would you like to come inside and look around? You can, if you'd like. It's quite a bit different, is what they tell me."

"Ah, no thanks," Kenny says, panicking. "I've got a thing I'm supposed to . . ." He makes a vague gesture toward the city as his voice trails off. In fact he would love to see the inside of the house; he just doesn't want to get caught having feelings, doesn't want anybody to see, not even this aqua stranger.

"Well, thanks," he says, though she's done nothing but allow him to look at the outside of the house. She would have done more, if he had asked. She's lonely, maybe. Kenny waves as he starts the car, slips it into drive, and slowly circles the dead-end to make his way out, tires slipping on the wet leaves. It's beautiful here; he's never coming back. Ache of a missed opportunity: knowing that he could have gone inside if he wanted to, wanting to, not being able to. I'm shy, he thinks, but that isn't the right word, either. Furtive, secret. The mess inside his chest, the tangle of this feeling and that feeling, and that's the main thing about the past, it seems to Kenny, its *insolubility*. You think that things are settled and then they come alive again somehow (a stray whiff of perfume, or the sight of her house) and you realize that things were never solved or settled. I have these feelings, Kenny thinks, useless and heavy as uranium. But he doesn't even *want* to get rid of them.

He lightens up as he turns onto the avenue, his mind drifting forward to the evening, when he is supposed to meet Kim Nichols for dinner; his last official friend in town. Everybody but Kim lives somewhere else now, Kenny included. He's thinking about the Dog Lady. *Whatever you're looking for, it isn't here.* Kim will like that, maybe or maybe not. Kim is in about her seventh year of graduate school, an art historian. She has a nose ring and a girlfriend, really she's having a pretty good decade, and Kenny—who has been mired in life for years, who has come to think of himself as a solid nowhere brown-fading-to-gray kind of person—feels flattered that she is interested in him, interested enough to go to dinner, anyway, and maybe more, he isn't sure. Last time he was in town they came within an inch of sleeping together.

Last time: he remembers the moment when it was decided that they wouldn't sleep together, the moment after dinner, over coffee, when he asked Kim if she and Junie were lovers for real. He knew this was out of bounds, knew she wouldn't answer, but he couldn't stop himself: and then he asked, and saw her soul retreat from her face, her eyes closing down and the old closed Kim instead, saying: maybe you'd better ask Junie about that. I don't really want to talk about that. She's not dead, you know.

She's just in California, Kenny said, the next best thing.

That isn't funny, Kim said. She called me from the hospital last time.

Is she OK?

She went *back* to him when she got out, Kim said; and then the evening was over, and each of them gone inside. Better to live in the present, better to live in the flesh: to stay faithful to what is, and not what might have been. Maybe he was making it up; but there was something when he telephoned Kim to arrange things, a faint, flirtatious . . . Time will tell. A dinner at one of the new restaurants on Columbia Road, they will eat Indian or Thai or Mexican or Ethiopian, the world spread out before them. The Ethiop will make us dinner, Kenny thought, and I shall pay for it with my Visa card. Artistic conversation—Kim kept up with her poets and painters— and then at some point she would enforce dancing or maybe just drinks or a retreat to her apartment or maybe the sanitized motel room, house of loneliness, and suddenly he is back in it, the words *motel room* triggering a dive into the insoluble past.

I belong here, Kenny tells himself. I love the present: a girl with a nose ring (a *woman*, he corrects himself), dinner, money in my pocket, and a full tank of gas. God bless the Ground! Then remembers the way the silences would fill up with the memory of Junie, his last evening with Kim; how they sat—not all through dinner, but once or twice—like orphans waiting for a bus, motherless children; her name unspoken. The thing is, he can go for years without remembering; or rather he remembers it safely, a youthful folly, the public joke of first love, moon June croon. The official story, official sentiments: time works its slow erosion on us all, all passionate feeling . . .

It's only here that it comes alive again. Here: driving down Massachusetts Avenue at a quarter to four in the afternoon, beautiful sunlight and golden leaves, the traffic already stacking up in the other direction; but Kenny is elsewhere, riding down this same road in the moonlight, dead of winter, the only car on the road. It's maybe three in the morning or four, coming back from her house. He's wearing Junie's pants. What? Just the silence of the houses, the families sleeping inside them and Kenny the only one awake, King of the World. The stoplights blink for him alone. His dick is still warm from being inside her. The phantom Kenny, the adult one, shrinks from the word *dick* but that's the only word for it. They were literal, both of them. She made his dick hard. He made her come, he made her bleed. She made Kenny bleed; but that was later, the continuing train wreck . . . A winter's night, anyway. He's wearing her pants. King of the World. Not happiness, exactly, but something close, a place in the world, it was hard to find the words for it, then remembers the words: he loved her. He loved her and believed himself loved and then she was gone. My *tragedy*, Kenny thinks; but the loss would not be laughed into silence. The voice inside: *Where are you?*

Kenny is standing at the dock, looking out over the lake toward Jacob's island, and the clouds rushing through the sky overhead and reflecting in the water make him feel like he is still driving. The sky is narrow, between forested hills, which makes the clouds look like they are moving at a tremendous speed. He honks the horn of Junie's father's Jeep again, and the noise echoes across the water and loses itself in the dark pines on the far shore.

Then Junie comes out of the house and waves to him across the water and he waves back. There's something strange about her. He can't figure it out and then he sees: she has a cast on her arm. This is news to Kenny, but everything is so strange to him right now—he's been driving for four days, all the way from Maryland—that the cast is just one more item. He watches her start the outboard and pilot the little aluminum boat across the water, trailing a stream of blue oil smoke and a shallow V-shaped wake, calling to him over the ring-ding of the motor: "Kenny, Jesus, it's you!"

Kenny can't think of what to say. She has been stuck in his dreams all summer and now she has emerged in the flesh, made out of things, wearing clothes. He thought a summer in the Rocky Mountain sun would change her more but no, she looks the same: dark hair, pale skin, not quite the fresh-dead look but still . . . Her hair is grown out to a boy's length and she's tall, Kenny knew that in an official way but seeing her reminds him. It would help if she were more different. He helps her beach the boat on the pebbly gravel shore, hauling it up an extra foot before they embrace, clumsily, the cast in the way. They don't quite fit. The cast is everywhere, cold white plaster.

"Junie," he finally says. "What did you do to yourself?"

"It was so stupid. I broke my arm," she says, laughing but embarrassed. She shows him the cast, first the top, then the bottom, like he needs to see both sides to make sure it's really broken.

"When? What happened? You didn't tell me."

"It just happened the day before yesterday. Come on, let's get your stuff."

"I can get it," Kenny says. "I don't have much." It's true: the Jeep is bulging with junk, books and clothes and stereos, but it's all Junie's. He opens the back, which pops open from the pressure of all the stuff, and takes out a tiny comical suitcase.

"That's it?" Junie asks.

"There wasn't room," he says, and shrugs. "What happened to your arm?"

She's embarrassed, she's blushing: "I was diving off the dock, on the other side of the island. You have to dive, the water is too cold, you can't just gradually make your way in. This is so stupid."

"What?"

"No, it's just that I thought the water was deeper than it was. You can look, you can see the bottom, but I thought it was some kind of optical illusion that made it look so shallow. And then Jacob had to take me all the way into Kalispell to get it set."

"Are you going to be all right?"

She looks at him sideways. "I've got to have this thing on for six weeks," she says. "After that I'm going to be just fine."

Jacob, Kenny thinks—the familiarity of his name in her mouth, a well-worn feel . . . Jacob van Wechs is the master photographer she came to study with, to be his assistant. Master and servant and what else came in the package? But Kenny knows better than to think about this. He's tired, he's not sure if he's even supposed to be here and Junie won't tell him, past their initial relief at the sight of each other.

She shoves the boat off until it is just floating, then hauls it parallel to the shore, holding the yellow nylon rope in her good left hand. Kenny embraces her from behind, not knowing if he has permission, or needs it. He takes her breasts into his hands, staring over her shoulder at the lake, which is shining like a giant Kodachrome in the evening sun. Her breasts feel familiar and warm. "We missed you," Kenny says softly. "Me and Little Kenny."

But Junie shakes herself free of him, stands watching the house, which seems to be watching her back; watching both of them. When Kenny turns her neck, her beautiful neck, to kiss her, he sees that her eyes are tightly closed. He hasn't got her. Junie's kiss, this time, is dry and quick: *perfunctory.*

"It's complicated," Junie says, stepping into the boat.

Kenny shouldn't be here. Junie's gone; this summer's apprenticeship to Jacob is only a stop along the way. And since the miscarriage they have been wary with each other, careful. He wonders if they would have lasted this long, if she wasn't leaving anyway.

But someone had to drive the car out with all her things, and Junie's father—opaque as usual, he's been kind to both of them— offered to pay all the gas and the plane ticket back and a month's wages besides. Either that or spend the rest of August laying sod around office buildings in suburban D.C. The problem is that now, as they slowly motor toward the island, water slapping at the tin sides of the boat, darkness settling into the hills around them, now he feels like a trespasser. He wants to touch her and be welcome; wants to put the toothpaste back in the tube, to unsay the things that have been said, to undo things. Where would you start? Consequences, take your chances.

"It's beautiful here," Kenny says, to fill up the silence.

"It's unbelievable," Junie says. "I am completely in love."

But Kenny doesn't know what to say to that, either; the word *love.* A pair of golden retrievers scramble around on the dock, chasing after a tennis ball, until the ball rolls off the dock and the larger of the two dogs leaps into the water, splashing all over Kenny and Junie.

"Psyche!" Junie yells. "Jesus! Cut it out!"

"Psyche?"

"The other one's Cupid—Psyche and Cupid—get it?"

"Cute," Kenny says. "This is Jacob van Wechs's idea?"

"Jacob has an assistant," Junie says. "A majordomo—Syd, she's really nice."

Kenny takes the warning and shuts up. Psyche has forgotten the tennis ball and is trying to chase down the boat, paddling frantically in the wake while Cupid barks from the dock.

"A *minor*domo," Kenny says. "Those are some stupid dogs."

"They're good dogs," Junie says. Apparently he's not supposed to criticize. She ties the yellow rope to the dock, which is actually the porch of the house, and they clamber out. Jacob's house is a Lincoln Log extravaganza: gables and picture windows and stone chimneys piled a couple of stories high, some sort of dream of rugged Western-ism. Kenny knows it's a fake but can't quite figure if it's *supposed* to be fooling anyone. He takes his tiny suitcase and follows her down the deck that faces the garden, feeling the cool night air starting to creep down from the mountains.

"He might be working," Junie says, her hand on the door. "We might not see him till tomorrow. He does that sometimes."

"Doesn't matter," Kenny says. "I'm a vegetable myself."

"Poor thing," she says, and these words echo around for a while inside his brain as she lets him into the house. It's all one big room on this floor, a kitchen at one end and a fireplace at the other, where a woman in black is striking a match to a pile of kindling just as they come in—a witch, as near as Kenny can tell. All in black, sharp-featured. She glances at them when they come in, then back to the important business of starting the fire. I like being invisible, Kenny

212

thinks. He turns back to where Junie was and she's gone. A moment of confusion, feeling the miles, the long drive.

"Do you want a beer?" Junie asks, coming out of the kitchen with one anyway.

"Thanks," he says.

"Sit down," she says, pointing him toward a couch. "You must be tired."

"I'm all right," he says, and goes and sits, but when he leans back in the couch he realizes that he's still got the little suitcase clutched in his hand. He forgot.

"Poor thing," she says again. "You can stay a couple of days, then? You've got time?"

"I'm not on any particular schedule," he says. He drops the little suitcase on the floor beside him. Junie sits. They look at each other like strangers, like a boy and a girl on a blind date. Where will they start?

The witch walks across the room toward them, preoccupied. "Junie," she says, "did you manage to make a copy of that video Jacob wanted?"

"It's running right now," Junie says. "I took the other deck down from the bedroom."

"Good," she says; turns to Kenny and sticks out her hand. "Syd Beasley," she said. "It's a joke of a name, I'm sorry, I'm stuck with it."

"Kenny Kolodny," he says, pumping vigorously. Syd has a manly handshake.

"I know," she says. "OK. You're taken care of, Junie knows where you're supposed to sleep. What else?"

She's looking at him, through him, and at first Kenny feels like he's supposed to answer. I don't know what else, he thinks. You tell me. It's the black hair streaked with gray that makes her witchy, that and her all-black clothes, artist clothes, Chinese slippers . . . She's beautiful, though, in a ravaged and wrecked sort of way. She might be in her forties still, her fifties, Kenny never can tell. He's just turned eighteen, he's never going to get any older than this.

Syd turns the headlights on Junie: "Are we going to see him tonight, do you think?"

Junie says, "I don't know. He's printing."

"We won't, then. Good. Is there anything you need to do? I know you're leaving in a couple of days."

"I've got some printing I want to do myself."

"God knows when you'll see another darkroom," she says; then turns pensively and gazes into Kenny's face. "Shit!" she says.

"What?" he asks.

She looks at him like he spoke out of turn, a sleepwalker awakening. "Nothing," she says. "Shit! I just remembered what I've been trying to remember all day."

"What's that?" Junie asks.

"Some stupid, stupid fashion shoot in Dallas," Syd says. "I was supposed to talk to Jacob's agent about travel arrangements and I forgot." Again she turns to Kenny, like he was the one who needs convincing. "It doesn't matter what you do," she says. "It doesn't matter what you tell them, they send you plane tickets anyway."

"Jacob doesn't fly," Junie says.

"He will if he has to," Syd says. "He just hates it, is all. You two have fun, if you can."

"What are you doing?"

"I'm going to hide out in the basement and pretend to sort negatives," she says. "There's an Orioles game on."

"Jacob has a satellite dish," Junie says.

"Jacob has one of everything," Syd says. " 'Night, all."

Leaving them tonguetied, blind-date hell in the big living room, side by side. "Everybody's busy around here," Kenny says.

"Oh, yeah," Junie says.

A small sparsely furnished cell somewhere on the ground floor: a single bed, Navajo blankets, a ladder-back chair; she never left her mother's house. That's the feeling Kenny has, anyway. He hasn't seen his own father since he left him in the road, which is something he thinks about. There's a double glass door at one end of the room and a small patio outside and past that the lake, which is still not dark yet. He takes his watch out: ten-thirty.

"We're at the edge of the time zone here," Junie says. "Plus we're so far north, sixty miles from Canada."

The lake is turning colors in the last of the day, basically dark gray but with dark purple shades hidden under the gray or dark green. The forest looks solid, gloomy. This landscape looks *depressed*. "You like it here, don't you?" he asks.

"Oh, yeah," she says. "It's different—you don't realize, living back east, the kind of variety of life you get. There are never two trees of the same species standing next to each other. Here it's simpler."

"Nature girl," Kenny said.

"I *like* it."

"I believe you."

"Don't make fun of me, Kenny."

"I don't mean to," Kenny says; and he doesn't, but he can't seem to stop himself. He wants her so badly—or thinks he does, which is no difference—that it makes him edgy, angry: *Tantalize*. She sits inches away from him, unavailable. A bumper sticker he saw, shortly after he passed the Montana state line: IF YOU LOVE SOME-THING, SET IT FREE. IF IT DOESN'T COME BACK, HUNT IT DOWN AND SHOOT IT.

"I'm still buzzing from the drive," he said. "This is a big country when you have to drive across it."

"Well, thanks for doing this."

Prim, official. Kenny feels like an emissary from the Department of Normalcy, the Department of Heterosexuality, come to claim her for the family again. Don't be grateful, please, he thinks. Be glad to see me, overjoyed, oversexed.

"I'd love to spend a winter here," Junie says. "Syd did it, two years ago. I guess there's a month in the spring and another one in the fall when there's too much ice to use the boat and not enough to walk on. Completely isolated. She had a radio, I guess."

Another silence: her face in the reflected light off the lake, soft outlines of the fading sky. Beautiful, Kenny thinks. Out of my price range. Hard to remember that he touched her once. He asks, "How have you been?"

And she says "I'm *fine*" in an aggrieved tone, to tell him he was wrong to ask.

And the silence falls over both of them again. The magic words, Kenny thinks, knowing they don't exist. Junie is keeping herself from him, which she has every right to do. *Privacy*, Kenny thinks. The core of unhappiness around which she is spun.

"You look tired, is all," he says.

"We've been working."

We: Kenny hears it but he doesn't know what to say.

"I'm tired myself," he says. "There's more South Dakota than there ought to be."

"I just flew over it," Junie says. "Next time I'll drive. Flying feels like cheating to me. You blink your eyes and suddenly you're there, magic."

"You want more *suffering*," Kenny says. She blinks at him, annoyed again.

He changes the subject: "I found the place I want to live," he says. "Coming across the border, up out of Wyoming, the first thing in Montana is a big green sign that says EXIT 0 and then a ramp that goes off the highway and there's nothing there, nothing at all. It's just like these grass hills and then the mountains off in the background. There was snow on them."

"In August," Junie says; and by some miracle Kenny has said the right thing again, and they're all right. A truce. He takes advantage by reaching out to touch the soft skin of her arm, just above the top of her cast.

"You've damaged yourself," he says.

She takes his hand in both of her own, holds it in her lap, examining it: a workingman's hand these days, rough from the shovel handle, a carapace of hardened skin.

"Where have you been living?" she asks.

"I'm apartment-sitting," Kenny says. "I feed the plants, I water the cat, it's tough."

"Whose apartment?"

"A friend of my family's," Kenny says; which is not only a lie but a very lame lie, which Junie would see through in a minute if she could spare him her attention. Kenny doesn't have a family; and even when he did, they didn't have any friends. In fact he's watching Mrs. Connolly's apartment but he doesn't want to tell Junie. Not exactly a guilty secret but hard to explain.

Fortunately Junie is preoccupied: her little light of sadness, Kenny thinks. Feeding the flame, Scandinavian sunsets, the dripping pines of Oregon.

"It just feels different here," she says. "It's like being in love or something, I just wake up in the morning and I can't believe I'm here."

"Even better than camp," he says.

"Don't be an asshole, Kenny."

"I don't mean to be," he says; but as he says it, he realizes that he is angry with her, a little tired of the aesthetic fussy-wussy, all these gray skies and silences. Somewhere outside of this little valley it is still summer. Somewhere out there is beer and corn and hamburgers, baseball games on the radio when you drive across Iowa at night.

The life they would have lived: scraping by, the young catastrophe with the baby and the tiny ugly apartment, green shag carpeting, Kenny still wants this. Young Americans struggling. He would love to feel her beside him, love to fight with her about who would go down to the courthouse and sign them up for food stamps; one of those American biographies, falling down to the bottom and then rising stronger than ever. Instead he's having to do it alone, which is lonely work. Maybe he's been listening to too much radio, country-and-western sermonettes and John Cougar Mellencamp, but Kenny wants to be an American again, join the navy, drink Budweiser. He wants to dive into the thing, bring her with him. It's not too late, he thinks. We can try again.

"How are you?" he asks. The last light is fading from the room.

"I'm the same," she says.

She takes his hand and holds it over her breast; an invitation, he hopes, but also a ritual gesture of friendship or solidarity. He sits behind her on the bed and kisses her neck and they watch the light disappearing from the sky, from the lake. This is where I started, Kenny thinks. This is where I should come clean, tell her everything, try to reanimate. Her lovely body. Her complicated brain. She's all right now, she came through the miscarriage without breaking up and now she's better, or something—contained within herself, anyway, no more loose threads and rough edges. She's learned survival, as Kenny has. He should be glad for her, and in a way he is but he misses the other: the open heart, the daring, the carelessness. Come on, he thinks. Come along with me.

"Junie," he says.

"Ssshhh," she says. Turns and stares at him, her face indistinct in the twilight, and then what? Something will happen next. She is not weeping, for him or for anybody else. "I'll be back in a minute," she says.

———

"Living and dying," Mrs. Connolly explains. "Don't you see they're both the same?" In this dream she's in the schoolroom still, she's angry with Kenny but she won't say why and she won't stop smiling. After that he's in the all-night drugstore again, trying to buy maxi pads but the clerk keeps telling him he's got the wrong size and he knows that Junie is bleeding to death back in the motel room but he can't seem to get the right size, he thinks he's got it and then the clerk says no, I'm sorry.

Kenny wakes up alone, late in the morning, the sunlight streaming in. He can still sense her in the bed, sex and another smell he can't identify at first, something rude and chemical: diaphragm junk, he remembers. They're being practical now, prudent. He feels the loss.

Thirteen or fourteen hours of sleep, and the highway buzz still faintly under his skin. He gropes under the bed for the glass of apple juice she left, heavy, sweet, all-natural, and lies naked in the bed remembering the exact answering shape of her body. Just thinking about her gets his dick stirring again. Nothing worried, nothing married, nothing hesitant. Maybe that's it: maybe it's just body to body, straight animal lust, and their brains can go fuck themselves. When did she leave? At night or did she wait for morning? It doesn't matter, he was asleep anyway, but he wishes he knew.

Outside the sun is shining upon the mountains and the lake, a greeting card except that Kenny is stirred by it. Why not? It seems like he is falling for it, but really nobody made this, nobody is trying to sell him; and the air, where it comes through the open screen, is bright and clear and warm. He throws the covers off and fishes around in his suitcase for the cutoff jeans, his only shorts, his asshole angling toward the ceiling, thinking about hidden cameras. Maybe he's seen one too many spy movies but he feels like he's being watched; shakes his ass one last time, thinking *Rosebud*.

In his shorts and sunglasses, then, his lifeguard regalia, he sits on the little patio and rolls a morning cigarette. The sound of a single chain saw echoes from across the lake somewhere, muted, insectile. A moment of luxury. The heaviness of a long sleep, the sound of bees, feel of the sun on the bare skin of his chest. He's been working all summer without a shirt and he's got a tan, a few muscles. He was prettier when he was a lifeguard but he's stronger now. He has not come begging to her. Why this is important, he can't figure out, but he has brought his own resources with him, his own stock of secrets. Kenny has a future, for instance; nothing guaranteed but Mrs. Connolly arranged for him to take the high school equivalency test, which he passed, then called a friend who taught at a small college in Florida. It was too late for the fall but he's apparently going there spring semester—a pleasant prospect but dreamlike. Kenny is going to sit in this chair in the sun until something happens. He can wait. *You should have called me a few weeks ago*, Mrs. Connolly said. Circumstances had changed: a boyfriend, with whom she was bicycling through France. She invited him to her apartment anyway, invited him to stay while they were gone. She kissed him, too, and Kenny knew that she would have gone farther if he had pressed her but he didn't, afraid of upsetting the balance. Now that he's got a future, he's gotten attached to having one, even if it isn't quite as bright and shiny as Junie's.

"A smoking criminal," Syd says. "I knew there was a reason I liked you." Kenny looks up, startled, and loses her face for a moment in the sun; a presence, another body, and when he gets over the surprise he's glad for the company.

"Can I have a cigarette?" she asks.

"It's just these Dutch things. You have to roll them, I mean, I'll do one for you if you want."

"I can do it," Syd says; perches on the arm of his chair and expertly, easily rolls a cigarette. She's wearing shorts today, baggy nondescript girl-shorts but her legs are long and brown, girlish. Wide

World of Sex, Kenny thinks. Beware. He hands her a lighter rather than lighting it himself.

"When did you get up?" she asks, around the wreath of smoke.

"A few minutes ago," he says. "Is it late?"

She shrugs. "The crack of dawn by New York standards. Out here, though, we get up with the pioneers. Jesus, I'm glad you came. I love to smoke but I like to have somebody to do it with. Otherwise it feels sordid."

"A solitary vice," says Kenny.

"That's right," Syd says. She holds the cigarette in the air in front of her, and both of them watch the smoke drift up through the sunlight. Curlicues, Kenny thinks. Arabesques. What am I doing here?

Without looking at him, Syd says, "We're all pretty interested in June around here."

"I'm glad to hear it."

"She's got this kind of, I don't know—daring, I guess. She takes a lot of risks when she takes pictures. It's very strange, very personal stuff, I don't know where she gets the nerve, especially at her age. I mean, I was thinking about what sorority I wanted to go to in college or something. That picture of you, for instance."

Kenny didn't know there was one. He makes a small noncommittal noise.

"You look so innocent, lying there asleep," Syd says. "At the same time there's this whole other not-so-innocent side, you look kind of bruised and worn. And it's still unusual, that kind of nakedness. I mean, women's bodies are a dime a dozen but men are still taboo."

She's seen his dick, that's what she means. He tries to cobble together an image from the hints that Syd has dropped, can't quite. Junie didn't trust him enough to show it to him. At the same time here he was in Syd's confidence, a circle of knowingness, unshockable—adult-world and beyond—and Kenny likes it here. *A whisper of steam goes up from that porcelain eurythra . . .* and realizes somewhere in here that Syd is gay, or partly gay, or something. Dark imaginings, ménages à trois.

"It has to come from somewhere," Syd says. "I mean, I don't know. I just have the feeling that something has to be driving her to it."

The common fascination, Kenny thinks. Everybody loves my baby. "She's an American girl," he says.

"What is that supposed to mean?"

"I don't know," he says. "It's a Tom Petty song, I was listening to the radio a lot on the way out here."

Syd stubs out the cigarette and looks at him, trying to gauge how much she can trust him, how far to let him inside the circle; which is where he needs to be, inside, and not out playing with the other children . . . Junie has made it inside, he sees that, and now he needs to follow, or get left behind.

Kenny says, "I know the words to all the Tom Petty songs by now, and all the Bruce Springsteen."

"You want to keep that crap out of your head," she says. "It won't go away. You'll be walking up some mountaintop somewhere, or swimming in the river, and this voice will pop up in your head going *You deserve a break today . . .*"

"It's too late for me," Kenny says.

"It's avoidable," Syd says; but now she's giving advice, looking down from on high, and Kenny is outside again; a disappointment. "They're working this morning," Syd says, "which leaves you at loose ends. I imagine we'll see everybody at lunch. There's coffee and so forth on the counter in the kitchen, and if you run out of things to do come down to the garden and I'll put you to work. You're leaving tomorrow, right?"

"That's the plan," Kenny says.

"Jacob will be pissed," she says. "Just get rid of your TV, turn the radio off, quit reading the newspaper. It's like the all-junk-food diet."

"I had a buffalo burger in Arlee on the way up here," Kenny says. "It was all right."

Syd smiles; he has won again, temporarily. She touches his arm as she leaves, ambiguous gesture, glad to see you. Kenny eases back into his chair. Sunlight, mountain air, the sound of water lapping at the pilings of the dock. Eyes closed, he tries to imagine the photograph that Junie took of him, the nude or naked. *I'm beautiful*, he thinks, and feels it, stretched out in the sun in only cutoffs. A faint persistent buzzing draws his attention to the leg of his chair, where a crippled wasp is wrestling with a crumb of toast, a souvenir of somebody else's breakfast. The small things, bliss. *I'm beautiful*, he thinks, and rolls another cigarette.

Jacob comes as a surprise. His work—it's everywhere, calendars and book bags—is woodsy and reverent, temple-of-nature stuff with the occasional French landscape thrown in, the occasional naked. Kenny is expecting what?—some hearty, outdoors . . . gray longish hair and an *aquiline* nose, maybe even turquoise jewelry.

Instead a man resembling his father sits at the head of the table, drinking not sipping white wine: fat, bald, dressed in white shirt, black slacks, black businessman shoes. Holding forth, charming. Kenny remembers the touch of the yellow antique fat on his father's sides. Where are you?

"This *complete* asshole," Jacob says. "I didn't know it was Winogrand till somebody told me, the next day. So of course I'd just driven four hundred miles in the rain for nothing."

Syd clucks her tongue, shakes her head in a pantomime of sympathy; she's heard the story before, obviously. A performance for Kenny's benefit, or Junie's. Kenny is unmoved.

"I guess there's a moral to that story somewhere," Jacob says;

then turns the headlights directly on Kenny. "How long did it take you to drive out here?" he asks.

"Four days."

"That's good time. Which route did you take?"

"Chicago, South Dakota, Wyoming, mostly on 90."

"It's quicker if you skip Chicago," Jacob said. "You cut down around Indianapolis, then north around, what? I guess it's Rock Island, Illinois. Pick up 90 around Madison."

The house of the father, Kenny thinks—that same ability to judge, though with more of a place to stand than his own father ever had. A tiny planet, a long lever. The women are saying something to each other and Kenny longs to be among them; tiny glimpse of what is slipping away from him, the possibility, the company of women . . .

"There was a full moon on the way out, across South Dakota," Kenny says; they stop talking, listen, which he was hoping for. "I took the cutoff through the Badlands there, I wanted to see it anyway so I went through in the moonlight. It was very strange looking anyway, like another planet."

Kenny stops. A silence. He realizes that he doesn't have the words to translate the feeling of being there, the desolation in the blue moonlight and the perfect loneliness, the last man on the way to outer space, looking back at the blue Earth . . . the way he thought of Junie's baby the whole time, the baby that was never going to be, stuck in purgatory. An idea that would never become a body; and Kenny was jealous, a little—pure possibility, free-floating, free-falling, disembodied. Kenny was coming into his own life and it felt like a loss, all the things he would never be. He was growing the carapace of his own life, as Jacob had: the continuing performance of his Self, performed by Himself. As opposed to driving, floating, the air so clear it filled the windshield with stars. He shut the lights off for a while and drove by moonlight only.

"Then what happened?" Jacob asks.

"Nothing," Kenny says. He doesn't want to sell this part of himself to Jacob. He says, "I went to sleep for a couple of hours at this rest stop, and when I woke up there were three busloads of Japanese tourists all around me."

"Fucking Japanese," Jacob says.

"Fucking Japanese," Syd says. "Fucking Germans. Fucking Australians. Fucking Mexicans."

"OK, OK, OK," Jacob says.

After lunch, Jacob and Junie take Kenny downstairs to show him the work space, a complex of rooms—darkroom, office, storage, a spare bedroom—that run the length of the house underground. The first room is the only one with windows, a bright room lined with gray, steel print files. A continuous easel for looking at prints runs around the three solid walls, a slanted board with a gutter at the bottom and an elastic strip across the top to hold the pictures in place. The first thing Kenny sees, on the far wall, are three large prints of the same famous picture: a black branch in spring, dark with rainwater, a few slow buds beginning to flower. More green peppers, Kenny thinks. Funeral Home of Dead Art.

Junie looks at him warningly. She knows what he's thinking. A quick instinctive sorrow, to think of how much they know each other and how little it's going to count. A million dollars in Confederate money, buggy whips, adding machines.

"I took that here on the island," Jacob says, "right after I bought the place. Two years later we cut that tree down for firewood."

Performance, Kenny thinks. What is there to say? I like your work? I *love* your work?

Jacob says, "One of those three is a reject. Which one?"

Kenny sticks his nose right up to the easel, really looking at each one: the delicate shadings from white to gray to deeper gray, the gloss of water on the petals. They look identical to him. "I can't tell," he says.

"June?"

"This one," she says, pointing to the left-most print, the one nearest the window. She points to a half dozen pinpoints of white among the dark wet leaves in the lower-right corner of the picture.

"Cause?"

"Dust on the negative carrier."

"Good," Jacob says. "But that's not the one—that can be spotted." He turns to Kenny. "I don't mind marking out flaws like that—makes every print different. Now watch this."

Jacob takes a scrap of white exposed printing paper and holds it next to the white blossoms at the tip of the branch. "See?" he says. "Just a little bit darker than white, just enough to give it texture. The only paper-white is in the highlights on the raindrops. If you look at this one"—he moves down a print, holds the scrap of paper in the same position—"you see that print is overexposed."

The white of the leaves, in this print, and the white of the blank paper are the same. "That's interesting," Kenny says.

Jacob takes the middle print from the wall and rips it in half, then in quarters, then stuffs the shreds into a trash basket.

Performance, Kenny thinks again. It's hard to imagine a life in which a shade of gray would make that big of a difference. He looks around the room at the pictures on the other two walls: leaves, flowers, aspen, models. Then others tucked behind, out of the way.

He sees the bare foot at the edge of one, and the black line of the shutter release, and at first he doesn't recognize it though it fills him with a powerful sadness, a dense, crushing . . . It's one of her nakeds, he sees it, one of the pictures with the sleeper's eyeshade. A flicker of jealousy but mostly this other feeling, this sadness, loneliness. Maybe it's the smell of developer and fix from the darkroom next to them. *Smell is the sense of memory.* That feeling of being back at the beginning, free, full of possibility. Nothing has happened, nothing will ever happen.

Jacob says, "That's all I'm trying to do. I'm trying to make some small perfect thing, you know? A little battle against entropy. You can only make perfection where you have control, so it has to be small."

"Let's go look at the darkroom," Junie says.

Out on the water, two hours later, Junie sits in the bow of the canoe trailing her good hand in the water while Kenny paddles in the stern. The wind blows them sideways, the waves make watery battering sounds against the aluminum sides. She sets a course for straight across. Halfway there, she points solemnly behind them, and Kenny puts his paddle up to look: a line of mountains had cleared the trees, the usual, majestic . . . It's beautiful, there's no other word, the way the granite stands against the clear dark blue of the sky, pockets of snow. Kenny won't surrender to it, though. It's only scenery.

"Glacier Park," she says. "That's thirty miles away."

"That's nice," he says, and starts to paddle again.

"What are you mad at me about?" she asks. "Why are you being an asshole?"

Kenny doesn't say anything, keeps paddling, listening to the slap of water against the canoe. At the far shore they beach it onto the pebbles, the metal noise sends a deer running for its life. Kenny catches a quick glimpse, more a motion than a thing: escape. Best wishes, Kenny thinks.

They lug the canoe into the brush and start up the trail, Junie first, to point the way. The afternoon is dry, and hot, and still. Nothing is moving but the two of them. The trail runs along a creek for the first part, a damp spongy bottom of cedar and ferns—hobbit-land, Kenny thinks. All charity has deserted him. After twenty minutes or so they turn, and start to switchback up a hillside of tightly closed forest, pine of some kind, he guesses. Kenny is still weak from driving, he can feel it in his hard breathing as he tries to keep up with Junie, driving and cigarettes. She walks ahead of him up the steep trail, silent as an Indian, swinging her cast.

He can't help imagining them together, his bald head and perfectionism. His belly against hers, his mouth on Junie's breast. Other things. Jacob calls her June, a new name. Kenny feels a specific weakness when he thinks of this, an emptiness down in his belly, lower then his navel, inside.

Junie waits for him an hour up the trail, in a little ragged clearing. She sits in the sun at the edge of the woods, on a fallen log that rain and winters have bleached white. Buffalo skull, Kenny thinks. Take a picture. Kenny stands next to her, but looking out over the meadow. The grass here is luxury green, a grown-out golf course, long and soft. A few wildflowers persist, big floppy yellow flowers and little purple ones. He sips from the canteen, then hands it to her, and she drinks from it.

"I've been wanting you to see this place," she says. "I thought we might see some elk up in here—there's a herd in this meadow all the time. Once I saw a bear."

You're fucking him, right? He almost says it; but what good would it do? He's almost certain anyway. And Kenny can't tell if he's got any rights at all in this matter.

"You've changed," he says instead; just a noise to make with his mouth but she takes it seriously, considers before answering.

"I had to," Junie finally says.

He waits for more but that's all she has to say. The air is still but changeable, the cool breeze coming down out of the forest and then this other, warmer air that smells like pinecones and sunlight. Kenny takes his shirt off, slides down in the soft grass.

"What have you been working on?" he asks, eyes closed.

"Just the same," she says. "More of the nature stuff. It's not so much Jacob's influence as that's what he does, you know? As long as I'm here I might as well learn it."

"Are you sick of it yet?"

"It's more interesting than you might think," Junie says. "You're mad at me."

"Yes, I am."

"Why?"

Then Kenny has to decide whether he wants to talk about the missing photograph, the naked of himself; has to decide whether he wants to accuse her of lying, when he hasn't been 100 percent himself, what Mrs. Connolly would call *bad faith*.

"You're leaving me," he says; a lie and a truth, all at once. "I love you. It's not a lot more complicated than that."

"I love you, too," she says; immediately, without question. Kenny sees this with pain: they do, they love each other, and they are still going to manage to fuck this thing up.

"This is idiotic," Kenny says.

"What?"

"The *waste* of it," he says. "A perfectly good feeling."

"I'm still here," Junie says.

What percentage? He doesn't ask. Part of him is elsewhere, too, although the best part of him is here.

"Let's just stay here," Junie says. "We can build a little house out of branches and leaves, send away to Kalispell for groceries."

"A *wikiup*," Kenny says.

"Think about it: just coming out in the morning and two feet of snow on the ground, and then you could build up a fire. The Indians used to do it."

"Grubbing around in the dirt," Kenny says.

"I'm not unhappy," Junie says. She comes down off her perch on the log, comes over to sit next to him in the soft grass, takes his hand. "I miss you all the time," she says. "That's not what I mean. But I've got my own life moving, Kenny, I feel like it belongs to me."

"OK," he said. She was lying about something.

"This isn't against you," she said. "You don't have to be angry with me."

"I don't know," he said; staring into the blank face of the fact again, she was going, he was gone. *Implacable,* he thought; and leaned toward her, and kissed her, and started to unbutton her shirt.

"What are you doing?" she asked.

"That seems kind of obvious."

"I don't want to do anything," she says. "I didn't bring anything."

"We could improvise," he says.

"Not now. We can lie here if you want to, though, I do it sometimes just to feel the sun. If you just want to lie here."

"Whatever."

"I don't want to torture you."

Kenny shrugs; she looks at his face, looking for something, not finding it. She unbuttons her shirt the rest of the way, lays it carefully out on the silver-bleached log, takes her brassiere off and then stands and steps out of her shorts. Standing naked above him and awkward, in and out of the sun. Her cast seems to be unbalancing her. Then she lies face down in the grass and says, "Your turn."

All that has been given to him, and all that has been lost: he stands to take his own clothes off, remembering what was permitted at the Girl Scout camp, that delicate torture, swell of her back . . . He lies down next to her in the grass, feeling the sun on his own body, the soft bent blades of grass rising again to tickle his neck. What? He's trying not to get a hard-on, trying to make this OK. He wants to be inside her again, unprotected. Instead she's turning into a nude beside him, a beautiful body, a commodity. Kenny doesn't know: he's in love, he's angry. I'm no good at this, he thinks, and this makes him even angrier; and then out of his anger he finds his dick rising again, thinking *I want to fuck you,* thinking *fuck you.* He doesn't know. The wind blows through the pines. He turns his thoughts deliberately toward the one thing that can always dispel a hard-on, the thought of his mother, trapped in Baltimore, staring out the window, waiting for Kenny to come and keep her company.

"How much work do you have left to do?" Kenny asks. "Are we going to see you again tonight?"

Junie gives him a look, and so does Syd, but it's a legitimate question. "We'll work till we're done," Jacob says. "There's no telling how long that will be."

"Oh," says Kenny, and watches them descend into the darkroom. "Good luck," he calls after them. "Have fun."

OK, I'm an asshole, he thinks to himself. What do I do now?

He helps Syd with the dishes, which isn't hard because there's a special way to do everything and he doesn't know any of it, so she does everything. He takes a shower. He sits in his room, drinking a beer, reading Frank O'Hara and trying to concentrate but the sex keeps getting in the way, *a tongue given wholly to luxurious usages*. Junie is downstairs with Jacob and Kenny is left out. It's only partly simple jealousy. What? This fantasy, this tiny marriage . . . Maybe she's right, maybe he only wants her to belong to him. This is a *step forward* for her . . .

"Shit," he says aloud.

"What?" Syd asks him.

"Nothing," Kenny says. "I'm going for a walk."

"You want some company?"

"No thanks," he says; and Syd blinks, he's hurt her feelings; or maybe not, maybe she's staring at him, measuring him for the clown outfit. Everybody knows, he thinks, even I know for once. Kenny says, "I just want to think about something, I'll be back in a little while. We can smoke cigarettes."

"No hurry," Syd says, and waves him off. "There's a lot to do."

Kenny grabs a tennis ball on his way out and bounces it on the deck near the sleeping dogs, who bound into action, following him down the beach, panting and slavering and nipping at each other's ears. His sneakers crunch in the smooth pebbles of the shore. Kenny tells himself small meaningless lies, trying to calm down: he is on vacation, everything is fine. A hundred yards down, out of sight of the house, he throws the tennis ball as far out in the lake as he can, expecting the dogs to chase it down, which they don't. They stare at his face, while the ball bobs greenly up and down in the water fifty yards off shore.

"Stupid dogs," he says. "Bad dogs, bad dogs."

They look up expectantly at him.

"I don't know what you expect me to do," he says. "I threw the damn thing."

Cupid starts to whimper, or maybe it's Psyche. Dogs: an alternative to humans. I think I'll just go out and *buy* a friend. The other one starts to circle him, sniffing his hands, looking for the ball. Kenny clambers through the brush at the edge of the trees, looking for a stick. Both dogs stand at the edge of the brush, yelping at him. He finds a two-foot pine branch and hurls it out next to the tennis ball. This time they both leap after it, splashing into the water then swimming out, with only the tops of their heads above water. They look earnest and purposeful and easy in the water, like golden red beavers, but neither of them can find the stick. Nor can they find the tennis ball, which is two feet from one dog's head.

But they *have* to chase it, no reason known or needed. It's just a reflex: fetch! And then there's Kenny, throwing the stick for them to get it, a little closed circle of pointlessness. While up in the house, Junie and Jacob are alone in the basement. Kenny is supposed to stand clear, stay out of the way. Jacob with his shirt off. Suddenly he feels like weeping, screaming, something. It's hard to imagine what, exactly.

The first cool breeze of evening descends from the mountains, starts a faint shiver in his spine; not from cold . . . Kenny gives up on fetch, starts skipping rocks. Some of the shoreline pebbles are perfect for it, smooth, round, and flat, and the lake is flat where the dogs aren't churning it up. He's killing time. Junie and Jacob are alone in the basement. What am I doing here? he wonders; and asks himself again and again, with each rock he skips into the water, what am I doing here, what am I doing here, what am I doing here . . . A reflex, maybe—he can't let go, doesn't want to let go. And then the idea comes to him, the one he's been avoiding, the idea he didn't want to have: it's over.

It's over: three thousand miles to find out a thing he already knew. And lots of trouble all around, trouble for everybody. The water seems to be glowing with a light of its own. Kenny throws a big rock into the water, to end the game, but the dogs come furiously paddling over and start to search around the splash. She's gone. She's outgrown him, or the other way around, or something else completely. It doesn't need explanations. He sits on the ground and watches the light slowly leave the water, the sky turning a delicate transparent gray but never completely dark. He lights a cigarette, another small betrayal but this time of Syd, and after a while the dogs get tired of the chase and come to shore. With the water slicked down onto their bodies they look skinny and embarrassed, until they fluff themselves up again with a big luxurious shake. Two weeks ago Kenny was sitting in another patch of dirt, outside of Baltimore, splitting a pint of lime vodka with Severin Watkins. Friday afternoon with the landscaping company, and everybody was fucking off, which was traditional. Severin was black, twenty-three years old, fresh up from Hampstead, North Carolina. He and Kenny tended to get the pick-and-shovel jobs, the ones the foreman unapologetically called "nigger work." They were what?—not quite friends, or like the kind of friends Kenny imagined you would make in a foreign country if you were just passing through. Severin was country, he said so himself. He was always talking about shooting squirrels and raising tomatoes, outboard motors and so on. But that last Friday—it was the day Kenny quit—Severin was talking about pussy. Specifically he was saying that there was a lot of pussy two thousand miles closer than Montana and Kenny was crazy to drive all that way.

And now Kenny is sitting in the pebbles at the edge of a strange lake, a long ways from familiar, and Severin was right; and Kenny left Severin behind and the job and the apartment and everything else to come dragging out here, for no good reason. He saw himself as he imagined Severin saw him: a kid, inexperienced, dumb. Kenny measured himself for the clown suit and saw it fit. He should have known better, should have been a man about it: suck it in, take the loss and get on with it. Instead of this pissing and moaning, O my poor sad feelings! Put on the manly armor.

No: that isn't the way out of here either. Something will happen, one way or the other. In a week, two weeks, this will be over. He wishes for company, then; wishes that Severin was beside him, Candy Connolly, anybody. Born damaged, Kenny thinks, misaligned (and the small voice in his ear, reminding him of his parents' failure, his own inevitable . . . They were beautiful once themselves, intelligent and young, there's no way out for him). He gets up, brushes his pants off, and heads back to the house.

Nothing has changed, not even Syd's position in the chair. She sits composed, relaxed, with one leg crossed under the other. Kenny, a born fidgeter, admires anyone who can actually sit still.

"What were you doing down there?" Syd asks.

"Torturing the dogs."

"Oh, well, they deserve it. Let's go smoke."

"I think I'll go downstairs first, see how they're getting along," he says experimentally.

"Not a chance," Syd says. "That's a no-trespassing zone, Jacob would kick my ass."

"Till when?"

"Whenever they're done," Syd says. "Probably three in the morning. Once Jacob gets started he doesn't like to quit."

Kenny gives himself away. He doesn't even know himself what he's feeling but he can see it reflected in her face: the trouble.

"Look," she says, "get yourself something to drink, let's go out onto the deck, relax. The summer nights here are like no place else."

"People keep telling me that," Kenny says, sulky. But he goes into the refrigerator and fetches a beer, meets her outside, where she rolls a cigarette for herself and one for Kenny.

"My cigarette, my friend," she says, lighting up. "Twenty friends for two dollars, not a bad deal."

"These are even cheaper," Kenny says.

"It's going to be lonely around here when June leaves," Syd says. "Jacob is a gigantic pain in the ass, and he's not even here half the time."

"You're going to have to pick one of those to complain about," Kenny says. "I don't think you can bitch about both."

Then realizes that she has made some kind of confession to him, something about Junie. She will miss her, too. We're all jilted, all lonely, let's all do the loneliness dance . . .

"What?" she asks him.

"I was just thinking," Kenny says. "I didn't mean to say anything."

"I keep having this urge to give you advice," Syd says. "How old are you, anyway?"

"Eighteen."

"That explains it. Everybody wants to give you advice, I bet. Anything in particular you'd like to hear my accumulated wisdom on?"

"I'm OK for now."

"I think you should go after her," Syd says. "She's a beauty, and she thinks about you all the time. She talks about you. That's all I wanted to say—I don't know if it's any use to you or not."

"I'll think about it," Kenny says, wishing she would go away.

"What are you afraid of?"

Then Kenny is angry for real—she's trespassing, walking all over him where she shouldn't be. Presumptuous: and, worse, she's probably right, Kenny can't tell. *Afraid:* not a word he would have chosen for himself. But maybe that's the right word for the feeling he has, this wanting to draw back into the safety of the past; really he just wants to set the clock for November again, ride the Wayback Machine to when his father was all right and Junie was all right and high school hadn't blown up in his face—not that there was ever a single day that was like that, his timing was off as always. Not a single day. A sympathetic silence from Syd, the glow of the coal of her cigarette, orange firefly, a half-moon over the lake. Still he feels misbegotten and alone, born damaged.

"I'm sorry," she says. "It's none of my business."

"It's OK."

"She told me about the baby, is all. You don't want to let something like that drive you apart."

"The baby," Kenny says; and all of his own sympathy drains out, and he thinks that Syd is upstairs talking to him about their baby while her boss is downstairs screwing Junie, maybe at that moment, while they are talking; and he was foolish to come. Whatever joke this turns out to be, Kenny will be the punch line. *Faithless*, Kenny thinks. The whore. And of course the stupid husband, unsuspecting . . . Kenny's had enough.

"Just take her with you," Syd says. "Take care of her."

"You're missing your lines," Kenny says; and his voice is harder in his ears than he means it to be, but he can't seem to control it. "You're supposed to say it's *all right*. You're supposed to say *you'll get over it*. There are lots of other girls, and you've got plenty of time."

He stops, because he's afraid that tears will overtake him. Why is he quoting his father's clichés at Syd? She looks on, unsure, unsteady. A stitch in time saves nine, he thinks. A penny saved is a penny earned.

"I'm sorry," Kenny says, "I'll . . ." But the rest of what he's got to say is gone, maybe it was never there, a hot, burning emptiness: nothing. She's gone and there's nothing. Kenny stubs out his cigarette, goes back to his little room without further explanation, pursued by the knowledge that he is a fool and everybody knows, the little husband, the one who almost made the mistaken baby . . . He puts his little foolish belongings into his little foolish suitcase and slips out the side door, where the two wet golden retrievers come hammering down the deck toward him. Cupid has the stick in his mouth, Psyche the bright green tennis ball, or the other way around. They dance around him like fools around a Maypole, prancing and leaping, hitting the back of his knees with the stick as he walks toward the dock, rubbing the wet fur of the tennis ball on his leg.

"No," he says, but he can't shout—he doesn't want to answer any more of Syd's questions—so it comes out in a stage whisper. "Bad dogs, bad dogs."

They bark nonstop as he lowers his little suitcase and then himself into the canoe. As he casts the yellow line off and starts for shore he hears the little splash of the tennis ball in the water, then the bigger splashes as the two idiots dive in after it. They crash around in the water, losing the ball immediately, then settling in to swim next to the canoe. Kenny feels like the admiral of the idiot fleet, piloting his idiot canoe.

He grinds the aluminum canoe into the rocky shore and beaches it, feeling red-handed, guilty. The two dogs sit at the edge of the water and start to bark. Kenny sits on the hood of Junie's father's car and wonders where he will go next, now that he has escaped. No direction known. Although he is in shadow, where he sits, and cannot see the moon, its light is shining over most of the lake, and onto the island, making a dim sketch of the house. The heat of his anger drains out of the hollow in his chest, which slowly fills again with some kind of sludge that makes him feel heavy and stupid. Kenny says to himself, What's done is done—as if that explains anything. What's done is done.

The two dogs curl up into little wet balls and go to sleep.

In the quiet Kenny hears the slam of the screen door, footsteps on the deck, a man and a woman talking. The water carries the voices to him but garbles the words. Kenny listens hard, trying to make it out, then realizes that he doesn't want to know what they're saying. What's done is done, he tells himself. Ignorance is bliss. Kenny is grateful when they go back in.

He finds the cooler in the backseat of the car with two cans of beer still in it. One of them he puts in the lake to cool, one of them he opens. The foaming, fizzing beer is blood-warm and sweet as Coca-Cola, not that it tastes particularly good but drinking a beer strikes him as something that a man might do in this situation. It seems plausible, which is enough for Kenny. His ambition is to get through the night and sort it out in the morning, if he can.

Slowly the tension passes out of his neck, out of his shoulders. He sits on the hood of the Jeep and watches the moonlight creep toward him across the surface of the lake, catching in the hollows of the little waves. OK, he thinks.

Then the door of Jacob's house opens again. Kenny can see it's her, silhouetted against the lights of the living room. She calls to him: "Kenny?"

The two dogs stand up and face the island, shivering themselves awake. Kenny doesn't move.

"Kenny?" she calls again. "God damn it, Kenny."

The golden retrievers rush into the water and swim toward Junie, their heads trailing a wake in the bright water. Kenny wishes there was something he could tie himself to. Her voice sounds sweet to his ears, and he remembers holding her in his arms and kissing her beautiful neck. She won't go away.

"God damn it, Kenny," she says again, not shouting anymore, but relying on the water to carry her voice.

This goes on forever, her standing on the deck, him on the shore. Then he sees her walk away, around the back of the house, and she is gone and it is over. He was wrong to come at all. Kenny feels a door swing shut inside him, a lock turning, not just Junie on the other side but the books they liked, music, winter afternoons alone in Junie's bedroom. He can remember the day, the hour, the windswept newspaper in the street outside her window. The wheel has made a complete turn, a revolution. She's gone for good.

So when he hears the rattle of oars in metal oarlocks, the slap of water against the aluminum hull, when he sees her row around the corner of the house toward him he feels more exhausted than elated. No more, he says to himself, no more. I am just plain tired. The dogs watch silently from the deck of the house as she splashes loudly toward him, veering left and right, clumsy with her cast. Kenny wades out to help her beach the boat but keeps a careful two-foot cushion of air between them, like opposite magnets. Junie stands in shadow against the bright water of the lake. She asks, "What was that, Kenny?"

"I don't know."

"You scared Syd halfway out of her skin."

"I don't care."

"You ought to, Kenny. She never did anything to you."

"Look, let's just say that I'm sorry, OK? You can tell them I'm sorry and then we'll drive the rest of the way out tomorrow and then we can just forget about it, OK?"

"What's this about, Kenny?"

"You know," he says. "You know better than I do."

"Jacob?"

But just to hear his name in her mouth is hateful to him. Kenny turns his back on her and walks quickly down to the shoreline, picks a heavy rock and hurls it as far out into the lake as he can, and another.

"What do you want to know?" Junie asks.

"I don't want to know anything," he says. "I think you ought to go back in. I'll sleep in the car. We can go in the morning."

"We started as lovers about a week after I got here. It's part of the deal," she says. "I don't know if it is or not but I know I'm a long way from the first."

Kenny can't face her, can't seem to turn. He holds a heavy, night-cold rock in his hand but can't throw it.

"I thought he was interested in my work," she says. "I was such a little asshole."

"He wasn't?"

"No, I think he really was. But then he's got to prove that he's better, I don't know. It's all such a game to him."

"And Syd knows all about it?"

"Sure," Junie says. "As much as she wants to."

Kenny takes the rock in his hand and sails it out over the lake, aiming for the reflection of the moon in the water, so when it hits the moon is shattered into a thousand concentric splashes; then turns quickly to face her.

"Are you pregnant?"

"What makes you want to ask that?"

"I don't know. Are you pregnant?"

"No, Kenny. I don't think so."

"You don't think so or you're not?"

"I'm not pregnant, Kenny, OK?"

"You're not pregnant?"

"I'm not pregnant, OK? Look, Kenny, what's this all about?"

"I don't know," he says. "I can't figure it out. Why don't you come over here?"

"Where?"

"Here by me. Where you were before."

"I can't do it, Kenny. I'm not your *girlfriend* anymore," she says. She takes a seat on a driftwood log, facing toward the water, and Kenny can't help coming to sit beside her, that same magnetic resistance keeping them connected but apart.

"At least with Jacob, it's something different," she says. "Something new."

"Tell me what you mean."

"I don't want to be that little girl anymore, Kenny, no matter how much you might want me to, or my dad might want me to."

"What does your dad have to do with it?"

"Whose car are you driving, Kenny? Who paid for your trip? Who sent you out here?"

She's right. Kenny feels caught, corrupted, a coppery bitterness at the base of his tongue. The glad hand of Junie's father on his shoulder: good boy, good boy. "There's nothing much to say then, is there?"

"Maybe not," Junie says.

"Then I think I'll go to sleep." But he doesn't go, not yet. He watches her for a sign, a revelation, but she keeps her eyes from him, staring out over the water toward Jacob's house, cradling her cast in her good hand. Kenny sees that empty white plaster and wants to write his name on it. He wants a flaming angel to descend from the skies, the earth to open and swallow the water from the lake, anything to break this deadlock. But nothing will come of it.

"Well," he says slowly. "I guess it's good night, then."

"I guess it is."

"What are you going to do?"

"I don't know. Go back out to the house, I guess, in a while. I'll figure something out. Good night, Kenny."

"Good night," he says. "Good night, Junie." Kenny leaves her by the lake, takes his flashlight and his sleeping bag and her father's fancy foam sleeping pad from the backseat of the car and thrashes through the brush of the lakeshore, looking for a level spot. He settles in against the base of a tree, snug in his bag, although the night is still warm and there's no wind. When he turns the flashlight off, the darkness comes alive around him: flickers of moonlight through the limbs of the firs, wing beats in the dark air. He hears a screen door creak open and footsteps on hollow wood, the deck of Jacob's island most likely, although it sounds startlingly close. No voices, no calls except the sporadic dry sound of insects calling to one another. Kenny's biology teacher had joked once that all the varieties of insect sounds, and all the birds as well, had only one thing to say: I'm here, make love to me, I'm here, make love to me, I'm here . . . He listens for Junie to make some noise, listens for the rasp of aluminum on gravel, waiting for her to go back but she doesn't. After a few minutes, three or five, he hears Jacob's footsteps again and then the screech and slam of the screen door closing behind him. A yellow bug-light, a beacon, clicks on.

Alone in his cheap sleeping bag—the kind with cowboys and cactuses on the flannel liner, a treasure—Kenny is filled with the calm of a survivor: the crash came, the crash went, he is still around. Only Junie, sitting silently in the nearby dark, disrupts this queasy calm.

Why won't she go? What good can she do him now, or even herself? Kenny has made a fool of himself, isn't that enough? He wants her gone, wants the collapse to be complete, just so it will be over.

Still she won't go.

Kenny tries to imagine what she is thinking but can't. All that comes is a picture of her, sitting on that bleached log, staring out at the water, at the long yellow reflection of Jacob's beacon. Her face is closed to him now, a house where he once lived but no longer can enter. Kenny sees that he has *not even started* to miss her yet. Why won't she go?

Finally he hears her stir, not toward the lake but toward him, the snap of twigs and rattle of branches. Just go, he thinks, and then says it: "Junie?"

"What?"

"It's late. I don't know what you want."

A long silence, filled with wind and crickets. He can almost see her, a few feet from his plain bed, a darkness against the deeper, mottled darkness of the forest. He feels her with some other sense, maybe his skin, receiving the closeness of her like radio waves.

"I love you," she says.

"Don't give me that." Kenny's anger spills out of his throat, fills his mouth, surprises him. "I'm not some goddamn bug you can pull the legs off, he loves me, he loves me not, he loves me."

"That isn't what I meant."

"I don't care what you meant. Why don't you go?"

"I'm going to," Junie says, her own blood rising. "I will in a minute."

"What do you want with me?" Kenny asks; and in the silence that follows his question, he discovers that he is no longer angry. Neither is she.

After a minute she says, "I didn't exactly plan this. Any of this."

"No."

"I just wanted you to know. It would have felt like a lie if I didn't tell you. I love you, that's all."

"Let's just stop talking, OK?" Kenny looks over into the darkness where she sits, silhouetted against the dark forest, then slowly unzips the length of his sleeping bag and crawls toward her across the pillowy nylon, takes her hand and pulls her to him. She comes to him, slow but willing, and they lie close and kiss once and then hold each other. Junie is awkward, resistant, all angles and projecting bones. Kenny traces the outline of her head with his fingers, touches the hollow of her throat, lightly. Then slowly starts to unbutton her blouse.

"Kenny," she says.

"What?"

"We can if you want to, but . . . Well, you wouldn't be the first."

But I *was*, he thinks; then realizes what she is saying: Jacob fucking Junie, down in the darkroom. Mr. Mustard in the library with a knife. His hand freezes onto her blouse. Falling, spinning, sinking. Kenny has no idea what to do; he never quite imagined that he was *right*.

"I'm sorry," she says, and sits up, cross-legged at the end of the sleeping bag, facing away. "I didn't mean for things to happen this way. I didn't mean any of it."

Kenny has his flashlight in his hand, ready to run, just get in the car and go, anywhere but here. Then looks at the flashlight, then puts it down. He can just barely see her. Kenny comes to her on his knees, rests his head against her neck, and wraps his arms around the angles of her stiff shoulders, so they are together, staring off into the darkness. Slowly, like always, he feels her relax into his embrace. "I don't care," he says.

A lie; but one that will get them through the next few hours, he hopes. The wheel, the big motor pushing them forward and forward. They lie nestled into each other on his sleeping bag, listening to the darkness around them, wondering what will happen next.

"Superb. . . . These tautly
structured stories breathe with sharp, distilled
intelligence, mingling recognition with surprise."

—*The New York Times Book Review*

A STRANGER IN THIS WORLD

The men and women in this mesmerizing collection of stories
walk a thin line between alternative lives. On one side are
well-lit homes, steady jobs, love, or its approximation. On
the other side lies chaos. To step across takes only one false
move, one bad choice. Kevin Canty has the rare power to
re-create the chain of thoughts that take his characters over
the edge.

In *A Stranger in This World*, the summons to do the wrong
thing may come from a neighbor with the body of a grown
woman and the mind of a submissive child. It may come from
the ex-wife who shows up just when you've gotten over her.
Disaster may take the form of a drunk driver who carries
a gun in his glove compartment. Canty gives us an entire
catalog of risk, in stories that unveil the hazards at the heart
of American lives.

Fiction/0-679-76394-5